A MARGIN OF LUST

GRETA BORIS

Cover design by Michelle Fairbanks/Fresh Design
Edited by Mary-Theresa Hussey

Print ISBN 978-1-945419-21-8
ePub ISBN 978-1-945419-22-5

Library of Congress Control Number 2017935084

To my husband and my dad who've shown me such vivid pictures of loyalty I was able to write about its opposite.

The infernal storm is raging ceaselessly,
Sweeping the shades along with it, and them
It smites and whirls, nor lets them ever be.
Arrived at the precipitous extreme,
In shrieks and lamentations they complain,
and even the Power Divine itself blaspheme.
I understood that to this mode of pain
Are doomed the sinners of the carnal kind,
Who o'er their reason let their impulse reign.

From the Second Circle of *The Inferno*

***The Divine Comedy* of Dante Alighieri**

CHAPTER ONE

PROLOGUE

SOMETIMES IT'S BEST TO LEAVE A DOOR CLOSED. When I crossed the threshold of my father's house on Cliff Drive, it changed me. Some would say not for the better.

I could argue my behavior was justified. We all have the right to protect our property from thieves and swindlers. But, really, it came down to simple lust. I was captivated by possibilities, and I wanted everything. I should have known by the screech of rusty hinges that that door was better left shut.

I'd made an appointment to see the house as soon as it came on the market, about six months after my father's death. Sondra Olsen, local real estate agent, met me on the curb out front. She opened the gate I'd only passed through once before in my life. The old fig tree I remembered from that time was bigger now and mantled the courtyard like a vulture, obliterating the light and warmth from the late afternoon sun.

We traversed the walkway and came to the front door that had always been locked tight against me. She threw it open and ushered me in. The curved staircase that led to the part of the house reserved for the family—in other words, not me—rose before me without a barrier.

My initial feeling about Sondra was one of warmth. She and I were sharing in a momentous occasion. She dropped the drawbridge across the moat and invited me into the castle, so to speak. But as we toured the house, my opinion changed. Yes, she was pleasant, subservient even, but I began to see beneath the surface.

"It's a fixer, but it has so much charm, don't you think?" she asked with a dimpled smile.

"Yes to both."

"Come look at the ocean view."

I paused before I stepped into the living room I'd only seen in bits and pieces through doors and windows. I don't know what I thought I'd find inside; the meaning of life, some kind of Holy Grail maybe.

"What do you think?" Sondra asked.

I couldn't speak.

It was a disappointment.

A huge disappointment.

It was much smaller than I'd imagined. The lack of furniture revealed nicked and scarred wood flooring. Blank dirty white walls framed the space. I didn't notice the cool breeze kissing my cheek until Sondra said, "Look at this view."

I walked through French doors onto a cement patio and looked down on the beach where I'd so often stood. How many nights had I made my way across the sand or the water, depending on the tides, to bathe in the light emanating from these very doors? How many times had I sat on the rocks that looked so small from this vantage point, straining to catch a glimpse of the family within? My family.

"Leaves you speechless doesn't it?" Sondra said.

I turned to answer her and inhaled sharply. She was caught in a beam from the setting sun, just like another girl on another day. Her hair glowed like gold around her head and on the shoulders of her sky blue dress. The vision only lasted for a moment. She turned and entered the house, and it was gone. But I recognized it as a premonition of sorts.

"The master bedroom has a terrific view as well. Is there a missus? She'll love it if there is. Very romantic." She led me toward the foyer. Before heading up, I noticed a short, dark hallway to the left of the staircase.

"What's down there?" I pointed.

"Believe it or not, that's the basement. Most California homes don't have them, but this house stands on top of a series of small caves that tunnel into the cliff. The man who built this place in the forties was a shipping magnate and a collector of art, furniture, all kinds of things. When he found out about the caves, he commissioned an architect to create a warren of storage rooms."

"Is there anything in the rooms?" I said.

"Probably, but don't worry. They'll be cleaned out before new owners move in."

"Can I see them?"

"The door is locked. I don't have a key." A cloud passed over Sondra's face as she said those words. She lied. It was my second clue. There must be a treasure within these disappointing walls after all.

"Let's go up, shall we?" She tilted her head and glanced at me from the corners of her eyes coquettishly, but it had no effect. She might as well have spit in my face. Unlike most men, I'm immune to the wiles of women.

I fingered the box cutter in my jacket pocket, then moved so quickly I surprised myself. I pulled her close and showed her the blade.

"Down," I said.

"In the kitchen. The...the...cellar keys are in the kitchen," she said.

We shuffled into that room like geriatric ballroom dancers.

"The pantry." She gestured with her chin toward a door. A round key chain with several keys hung on a hook inside. We stumbled back to the foyer.

I found the correct key after three tries, and we descended the steep cellar steps together. Dim yellow lights revealed a long hallway with doors opening off it every ten feet or so. I twisted the knob of the first door on my right and nudged it open with my foot. A moldy funk wafted out.

A single bulb hanging in the center of the room exposed stone walls, slick with moisture and the shadowy outlines of furniture. Old tables, chairs, desks, and bureaus were stacked and jammed into every corner. Nothing looked particularly valuable. Just old oak.

We moved to the next door. I opened it and saw a mountain of cardboard boxes moldering on a damp floor. I stood Sondra in front of me, close enough to reach her if she moved, and opened one with my box cutter. I pushed aside the dusty cardboard and saw something that looked like peeling skin. I hesitated, then reached in and lifted the object. It was a woman's purse; or rather it had once been a purse. I dropped it in disgust.

"I told you. There is nothing here but trash," Sondra said.

I jerked her forward. The possibility she told the truth angered me more than her attempts to get me to leave off my search. I threw open door after door. The farther we went through the basement, the more enraged I became. My dream, the thing I'd longed for all these years, was nothing but a graveyard of old, decaying junk.

Sondra struggled against me. "Let me go. I won't tell anyone about this. I promise. Let's just go—"

"Shut up." I tightened my grip across her chest and nicked the smooth skin of her throat with the box cutter. She tensed, but stilled.

We came to the dead end of the hallway. I could hear the faint sound of waves throwing themselves against the cliff walls like they were seeking entrance. I kicked open the last door. The heavy wood bounced off the wall behind it. I dragged Sondra into the room, thinking I'd kill her here. Here at the dead end of my hopes. It was the first time I killed a stranger, but I couldn't very well leave her alive after holding a box cutter to her throat.

I pushed the blade of my knife higher in its case. She began to fight in earnest now, scratching and biting. I threw her to the floor and fell on top of her. Her head slammed against the stone. She went limp.

As I sat panting, straddling her body, I saw it. Something glinted in the spill of light from the hallway.

I stood to investigate. Joy dawned with realization. What was hidden here was better than I had ever imagined. It was an inheritance meant only for me. Maybe my father did think of me after all.

CHAPTER TWO

IT TOOK GWEN EIGHT PASSES to maneuver her Honda into a tight spot between a MINI and a Ford pickup. Cliff Drive in Laguna Beach bordered Diver's Cove, a popular dive beach in an even more popular tourist town. Parking was at a premium, but that wasn't the only reason it took her so long to settle in and turn off the ignition. Her excitement bordered on anxiety.

"Is this it?" Maricela said, awe creeping into her tone.

Gwen glanced at the elegant Mediterranean home she'd parked in front of. "No. It's at the end of the block."

She led Maricela up the sandy sidewalk until they reached a fence bulging from a jungle of vines and branches fighting to escape from the yard behind it. All that was visible of the house was a bit of gray, shingled roof rising above the fray.

Gwen directed her e-key at a lockbox hanging from the gate. "This isn't a mini-mansion like the rest of the houses on the street, but, hey, it's beachfront property."

The sound of the gate, hinges half-broken, scraping across the cement seemed louder than last time she was here. "It's been empty for a long time," she said, then mentally kicked herself. She'd done it again. She'd apologized for her multi-million dollar listing. This house, as dilapidated as it might be, was a game changer. She'd be damned if she was going to be embarrassed by it.

"The owner's father died about six months ago after living in a nursing home for years. She just inherited." Gwen picked her way up the broken walk around the gnarled roots of a large fig tree. Its fruit, in varying stages of decay, littered the ground.

"Have you already signed the listing agreement?" Maricela said.

"Yes, a couple of days ago, and it's already been shown. Sondra Olsen, First Team Realty, had somebody by yesterday. But I think I'll get more action if I spruce the place up a bit, which is why you're here." Gwen fitted the key into the front door lock and pushed it open. "I want your advice. Fiona, she's the owner, gave me a budget. It's not big, but it's something."

Gwen squinted into the dim interior, and her heart rate rose. It was an overreaction, but dark, enclosed places always made her nervous. Through the shadows, she could see a circular staircase dividing the foyer in two. A hallway opened to its left.

The hallway led to a basement of cave-like rooms. She'd never gone down to see them, and she wasn't planning to. Just walking past the entrance made her queasy. She planned to hire a cleaning crew to haul away the junk they were filled with. Milky sunlight beckoned from a room to the right of the stairwell. Gwen hurried toward it.

"Okay. This is nice." Maricela's voice echoed in the empty living room.

"Nice? It's fantastic." Gwen unlocked French doors that framed a panoramic view of the Pacific Ocean. The sight never failed to send a ripple of pleasure up her backbone. She'd been selling real estate for three years. Three years of tract houses in planned communities, attached townhomes, and condos. Then last week she got the call.

Fiona Randall, a woman she'd sold a three-bedroom to a few years back, had inherited the family home on the cliffs in Laguna Beach. This was a listing that made careers, moved agents out of the scrabbling masses and into the elite ranks of real estate brokers. Gwen had dreamed breaking into that echelon since she started in the business.

She and Maricela stepped outside onto a veranda of cracked cement and looked down onto a sandy beach. A crisp breeze carried the sounds of crashing waves, children squealing in the surf, and the clanking of diver's equipment. It was a symphony to Gwen's ears. She still had a hard time believing that she, Gwen Bishop, was representing oceanfront property in Laguna.

"Look. It has beach access." Gwen pointed to a rickety railing rising out of the ice plant at the end of the neglected garden.

Maricela folded her arms across her chest. "If you want to die young."

"I know. It needs a little work."

"This place needs more than a little work, *chica*."

"That's why you're here. You're a pro. If you had ten thousand to throw at it, what would you do?"

Maricela's dark hair reflected the sun as she shook her head. "I'd start by putting a barrier across the top of those stairs. If someone breaks their neck, it'll decrease the value."

"Sudden violent death has a way of doing that," Gwen said and pulled a pad of paper from her purse to make notes.

"Show me more," Maricela said.

Gwen reentered the gloom of the house and led the way through the living room to the foyer and up the carpeted stairs. "I've been looking at the comps, and nothing with beach access has sold for under twelve million in the past year and a half. Fiona has her hopes set on ten."

Talking about numbers like ten million and twelve million made Gwen feel like a child playing at real estate agent. When she was small, she had a toy cash register on which she rang up plastic food and empty cereal boxes. The prices she set then had no more meaning to her than the price of this house. There were too many zeros for it to compute. But, the zeros still made her happy.

A sweet odor, delicate at first, grew stronger with each riser until it overwhelmed the mold bouquet. "I'm afraid to ask what that smell is," Maricela said.

"Probably a dead rat in the attic. They love figs. I'll have it removed," said Gwen, keeping her voice cheerful. She needed Maricela's expertise. She'd been an agent for much longer than Gwen, and she was a successful one. She knew how to maximize a home's assets and hide its deficiencies. When she staged a house, it sold. But optimism wasn't on the short list of her wonderful qualities.

"I think you should get a cleaning crew, make the place smell better, and price it under market."

"Wait until you see the view from the master bedroom," Gwen said, ignoring Maricela's comment, and the reek in the air.

The hardwood floor groaned under their feet as they walked toward a room at the end of the hall. A triangle of light pointed outward from a partially opened door. She looked over her shoulder to monitor Maricela's reaction.

"Ta-da," she said and pushed the door ajar.

Maricela's eyes widened.

"It's spectacular, right?" Gwen said still looking at her.

Maricela's jaw dropped, but nothing came from her mouth.

"You can see Catalina on a clear day," Gwen said.

Maricela's caramel skin turned ashen. The stench was worse here. Was it making her ill? Gwen looked into her friend's eyes. They were focused on a spot over her right shoulder. Before she could follow her gaze, Maricela pitched forward and gagged.

CHAPTER THREE

AN AMBULANCE AND THREE POLICE CARS, all with lights blazing, blocked the house on Cliff Drive. There was nowhere to park. Art threw the minivan into reverse and backed up, engine grinding, then made a three-point turn onto one of the perpendicular streets.

He circled the North Laguna neighborhood, tires squealing, four or five times before giving up and crossing Coast Highway. He found a parking spot in the Boat Canyon shopping center and jogged back to the mayhem.

Gwen had called him a half hour ago, not hysterical like most people would be, but cool and steady. She explained that she and Maricela had stumbled on a body in the same tone of voice she would use to dictate a grocery list.

Art knew from fifteen years of marriage; it was the calm before the storm. His wife often went "into character" when faced with uncomfortable situations. It was a technique she learned in method acting and now employed in life. She was probably channeling a detective or crime reporter, but at some point, he knew reality would come crashing in. He wanted to get there before it did.

He slowed his pace as he approached the emergency vehicles. Two officers, a male and a female, guarded the street in front of the house.

"Stay back, please, sir," the man said.

"My wife is in there," Art said.

"Her name?"

"Guinevere Bishop."

The cop spoke into his radio. A few minutes later, a woman emerged. At first, Art thought she was young—too young to be the officer in charge. But as she drew close, he saw small crow's feet around her almond-shaped eyes. Her build and smooth complexion created the image of youth. She was slender, but well-muscled, with skin was so uniformly dark it looked like polished ebony against the white of her blouse

"I'm Investigator Sylla. And you are?" she said in a clip, British accent.

"Arthur Bishop. My wife, Gwen, she and her coworker found the body."

She nodded, and Art followed her into the house. He was hurried through an entryway, down a hall, and into a wide living room. The impression of the house was brief, but poignant, an Addams-family-goes-on-vacation kind of place. The woman ushered him out onto a sunny veranda, then turned and was swallowed again by the gloom of the house.

Maricela sat on the cement with a blanket around her shoulders sipping water from a bottle. Gwen stood with her back to him, looking out to sea. He walked up behind his wife and wrapped his arms around her. "You okay, honey?"

She nodded, but stepped out of his embrace. Apparently finding a dead body wasn't a sufficient distraction to end the frost she'd been leveling at him since their argument that morning. Now that he thought about it, her calm explanation on the phone might have been part of the same treatment. If there was one thing his wife was good at, it was maintaining a chill.

He decided to check on Maricela. She'd appreciate his concern. Her color wasn't good. Mascara streaked her cheeks. He squatted beside her and put a hand on her shoulder. She gripped it with damp fingers and held on tight. He was beginning to wonder how long he could maintain the position, his knees not being what they once were, when the detective came outside.

Art stood, stifling a groan of relief.

"I need to take the ladies to the station to make a statement." Sylla's tone was all business. "Follow us, if you like."

#

Five hours later, Art handed Gwen a glass of wine. She sat with her feet curled under her on the couch in the family room. She was a tall woman, but the pose made her look small and vulnerable. Like a child.

"Want to tell me about it?" he said.

She took a large swig of wine. He waited. She drank half her glass, stared at the wall for a full minute then said, "It was awful." Once the pump was primed, the words flowed. "I thought it was a joke at first. Can you believe it? I actually thought someone had dragged a naked mannequin into the house, slashed it, and put that fake blood from the costume store on it. She looked like plastic—white and shiny." Gwen shivered.

Art reached for her hand and squeezed it.

"Of course, that makes no sense when you think about it. They don't make mannequins that look like people you know. Or mannequins that have pink fingernails. Or nipples. Or pubic hair." Gwen breathed deeply through her nose like she was trying to calm her stomach. "It was Sondra Olsen. From Team One Realty. She showed the place last night. Her husband reported her missing, but the police weren't taking it too seriously. Hadn't been long enough, I guess."

"Did you know she was going to show the house?"

"Yes. I talked to her in the afternoon. I warned her it needed help, but she said she had a hot prospect—wanted to see the place right away."

"She didn't say—"

"No. She did not." Gwen snapped at him. "I have no idea who she showed it to. That detective, Sylla, couldn't seem to understand that. She must have asked me fifty times."

"She's just doing her job," Art said.

Gwen removed her hand from his. "She also said I'm not supposed to talk to anyone about what I saw, and look at me. I've already blown it."

"I'm not anyone." Irritation tightened his jaw. "I'm your husband."

"It must be okay to talk to you, right?" Gwen looked at him through tear-filled eyes.

"Of course it is." Art pulled her close, leaned her head on his shoulder and rocked her as she finally cried. He felt the iceberg that had been separating them all day melt.

Several years ago, the family had visited the Living Desert—a zoo in the Palms Springs area that featured indigenous animals. Emily, their youngest, only about two at the time, toddled past the mountain lion exhibit.

Art remembered the adrenaline-fueled surge of protectiveness that coursed through him when one of the lions charged the plexiglas of its enclosure. It was hunting his daughter. It couldn't reach her. She was safe, but his hormones didn't get the message. He had that same feeling now. When Gwen's sobs subsided, he said, "You should take a break from work."

She pushed damp, auburn hair from her forehead and took a shaky breath. "Yeah. I'll take a few days off."

"That's not what I mean," Art said. "Take a break until they catch this guy."

Gwen pulled away. She didn't say anything, just played with her wine glass and took another sip. After a minute she said, "What're the chances I'll run into another dead body? I mean, that seems like a once in a lifetime opportunity."

"This guy might be targeting agents, Gwen."

"Nobody knows who did this, or why. Most murders are personal. Maybe Sondra was having an affair with some nut case, and he flipped out on her."

"She told you she was showing the house to a client." Gwen didn't answer, just sat up a little straighter on her side of the couch. "What about Texas?" he said.

"What *about* Texas?"

"The murders."

"They happened in Texas."

"Maybe the murderer moved to Orange County."

Over the past ten months, three real estate agents had been found dead in vacant homes in the Dallas area. There'd only been one short article in the local papers after the last death, but the Orange County Association of Realtors had taken it seriously. Safety had been a featured topic in the newsletters Gwen brought home from the office. The concern Art felt when he first saw them now exploded into full-blown worry.

"I can't abandon Maricela. I'm the one who dragged her over there, and she's shook up. She has to work," Gwen said.

"But you don't."

Gwen was quiet. Pricks of color stung Art's cheeks. Her silence was a reminder that his statement wasn't entirely true. They had needed her income the past few years, but that could change. Soon. He stood, crossed the room and leaned on the mantel. "Hopefully, in March..." He let his words trail off. He didn't want to fight again.

Art had been acting principal at St. Barnabas Lutheran School since September. At the end of this month, he would be reviewed and either get the job permanently, along with the commensurate raise, or he wouldn't. Gwen couldn't seem to understand he needed her help. The job was political, and like any candidate running for office, his family was under almost as much scrutiny as he was. Gwen couldn't, or wouldn't, show up for school events, run for a position on the PTA, or do any of the things necessary to romance the board of directors.

That morning he'd made what he thought was a simple request. Could she, please, attend a school orchestra concert next Friday night? It was one of the year's biggest events and he was giving a short address before it started. She'd said she was busy.

When he reminded her how important the wife of a St. Barnabas principal was, she reminded him she had a demanding job too. Then he'd committed the unpardonable sin, he suggested she quit when he got the new position. She'd frozen over like a shallow pond in below zero weather.

"I can't believe you're using what happened today to manipulate me. I repeat what I said this morning. I need to work. I want to work. I love my career. I'm not going to quit, go part time, or stay home and be the little woman behind the big man."

Her words bit like hail, and the temperature in the room dropped to that morning's frigid degrees.

CHAPTER FOUR

GWEN TAPPED OUT HER FRUSTRATION on the steering wheel. "What is going on up there? You'd think they were being dropped off for a six-month tour with the Peace Corp instead of six hours of school."

The twice-daily traffic jam at St. Barnabas Lutheran School reminded her of a herd of cattle headed for a watering hole. Mothers in minivans rattled their horns and jostled each other to best position their young.

"Everyone have their backpacks? Lunch?" Gwen said when she was able to pull forward. Art was the principal at St. Barnabas, so he took the kids to school on most days. Gwen was only called upon to be the designated driver on Mondays when he had an early breakfast meeting with the board. This also happened to be the only day Humboldt Realty had a meeting. Mondays were stressful.

"Just keep driving, Mom," Tyler said. "We'll jump and tuck and roll." Tyler was eleven, and the funny man in the family.

Emily, never one to be outdone by her older brothers, said, "I want to tuck and roll."

"You'll mess up your hair," Gwen said. "I'll stop."

She jockeyed to the curb. Tyler and Emily tumbled out of the back seat and Jason, her oldest, exited the shotgun position.

"You have your sister," Gwen said when Jason came around the driver side. "Take her to her classroom, please." Jason gave her a quizzical look. Emily was in third grade and had been walking to her class alone all school year, but Gwen's protective instincts were running wild. She and Art had decided not to tell the kids anything about the murder, no reason to give them nightmares too.

Gwen had been plagued with them since last week. Some revolved around the basement of the Laguna house. She'd find herself walking down the stairs, terrified, but wake before she discovered the source of her fear. In others, she found Emily instead of Sondra in the upstairs bedroom. She'd even experienced a return of the recurring dream she'd had all through her childhood and teen years. It had been years since she'd had that nightmare. She was trying hard to maintain a business-as-usual front for the kids, but they were smart. They could tell something was up.

Her children turned to walk toward the brick front building.

"Hey. Goodbye." She called after them.

Emily returned and wrapped her arms around Gwen's neck and leaned in for a sticky kiss. Tyler, smelling like soap and cereal, was next. Jason stooped; the top of his red head entered the window first. He pecked her on the cheek. He was getting so tall.

Then they were off. Jason loped with the awkward gait of a teen whose brain hasn't figured out how to handle the extra inches. The two towheads jogged to keep up with him. Gwen watched until they reached the double glass doors of the school. A car horn sounded. Work. She was late.

By the time she arrived at the office, there was standing room only in the conference room. She found a piece of wall to lean on next to Maricela.

"Anything interesting?" Gwen whispered.

"Taryn's talking about the murder again." Maricela looked sick.

"She's been fixated on it," Gwen said. "It's sad, but it's over. Time to move on."

"We need to be on high alert. Especially the women." Taryn Humboldt, the owner of Humboldt Realty, addressed the room. "I called around. The Texas police recommend establishing a buddy system. It's working at Western State Realty and in Concord Realty's Houston offices. Nothing has happened since they began taking precautions."

"You really think that's necessary?" John Gordon, forty-something with a fringe of black hair encircling a balding pate, reclined in his chair and placed his hands behind his head. He was one of only three male agents in the office.

"Maybe not for you," said Caroline Bartlett—a teased blonde in leopard print pumps with a sweater that reminded Gwen of a shedding Pomeranian.

"I'd be happy to partner with one of the women. The men in the office should do what we can," Lance

Fairchild said. Gwen could have sworn she heard a sigh float up like a cloud of pollen from the estrogen producers in the room. Lance was handsome—extremely handsome. Eric Woo, the only other man in the room, stared at the ceiling.

"Everyone needs to use a little common sense." John bristled.

"The old rooster doesn't like the competition," Maricela said out of the side of her mouth.

"Take the most recent case." John liked to hear himself talk. "She met the guy alone in an empty house. Not the brightest bulb on the tree if you ask me."

"You probably meet people alone all the time." Caroline's over-painted lips pouted.

"In his dreams," Gwen said under her breath.

"Maybe I do. But I'm not a woman." John sneered ever so slightly.

"Anyone who is willing to buddy up please write your name on a slip of paper and put it in this basket." Taryn held up the container normally used for sweetener packets in the coffee room. "I've also printed up a new list of safety tips issued by the Board of Realtors. Take one and read it please."

Maricela leaned closer to Gwen. "Put your name in."

"Why?" Gwen said.

"Don't even ask me that."

"We've had our fun. Things like finding dead bodies in empty houses don't happen to people twice in one lifetime."

Maricela reached for a pen and a slip of paper and wrote her name. She handed the pen and another piece of paper to Gwen when she was done. "Write."

Gwen obeyed. "Now can I get to work, Mom?" She turned from the conference table and collided with a white shirt and striped tie. It was Lance.

"I'm glad you're being smart," he said. Then he winked, threw his name in the basket and walked away.

Gwen's face grew hot. The other women in the office might find him irresistible, but she found him insufferable. He'd only been at Humboldt eight months, but he strutted around like he owned the place. The fact that he'd bagged the top sales position for five of those months and Gwen, who'd been there for years, had never had the honor, only deepened her animosity.

She sank into the chair behind her desk, flipped her laptop open and logged into her email. Today was going to be busy. She had three listings. Two were nothing to write home about, a condo and a 1,500 square foot tract, but the third took some of the sting out of temporarily losing the Laguna Beach house. It was currently a crime scene, barricaded and off-limits. She didn't know when or if Fiona would put it back on the market. She wasn't sure if she could face it if she did.

Gwen had acquired the third listing a couple of weeks ago at the end of January. It was a five-bedroom, oceanview home in Dana Point. It wasn't oceanfront, but it was in mint condition. The owner was a builder, and he'd designed the place himself.

"Are you showing the Sailor's Haven house today?" Maricela asked, as if on cue.

Maricela's desk was next to hers, which was one of the great blessings of Gwen's life. Three years ago, Gwen had sat at her empty desk for the first time with a mix of pride and dread.

She wondered how, or if, she was going to get this new enterprise off the ground. Real estate seemed like such a great idea when she and Art had discussed it, but there she sat on day one staring at a phone that wasn't ringing and a calendar as pristine as a field after a snowfall. Then Maricela sat at the desk next to hers.

They'd seen each other at St. Barnabas events but had never spoken. Once Maricela found out Gwen was Art's wife, she lit up like one of those crazy neighborhoods that go all out at Christmas. She was a fan. He had lots of them.

Within hours, Gwen was out the door previewing other agents' listings, had two appointments to show properties Maricela was too busy to handle and was scheduled to hold her first open house that Saturday.

Since then Maricela had learned to appreciate Gwen for herself, and they'd become best friends. Sometimes Gwen felt life was a constant battle with suburban obscurity. Around St. Barnabas, she was known as Art's wife, sometimes Jason, or Tyler, or Emily's mother, but never as Gwen.

"Next week," Gwen said. "I have a couple coming in from Chicago. I'm trying to bump them up to that price range."

"*Bueno*," Maricela said and picked up her phone.

They worked companionably for about a half hour. Gwen, engrossed in updating her listings in the

Multiple Listing Service, didn't notice Taryn Humboldt's presence until a slip of paper dropped onto the calendar in front of her. Gwen picked it up and swore under her breath. Lance was her safety buddy. To her great annoyance, her heart tapped a few extra beats and her face grew hot for the second time that morning.

CHAPTER FIVE

I PULLED THE WRINKLED NEWSPAPER ARTICLE from my drawer and stared at it as I had countless times over the past week. It was illogical, but I hoped that if I looked long and hard enough the answer to my dilemma would leap from the page into my consciousness.

But I saw what I'd seen a hundred times before, a color photograph of the house with yellow, crime scene tape encircling it like a ribbon around a gift. I had handed it to them. Made a present of it. It galled me I'd been so shortsighted.

I could have disposed of Sondra's body anywhere, but no. I left her in the very place I least wanted to call attention to. Well, almost. I'd taken her upstairs. I would no more have bloodied that cellar than Howard Carter would have taken a piss in King Tut's tomb. But, still, I might as well have stood on the roof of the house with a megaphone and barked, "Step right up, gentlemen." I'd made a circus of the place.

The only excuse I can offer is that I was beside myself. It was, after all, a very eventful day. I'd scaled the castle wall for the first time, killed a gorgon, and found a treasure. Lesser deeds have had entire tomes written about them.

However, I was now stymied. How was I to proceed? The house crawled with police. They'd swarmed in like cockroaches, invading every corner. They were looking for clues to Sondra's killer, clues they weren't going to find. I'd been careful about that. But the fact they were there at all worried me. There were other things they could find.

I focused on the paper in my hands for a long while, willing something to happen. I was about to give up, fold it and stick it away when all at once a line I'd read countless times before changed. It morphed from normal newspaper font to bold, neon letters right before my eyes. The words screamed from the page. I couldn't believe I hadn't seen it sooner.

Investigators on the scene had no comment when asked if they believed the crime was related to the rash of murders committed against Texas real estate agents in recent months.

The investigators had no comment. What did no comment always mean? It meant there were many comments on the topic when no reporters were within shouting distance. It meant they were halfway convinced the statement was true. It meant they didn't have evidence to support their suspicions.

I saw an opportunity. I would give them the substantiation they desired. I'd been preoccupied with trying to protect what was hidden. I'd been so busy trying to come up with ways to either retrieve or bury my treasure deeper, I'd overlooked the obvious. The best way to make my house less interesting was to make someplace else more interesting.

I would create a distraction. Lay some cockroach bait elsewhere. It wouldn't be hard with attention spans being what they are these days. I dropped the paper, turned on my computer and typed in Texas real estate killings.

CHAPTER SIX

"DONALD IS ON LINE THREE. He's not happy, but that's nothing new. Don't let him drone on too long; you have a meeting with the fourth-grade teachers at 12:30. Here are the files you asked for." The ever-efficient Millie handed Art a stack of manila folders. "Don't let him push you around either. I'd give him a piece of my mind if I didn't think he'd send me packing."

Art grinned. Donald Pratt, president of the St. Barnabas Board of Directors though he was, wouldn't dare fire Millie. She'd become administrative assistant to the principal when Donald was still wearing shorts and swinging a book bag. She knew where all the bodies were buried—and all the best gossip.

And like Cerberus guarding the gates of hell, she was the first terror wayward children had to pass on their way to the various circles of punishment. That kind of intimidation wasn't something you easily got over.

Art opened his mouth to thank her for the files, but before he could say anything, she said, "Oh, and bad-boy Brian is sitting on the bench in my office. He needs a word of...encouragement."

"Send him in," Art said. Brian would give him an excuse to get off the phone quickly. He picked up the receiver. "Hello, Donald."

Donald had a talent for ferreting out problems where there were none. Today he launched into his ideas for rerouting the parents' cars during student drop-offs and pick-ups. Art listened with half an ear to the latest installment in his quest for a legacy issue.

The office door opened an inch, then a few more. A small, grubby fist shot through. A sneakered foot, laces untied, followed. "I hear you, Donald. I hear you," Art said into the phone.

A pair of worried looking brown eyes peeked around the doorframe. Art waved Brian in before he could run away. "I'll tell you what, Donald, I promise to look into it, but I have a student here now. You bet. You bet. Thanks for all your hard work." Pandering to the man turned Art's stomach, but it was temporary. He only had to make it to the end of the month when Donald would make his recommendations to the board.

Brian McKibben sat in the chair opposite Art, his chin hovering a few inches above the top of the desk. He looked small and nervous, not at all like the terror of the third-grade playground.

"Fighting again?" Art asked.

Brian nodded and ran his hand under his nose leaving a long, brown smudge on his upper lip.

"What's the trouble this time?"

Brian shrugged one shoulder and looked out the window.

"Was it Dwayne?"

Brian nodded again.

Dwayne Pratt, Donald's youngest, was a bully, not unlike his father. Brian McKibben was a scholarship student at St. Barnabas. He and his mother, Olivia Richard, a waitress at Enzo's Sports Bar, lived in the only HUD housing condos in Laguna Niguel. He made a big target for a kid who could afford a lot of darts, like Dwayne.

"Fighting isn't the way to handle it, Brian. You know that. We've had this talk."

Brian studied the floor as if it might hold a hidden escape hatch.

"I'm going to have to suspend you."

Brian's chin shot up. His eyes widened, and his lower lip quivered.

"Just for a week, but I want you to spend some time thinking about this."

Art's heart went out to the kid. Dwayne was an odious child who deserved whatever Brian had dished out, but this was the third time Brian had thrown the first punch. He needed to learn some self-discipline. If he didn't, Art might not be able to convince the board to extend his scholarship next year.

Besides, Dwayne was Donald Pratt's son and Donald had leverage. He was head of the committee tasked with hiring administrative staff including St. Barnabas' next principal. Art couldn't afford to tick him off.

At the end of the last school year, Steve Johnson, the prior principal, had been fired. There had been a sexting scandal involving the St. Barnabas football team and a cheerleader. The whole thing erupted when the cheerleader took a half bottle of her father's painkillers and wound up in the emergency room.

None of it was Steve's fault. He was a good guy, honest, hardworking. But families began pulling their children out of the school. The buck had to stop somewhere if the board was going to stem the financial tide. It stopped with Steve.

When Art had agreed to take on the interim principal position, he hadn't received a raise, only more responsibility, more hours, and the promise he'd be first in line for a job he wanted. He'd been working toward it for years. He started as a lower school English teacher, graduated to the high school, became the English Department Chair, and now the highest position in the school dangled in front of him, so close he could smell it.

Not only would the role change his financial status and relieve him of having to suck up to Donald Pratt it would enable him to do a lot of good for a lot of people. People like Brian McKibben and his single mother.

The agreement had been for six months and that time was almost up. His performance would be evaluated and he might, or might not depending on Donald's recommendation, be offered a permanent position at the end of February, only three weeks away.

A few years ago, he and Gwen had discussed Art making a move into the public school system where salaries were higher and benefits better, but he wanted to climb the ladder where he was. Gwen had supported his decision.

Since they needed additional income, she'd gotten a job. When she'd started at Humboldt Realty, they'd both thought of it as a stopgap measure. Now the opportunity for her to scale back her career, or quit altogether, was right in front of them. Not only wasn't she excited about it, but she got belligerent whenever Art mentioned it.

Thankfully, Lorelei Tanaka, the school counselor, had stepped in and taken on many of the jobs Gwen should have shouldered. Lorelei showed up at PTA meetings, assemblies, and bake sales and waved the flag for Art. She was in his camp, a real advocate. But it would look better, strengthen his position, if his wife showed some enthusiasm.

The door closed behind the small fugitive, and Art looked at his watch. He was already late for the teacher's meeting. No time for lunch. He'd have to stop by the cafeteria and grab some peanut butter crackers from the vending machine, again.

Millie held something up for him as he hurried past her desk—a white bag perfumed with the sweet smell of Italian sausage. "You have to eat occasionally, or you won't have the strength to sign my paycheck."

"Thank you." Art smiled and patted her shoulder. Gwen might not give him the support he'd hoped for, but he always had Millie. And Lorelei.

CHAPTER SEVEN

HE WAS A CRETIN. Gwen led Arnold and Etta Paul, in from Chicago, through the fifth and, thank God, final house of the day. She'd thought this would be an easy deal. They were motivated buyers—not much time and plenty of capital. But after spending two days with them, she wondered if she would ever be able to make him happy.

"What's this crack here?" Arnold bent over, held his bifocals away from his face and peered at a space between the wall and baseboard. Gwen looked to the ceiling for patience and, staying as far away from him as possible, moved over to inspect the spot. "That's where the molding attaches to the wall board."

"You could fit a small animal through that space." He straightened up to his full six feet, pushed his glasses onto his patrician nose and gazed at Gwen with disdain. "As you are a woman, I don't expect you to understand the basics of carpentry, but let me assure you this is sloppy work—extremely sloppy work."

"I can't imagine it would be very expensive to—" Gwen began.

"Maybe, maybe. But this could be the tip of the iceberg. If there's shoddy workmanship out here in the open where people can see it, just imagine what the foundation and studs look like."

In a timid voice, Etta interjected, "The neighborhood is nice, Arnie."

"How would you know?" Arnold glared at his diminutive wife.

Gwen thought Etta must have been pretty once. Her beauty was that of a brightly colored dress that had been through the wash one too many times. Everything about her was muted: her hair, her voice, her clothing, her personality. What Gwen found the saddest, however, were her eyes. They were the color of the ocean in the stretches of polluted beach near the Dana Point Harbor.

Etta twisted the fraying leather straps of her purse, "I mean it's pretty. The trees and..."

"Yes, well those trees would go up in flames right along with the house if the wiring is as poor as the finish work. No, no, this isn't for us." Arnold was sticking a credit card he'd pulled from his wallet under the wood around the doorframe. Whenever it slid in farther than a centimeter, he grunted in satisfaction.

"There are other places we can take a look at tomorrow," Gwen said and moved toward the door. She couldn't wait to put distance between herself and old Arnie, at least for a few hours. Her self-control was slipping.

Between his extreme negativism and the snide comments aimed at female agents in general, and Gwen in particular, she'd about had it. She would say something she'd later regret if she didn't get away from him soon.

"If they're anything like the ones you've already shown us, I'm not sure I want to see them." He examined his well-manicured nails for the imaginary dirt he'd picked up in the eight-hundred-and-fifty-thousand-dollar hovels she'd taken him through.

"The houses we looked at today were in the price range you quoted me, Mr. Paul. I'm sorry to say the average home price in Southern Orange County is quite a bit higher than in the bedroom communities around Chicago." A vein throbbed in Gwen's temple.

"You don't need to give me a lecture little lady. I'm well aware of the real estate market in California. I've been flying out and looking at houses for the past year and a half. In fact, I was here last week to look at some places in Laguna Beach."

"Then you know—" Gwen started to say.

"But I've never seen such a sorry bunch of houses in my life as the ones you showed us today. Come, Etta." He pointed to the door. He said the last like you would say, "Sit, Etta," or "Fetch, Etta." Etta jerked into motion and trotted toward the exit. Gwen wished Rocket, her family's retriever, were as well behaved.

Why women stayed with men like Arnold Paul was one of life's great mysteries. Gwen would have started peppering his dinner with arsenic on the honeymoon. Or, maybe she'd have clubbed him with a frozen turkey leg then cooked it up for the cops. Or, she might have slipped him a mickey on a cruise ship and pushed him overboard. The thoughts cheered her.

"I can show you some homes in a slightly higher price range if you'd like. It doesn't pay to be cheap when it comes to property," Gwen said.

"Cheap?" He spit out the word. "I'd hardly call any of the homes we looked at cheap in any way other than in their construction."

"I have another listing I haven't shown you because it's more than you said you wanted to spend. The owner is a builder. He designed the house himself. It's sensational." Gwen looked at Etta and added, "Nice neighborhood, oceanview, quiet well-landscaped street."

Etta looked at Arnold before allowing herself to smile.

"How much more?" Arnold narrowed his eyes.

"Thirty-five thousand," Gwen said.

"I don't know." Arnold folded his arms over his ample stomach.

"I think you'll qualify..." Gwen let the words trail off.

"Of course I'll qualify." He puffed out his chest.

Gwen smiled. "I can take you by tomorrow. The owners are getting ready to leave town and can't be disturbed today."

"Okay, we'll take a look at it." He strutted out the door, flattening his poor wife against the wall as he steamrolled by her. "But don't you get your hopes up, Etta."

#

After Gwen dropped the Pauls off at their hotel, she headed to Dana Point. A cool breeze tickled the hair on her neck as she walked up the stone path of 213 Sailor's Haven Drive. She inhaled. The delicious scent of wisteria riding on the ocean air reminded her of chocolate laced with sea salt. Rockroses and white hydrangeas popped against a backdrop of cool gray-blue siding. She couldn't imagine what Arnold could find wrong with this house, but he'd probably find something.

She rang the doorbell next to the crisp, white front door. Mary Beth Frobisher answered looking like a cover model from an AARP magazine. "So, show me this contraption you're hooking our house up with," she said, ushering Gwen indoors. "Tea?"

"No, thanks. It's nothing like the old lockboxes," Gwen began.

They walked through the dining area to a living room overlooking the Dana Point Harbor. Sunlight streamed through large, paned windows and fell in blocks on the hardwood floor. Boats bobbed on a crayon-box blue background. This was the kind of house Gwen dreamed of, not only to represent, but also to live in one day. One day, when she'd made it big.

"It's been so long since we've sold a house, I'm afraid I'm way behind the times." Mary Beth sat on a spotless, white sofa gesturing to a matching chair opposite. Gwen perched on its edge, fearful she'd smudge it. She could only imagine what the kids and the dog would do to this furniture.

"Things have changed a lot," Gwen said.

Mary Beth and her husband, Charles, had not wanted to put a lockbox on their home. They had expensive art and didn't like the idea of strangers tromping through their house when they weren't there.

"The new lockboxes," Gwen said, "are connected wirelessly to a security company. Agents have to have an account with them to get to the key inside the box."

"But how do they know you're an agent when you sign up? What's to stop any Tom, Dick, or Harry from creating an account?"

"We have to prove we're Realtors in good standing with the board. It's a very secure system."

Mary Beth crossed her legs, tapped her foot in the air and looked out the window. After several seconds she said, "You must think I'm a fuddy-duddy but there have been two break-ins near here recently."

"I'm sure they didn't use e-keys to enter the homes," Gwen said.

"They could have if they were agents," Mary Beth said with an intake of breath.

"Yes, they could, but whenever an agent uses their e-key, a message is sent to the security company letting them know the address of the box, the date and time it was opened and by whom. It would be like leaving a business card for the cops."

"Oh," Mary Beth's shoulders relaxed, and she looked out the window again. "So, it's safe? You're sure it's safe?"

"It's safe," Gwen said in a soothing tone. "I'll get a report of every agent who enters your house." Mary Beth continued to tap her foot and stare at the passing boats.

Gwen added, "If you want to sell your house while you're in Switzerland, you have to have a lockbox. Agents just won't show the house without one. It's too much trouble for them."

The Frobishers would be away for the rest of the month. They were disappointed they hadn't had an offer on their home before the trip, but Gwen had only had the house listed for two weeks. It was unreasonable to think it would sell that quickly, but now she had to talk them into putting a lockbox on the property.

"Okay, then. Let's do it." She uncrossed her legs and stood in one smooth motion. "I promised Charles I'd give you the third degree."

"I'll tell him you did an excellent job." Gwen stood with her.

Gwen snapped the box on the side gate and reassured Mary Beth several more times before the front door closed between them. She pulled her keys from her purse and hurried to the curb. She was running late, again. She had to pick up the kids and get Emily to ballet before four.

When Gwen had gone to work three years ago, she'd felt like she took on an avatar whose busy life had to be lived in the same twenty-four hour period as her own. The Frobishers were leaving for Europe the next day. Gwen wanted to have a buyer in place before they returned. But ballet and basketball, dinners and driving duty took as much of her time as ever. Even so, it was exhilarating to be in the race again. She loved her children, but she'd found being a stay-at-home mom claustrophobic.

"Excuse me. Miss." A breathless voice interrupted her rush to the car. It belonged to a painfully thin woman with a beak for a nose and gray hair that stuck up from her head in nest-like tufts. A loose, charcoal cardigan flapped behind her as she walked stiff-legged up the sidewalk like a sandpiper racing before a wave.

"Are you the agent?" she asked.

"I am *an* agent," Gwen answered.

"I mean the agent, the Frobishers' agent?"

"Yes, I have the listing."

The woman studied Gwen with beady eyes that were neither brown nor hazel. "I just wanted you to know I'll be keeping an eye on things for Mary Beth and Charles while they're out of town." She said the words as if Gwen were a teenager bent on partying hardy while Mom and Dad were away.

"That's a comfort," Gwen said.

"I'll be taking in the paper and the mail and making sure the gardeners don't skip days. They do that sometimes when they know people are gone. Just let the lawn go to heck in a handbasket, and figure they'll catch it up right before the owners come home." She thrust her head forward on her scrawny neck and stuck a thumb in her concave chest. "Not on my watch."

"The Frobishers are lucky to have you. I'm Gwen Bishop. You are?" Gwen donned her friendliest smile and stuck out her hand.

Maricela had taught her to find and befriend the busybody on the block. Every neighborhood had one. The busybody knew things like who was transferring across the country, who was getting a divorce, or who was planning to retire to a condo on a golf course. Nuggets of valuable information could be mined from a busybody. Gwen was pretty sure she'd struck pay dirt.

"Esther VanVlear. Been living in this neighborhood since 1969. Original owner," she said and shook hands.

"Glad to meet you, Esther," Gwen said and turned toward the street, rattling her keys for emphasis. She would have loved to talk longer, but time didn't permit. "I'm sure I'll be seeing you around."

"You will. I'm on the neighborhood watch committee. Can't be too careful. Crime is rampant." She tipped her head and gave Gwen a sidelong glance as if she was a suspect. "Rampant."

CHAPTER EIGHT

THREE DAYS LATER Gwen blew into the office to pick up her briefcase before heading to Dana Point to show the Pauls the Sailor's Haven listing for the second time. Maricela sat at her desk, unmoving.

Maricela was the most energetic person Gwen knew—a perpetual motion machine at work. Her uncharacteristic stillness brought Gwen to a stop, despite the fact she was running late.

"You okay?" she asked.

Maricela raised her eyes to Gwen's face. They were rimmed with red.

"What?" Gwen defaulted to her own worst fears and wondered if the problem lay with Maricela's daughter. "Is Julissa—"

"She's fine," Maricela said in a shaky voice. "They found another body."

The weight of Maricela's words took several seconds to fall. When they did, Gwen sat, her knees giving way.

"Who?"

"A San Clemente agent. Rachel something. They found her in her listing."

"It could be a coincidence," Gwen said without conviction.

"The police are being quiet. No details. But she was found in an empty, oceanview house. What do you want to bet she was naked and all sliced up? It's him again. I know it."

Gwen reached out a hand and squeezed her friend's arm. "Look, it's upsetting. It's bad. But forewarned is forearmed, right? We know he's out there. We can take precautions."

Maricela rested her head in her hands. "I'm scared. It feels personal. Like he's after me."

"But he's not. Who knows what he's after, but what this tells us is it isn't personal. Two different agents. Two different towns. He's an opportunist, and you and me, we're not going to give him an opportunity."

Maricela stared at her desktop without speaking.

"Look, I've got to go. I'm already late for an appointment. It's Friday. Let's go over to the Barrel and get a glass of wine tonight after work. We can talk more."

On her way to Dana Point, Gwen tried to shake off the sense of dread that followed her from the office. She needed to focus.

She wanted a strong offer on the Dana Point house before the Frobishers returned from Europe. Arnold and Etta were qualified, motivated buyers. She should be excited, but she disliked dealing with the man. She exited the San Diego Freeway onto the Coast Highway and wondered, as she often did when life was difficult, how different things might have been if she'd pursued her early dreams.

She remembered the exact moment she'd set her goal of an acting career aside.

She and Art had been engaged for two months. He was working at St. Barnabas, teaching high school English, and she was about to graduate with a degree in Drama from UC Irvine.

Gwen was performing in a montage of one-act plays at the college. Art attended. After the event, he took her out for a late dinner at a pub near the campus theater.

Gwen didn't notice his mood immediately. She was excited, riding the adrenaline high she always felt after a performance. But after receiving only monosyllabic responses to her enthusiasm, she stopped talking and looked more closely at him. Art loved to discuss all forms of literature, but tonight he was silent.

"Are you sick?" she asked.

"No," he said.

"What's with you then?"

"Hmph."

"Didn't you like the show? I thought you'd love it. There was humor, but it was thoughtful. When you realize, at the end, that the old man in the wingback chair is really the little boy from the first vignette, I mean, that got you didn't it? It got me when I read the script."

"Yeah, it was good."

"It was good? That's it? I thought it was borderline brilliant."

"Right." Art almost snapped at her. Art never snapped at her.

"Okay, maybe not brilliant, but the best thing we did all year," Gwen said, hurt.

A stony silence dropped between them. The waitress, a girl Gwen knew from the Dance department, walked up to the table with feet locked in first position. She placed burgers in front of them.

"How was the play?" she asked and leaned onto one leg so the other toe could rise to full pointe.

"Great, it went great." Gwen beamed an exaggerated smile in her direction.

"I'm coming tomorrow night," the waitress said. "I have to write papers about three live performances this semester."

Gwen waited until the waitress sashayed away. "Are you going to tell me what's wrong, or do I have to guess?"

Art looked her in the eye for the first time since they'd sat down. "I don't think I can do this."

"Do what?" A cold finger poked at Gwen's stomach. She pushed her burger into the center of the table.

"I know it's silly. Not sophisticated. Small minded."

"What is?"

Art drew designs in his ketchup with a French fry for an annoying number of minutes before he said, "I hate watching you kiss other guys."

It wasn't what she expected. Gwen had thought he was going to break up with her, ask for the ring back. In many ways, she felt he was too good to be true and maybe too good for her. He was smart, handsome, kind and five years older— just old enough to engender a schoolgirl crush. But this, this she didn't know what to do with.

"But, you've been to my perfor—"

"I know. That's why it's so miserable of me to say this now. I've known all along you want to be an actress. It's just... well, everybody wants to be an actor, you know?"

"So, you didn't think I would make it? Is that what you're saying?" Gwen's voice rose. A couple at the next table glanced over.

"No, honestly, I guess I didn't, or maybe I hoped you wouldn't. But, tonight, you were so good."

Gwen softened. "Thank you for your half-assed compliment, I think."

"That movie we saw Thursday, the love scenes, the actors were all over each other. I put you in that bed and me in the audience. I couldn't stand it, watching you rolling around naked with some buff actor. It was the first time I thought about it."

"I won't do nude scenes. I told you that," Gwen said, trying to lighten the mood.

Art's eyes lifted to her face, "Technically, it wasn't a nude scene. We couldn't see anything with them lying on top of each other."

Gwen nodded. Technically, he was right. "I couldn't work if I refused romantic parts, unless all I did was TV commercials."

Art looked hopeful.

"That's not going to happen." Gwen shut him down.

"You could teach," Art said. "St. Barnabas has a Drama teacher. She runs the school plays."

Gwen wasn't sure how she felt about that. She wanted to be in the spotlight, not buried backstage. But the conversation turned to their post-wedding plans, and she was saved from having to comment. As Art talked, an understanding of his vision of marriage and family dawned on her.

She got it. Frequent trips to L.A. for a soap opera role in which her character jumped from steamy bed to steamy bed didn't fit the plan. She also realized a good man—the kind of man she wanted—would be protective, would cherish her but would struggle with seeing her embrace another man, even if the passion was only pretend

In that moment, she loved him more than ever. The shallowness of tinsel town became so obvious; she wondered why she hadn't seen it sooner. Gwen graduated with her degree in Drama, but other than directing the church Christmas pageant each year, she never used it. She'd had Jason a year after they were married and settled into a life without acting.

Gwen turned onto Sailor's Haven Drive and pulled up to the curb in front of the house. Most days weren't as hard as today, and most of her clients weren't as difficult as old Arnie, she reminded herself. Real Estate wasn't a bad gig, and some of the acting techniques she'd used came in handy.

Over the years, she'd learned something about herself. She'd learned her chosen profession wasn't as important to her as success. She also knew it was more likely to get to the top of the real estate ladder than it would have been to climb Hollywood's slippery slopes.

The Pauls' rental car was already in the driveway. Great. She was ten minutes late, and sure she'd hear about it. The driver side door opened and Arnold unfolded himself from the compact vehicle. Gwen walked wide, around the passenger side, so she wouldn't interfere with Etta's exit, but the door didn't open.

"I thought you said three o'clock." Arnold Paul raised an eyebrow above his bifocals.

"I'm so sorry, traffic..." Gwen gave him her brightest smile.

"Well, let's take another look. Shall we?" He marched toward the front door. Gwen peeked through the tinted windows of the car on her way past. Empty.

"Where's Etta today?" she asked.

"At the hotel. Migraine," he answered.

Gwen popped the key from the lockbox and opened the front door. She shouldn't be entering the property with Arnold, alone. Especially after the conversation she'd just had with Maricela. There had been two Realtors murdered in Orange County in as many months. This was foolish.

What was she going to do about it now, though? After putting up with Arnold's insults and condescension, she'd be damned if she would risk losing the fruit of her labors. He was interested in this house. If he purchased it, not only would she have a buyer before the Frobishers returned home, but she would double her profit having both the buyer and the seller as clients.

The door closed behind Arnold, snuffing out the noises of the street and leaving the house dim and quiet. Gwen flicked a hall switch on and fumbled in her purse for her phone. She planned to text Lance. Even though she felt silly doing it, she'd promised Maricela she'd get on board with the safety buddy program. Her cell was buried somewhere in the bottom of her bag.

Arnold shoved past her into the living room and began examining the woodwork. Gwen didn't think he'd find anything wrong with this house, but you never knew with someone like him. He could ferret out flaws in the *Mona Lisa*. She gave up trying to find her phone and walked over to the beautiful, bright windows.

"The view is wonderful, isn't it? You don't find harbor views in this price range very often," Gwen said.

Arnold came up behind her to take it in. He stood close. Too close. His hot breath crawled across her shoulders. Gwen's pulse quickened.

Silly. Arnold didn't even live in California, and the chances of there being two murderers with a penchant for real estate agents was too much of a coincidence. Still. She slid past him and moved toward the kitchen.

"I wish Etta was here," Gwen said, and meant it. "I forgot to show her the oven yesterday. It's convection. That's a big plus if you like to bake. Does Etta bake?" Etta didn't look like a baker, she was too thin and spindly to be a cookie devotee, but Gwen wanted to keep the conversation going.

"Poorly," he said, opened the oven door and looked inside. "Is this the fan here?"

"Yes," Gwen said without coming close enough to see it.

Arnold flipped the door shut with a bang. "I want to see the bedrooms again. I need to make sure all our furniture will fit."

Gwen dropped her purse onto a side table holding a vase of dead roses at the foot of the stairs. The yellow petals, crumbled and fallen, looked like old lace on its dark lacquer. Gwen made a mental note to toss them when she came down.

"I saw a house I liked in San Clemente with another agent a couple of days ago. It's a strong possibility." Arnold sniffed.

Gwen's first response to that news was indignation. You didn't run an agent all around town one day, then look at homes with another agent the next. Then, on the sixth riser, she froze. He rested a hand on her back, probably to stop himself from colliding with her. San Clemente?

Hadn't Maricela said that agent was killed in a San Clemente listing the day before yesterday? And hadn't Arnold told her he was in town looking at houses in Laguna last week? That would put him in the right place at the right time for both murders.

She jerked away from his touch and sprinted up the last of the stairs. He followed with heavy footfalls. Gwen stood on the landing with her back pressed against the hallway wall.

"Which way is the master again?" he asked.

Gwen pointed. He looked at her with unreadable, reptilian eyes for a moment then walked the way she'd directed.

What had she been thinking to come into the house alone with him? Arnold was not a nice man. He was rude and demeaning. An egotist. His wife had been cowed and bullied until she was nothing but a wraith.

"Do you know the square footage in here?" He stuck his head through the bedroom doorway.

"No. No, not exactly, but I have that information at the office. Maybe we should—"

"I drove all the way down here to see this place again," he interrupted her. "I'm surprised you didn't come prepared."

Gwen bit back a retort. She felt the anger that percolated under Arnold's dissatisfied facade. She didn't want to fuel it. He huffed into the bedroom.

Anxiety slicked Gwen's palms. She rubbed them on her skirt. The idea he was the killer was absurd. *Shake it off, Gwen. Shake it off.*

If she even hinted that she was suspicious, he was sure to be offended. He was the kind of person who'd buy the San Clemente house instead of this one just to spite her. Then how would she feel? Losing a deal over nothing.

Gwen went as far as the master bedroom doorway and leaned on the jamb. She wiggled one foot in her pump and wondered how quickly she could kick her shoes off if she needed to run.

Arnold went into the bathroom. She could hear him turning on the tap, opening and closing the medicine cabinet, vanity drawers, and cupboard doors.

The Frobishers' things were still in there. Gwen knew she should follow him in and ask that he respect the owners' privacy, but she couldn't. Entering that small, close space with him was unthinkable. She licked her lips with a dry tongue. Her phone. She'd left it in her purse on the table downstairs.

"This'll work." He exited the bath. "Let's look at the smaller bedrooms. I'm planning to use one as an office."

It was his turn to gesture forward. Gwen had no choice but to walk down the narrow hall in front of him.

She almost jogged, but Arnold's long strides ate up the space between them.

"I like backsides." His voice was gruff.

Gwen leaped through the doorway she'd just reached and spun around to face him. Her heart rate went wild. What did he mean "backsides"? Her backside?

The room must have been one of the Frobishers' children's. They'd never redecorated. An old brass bed topped with a patchwork quilt took up most of the space. The framed posters on the walls were of things a young girl might enjoy: a Monet waterlily print, the feet of a dancer on full *pointe,* a kitten tangled in a ball of pink yarn.

Gwen scanned the space for a weapon. There was a lamp on a side table topped with a frilled shade. Like everything else in the room, it looked delicate. She needed something sturdier, wood or metal. Something blunt.

Arnold slipped a hand into his jacket pocket. Did he have a gun? A knife? He'd gone through the bathroom cabinets. Could he have found a straight razor? Gwen's mind filled with the memory of Sondra Olsen's bloodied corpse.

She heard the whine of a siren in the distance, and her chest tightened. No one was coming to her rescue. No one knew she was here with this man. She hadn't even told Maricela.

Stupid. Stupid. Stupid.

Gwen sidled along the edge of the bed toward the lamp with the lacy shade mumbling a prayer under her breath. She promised God she'd become more thoughtful, more cautious, that she'd slow down if only...

"The back side of a house is always quieter," he said. "I find street noise so distracting when I work." And out of Arnold's pocket came a tape measure.

CHAPTER NINE

"SO, WAIT, YOU WERE GOING to hit him over the head with a lamp?" Maricela asked, eyes wide over her wine glass.

"It was all I could find," Gwen said. "I almost fainted. I was so relieved when I saw that tape measure come out of his pocket."

"What did he say? He liked your butt?" Caroline had squeezed up to the table next to Maricela.

It was happy hour at The Leaky Barrel, a wine shop and tasting room a few doors down from Humboldt. It wasn't the most elegant spot in town—too dark and dim. It had been decorated to look like an old sailing vessel. Everything was lined with wood: wood shelving, wood floors, wood paneling on the little bit of wall visible between bottles. Gwen half-expected to feel the sway of waves beneath her feet when she stepped through the doorway. After a few glasses of wine, the illusion was known to cause seasickness. But it was convenient, and it was a Friday night tradition.

"No, I thought that's what he was saying. He said," Gwen lowered her voice in a fair imitation of the now infamous Arnold Paul, "'I like backsides.'"

A loud gong announced Lance's entrance. A ship's bell—large and brass and covered in a green patina as if it had been exposed to the elements for years—was affixed to the front door of the shop. It was another affectation; one Gwen found annoying.

Lance walked across the weathered floorboards toward the women. "What's so funny?" He glanced at their smiling faces.

Most of the regulars from the office had filtered into the Barrel between 5:00 and 5:30 to enjoy their T.G.I.F. celebration. It was now quarter past six, and their first glasses of wine had taken effect. Camaraderie flowed like the libations. The week's victory stories were more impressive, and the jokes were funnier. Humboldt agents had become "us," their clients, "them". Gwen wondered why she'd hadn't done this more often.

"Gwen thought the Real Estate Killer was after her," Maricela said.

"But it turns out he just wanted to measure her hips." Caroline giggled.

One-half of Lance's mouth turned up, and he raised his eyebrows at Gwen.

"It was nothing. That Chicago couple I've been carting around wanted to see my Dana Point listing again, but only the husband showed up. I let my imagination run away with me."

"Wait a minute," Lance said and raised a finger to summon the proprietor. "What happened to the buddy system?"

"I didn't have time—"

"She didn't think," Maricela said. "She's very impetuous. She's like my daughter, Julissa, always getting into trouble then telling me, 'Mama, I didn't know.' But, Julissa has an excuse. She's fifteen, not almost—"

"What was I supposed to do?" Gwen interrupted before Maricela mentioned her age. A vanity maybe, but she was feeling self-conscious about her fortieth right around the corner. "He was at my elbow the entire time. And he's very sensitive—not a chip on his shoulder, a two-by-four. I could see it, 'Excuse me, Mr. Paul, I need to call my office just in case you're a murderer. Can you hold up a minute?'"

"Mo, can I have another merlot please," Caroline said when the wine shop owner came over with Lance's glass.

"And are we having the Braided Vine or the Adele Cellar?" he asked.

"I had the Braided, but which do you like best?" Caroline asked and fluttered her eyelashes. Mo sniffed and pulled out the Adele Cellar.

Caroline was interested, Gwen thought with amusement. But why not? She was only a little younger than the man was. Gwen wondered what he'd look like without the omnipresent ship captain's cap he wore. His features were nice enough. He wasn't her type, but he had a refined way about him she imagined was attractive to some.

"I put an app on Julissa's phone," Maricela told Lance. "She turns it on, and I know where she is. She's very worried about appearances. She doesn't want to have to check in with me in front of the other kids."

"Ooh, I should get that. But who'd care where I was?" Caroline's expression went from excited to depressed in three seconds flat.

"So it works? You can keep track of her?" Lance leaned over Maricela's phone, and she showed him the features.

His profile was almost perfect. It reminded Gwen of a Greek bust she'd seen at the Getty Museum. If she were a director, she'd cast him as a young Caesar, or Pericles, or even an older Romeo.

He glanced up at her. She realized she'd been staring, jumped up and walked to the bar. Mo acknowledged her with a nod. She ordered more Cabernet. She hadn't been planning to have another, but it was the first deflection that came to mind. Now she would have to stay, not only until it was drunk, but also until she wasn't.

It didn't matter. Art wasn't going to be home until late. He and the kids were going to a school concert, then out for pizza. Gwen felt a little guilty she hadn't attended, but she'd promised Maricela she'd meet her for a glass of wine. Besides, she was making a point by her absence.

If Art wanted to be *el presidente* of St. Barnabas, God bless him. She didn't plan to be *la primera dama*. Her mother had been her father's wingman, the wind beneath his wings, his guardian angel, whatever. He'd had many names for her. All lovely. But none of them stopped him from abandoning her when a younger cherub flew into his life. Art would have to accept that he and she were a team with different, but equal, roles.

"So you were almost strangled with a tape measure." A warm voice close to her ear startled her.

"That seems a fitting death for a Realtor." Lance sat on the stool next to her.

"Better for an interior designer."

"True." He nodded. "I guess if I were going to kill an agent, I'd suffocate her under a mountain of paperwork."

"Or bludgeon her with a 'For Sale' sign," Gwen said.

"Seriously, though, that was a pretty stupid thing you did today, if you'll forgive me for saying so."

"Yes, but I want this deal. And," Gwen lifted her glass in a toast, "it looks like I'm going to get it."

Lance didn't return the gesture. "But what if he'd been the guy?"

Gwen shrugged. Since the shock and fear had worn off, the whole event seemed more humorous than dangerous. "What if you get hit by lightning when you leave here tonight? That's more likely than me becoming the Real Estate Killer's next victim."

"Lightning just struck twice in the same county." Lance sipped his wine.

That was another thing that annoyed Gwen about Lance; he always had to have the last word. A bubble of laughter burst at a high top table where the Humboldt agents sat. She slid off her stool and wandered over to the group.

"So I shove the panties under the bed with my foot while I try to distract my client with the view out the bedroom window, which, believe me, is nothing to write home about. I think she thought I was a nut case," John Gordon said.

Caroline, Maricela and two other women from the office laughed.

"You should have seen the backyard of the house I showed two weeks ago," Maricela said. "I never take people to a house I haven't previewed, but I had a busy week, and... well, anyway, the whole yard was covered in pink flamingos and dog crap. *Que lio*. The lady of the house had four Chihuahuas. I guess the flamingos were there to keep them company or something."

The-worst-thing-I've-ever-seen-in-a-house was a popular game among real estate agents, but Gwen was surprised it was being played tonight. Time hadn't had a chance to smudge the stark edges of their recent discovery. Gallows humor boosted bravado she guessed.

"The most terrible experience I ever had, hands down, was the cockroach house," Caroline said, and smiled at Mo as he handed her another glass of wine. She was on a roll.

"You win." Gwen groaned and placed her hands over her ears. "Please don't tell that story again. I don't even like to think about it."

"That's right, you're cockroach-phobic," Caroline said, pretending she'd totally forgotten. "Tell you what, I won't talk about it if you cover my bar tab." She smiled sweetly.

"I haven't heard it," John said. "How do I know if it's worse than my panties if I don't get to hear it?"

"Trust me," Gwen said. "It's worse than a pair of panties on the floor."

"They weren't clean."

"Yuck, and it's still worse."

"Caroline's on her third glass of wine. That's a lot of money to cough up." John's words were fuzzy. It sounded like he'd had more than three himself.

Several nasty comments popped into Gwen's mind. Before she had a chance to choose the perfect one, Lance appeared at her side. "Tell you what, John. I'll pay Caroline's bill if I don't have to hear about it. I'm with Gwen. I can't stand cockroaches."

John's jaw jutted forward. "You can't leave it alone, can you? Always gotta be the guy. The guy with the ladies."

"Come on, John. That was uncalled for."

"Seriously." John's "s's" slurred together. "You got like a Prince Charming complex or something? It's getting under my skin."

"Hey. Sorry. I haven't been trying to get under your skin." Lance's voice was soothing. He pulled his phone from his pocket and began typing.

"No." John pushed away from the table and swayed on his feet. "Not my skin. The ladies' skin. That's what you want to get under."

"Shut up, John," Caroline said.

"Whassa matter? You got the hots for Lancey boy? Little young for you, wouldn't you say?" John walked to the bar and slapped down his credit card. "Mo, my man, I wanna pay. It's getting stuffy in here."

Lance reached John in two long strides. "You owe Caroline an apology."

"I owe Mo some money."

"You're making a fool of yourself."

"Yeah? Well, least I don't make my living on my knees," John said.

Lance became as still as stone except for the clenching of his right fist. Gwen took a step toward the men. What she was planning to do if a fight broke out, she didn't know. Lance's hand jutted forward. Gwen flinched, but he didn't hit John. Instead, he snatched the credit card off the bar and stuffed it into John's shirt pocket. "An Uber is on its way. Let's go wait outside." Lance gripped the other man's arm and steered him toward the door.

John yanked away and held both hands up in mock surrender. "I'm flattered, but, sorry, you're not my type."

"You need to leave," Lance said.

"I was on my way."

"You're not in any condition to drive."

"Doesn't your flock of hens keep you busy enough? You gotta be all up in my business too?"

Mo came around the bar and placed himself between the men. "You can’t drive, John. Sorry. But my license is on the line."

For a moment John tensed as if he was readying himself for a battle, then realizing he was outnumbered, or maybe that they were right, his shoulders slumped. He got the Uber info and slammed out the door. The brass bell clanged a jarring note.

Nobody said anything for a long moment. Caroline broke the silence. "Talk about a buzz kill. I guess I'm headed home to the cat."

Lance put a hand on her shoulder. "Sorry."

"Hey, it's not your fault. Wife left him for another guy last year. He's mad at the world."

Gwen hadn't known that. All she'd known about John was that he was difficult, prickly and proud. And, she didn't like him much.

Lance handed his credit card to Mo. "Take care of the table."

"You don't have to do that," Gwen said.

"I feel like I kind of ruined everybody's evening."

"How was this your fault?"

"I know how John feels about me. I shouldn't have gotten involved. Should have let Mo handle things."

"You were chivalrous, defending Caroline's honor." Gwen was surprised to hear herself defend him.

"And protecting you from cockroaches. Don't forget that."

Gwen laughed. "Right. How could I forget?"

"You can't if I keep reminding you."

"Ready to go?" Maricela hefted her purse strap over her shoulder. "I'll walk you to your car."

"Sure." Gwen smiled once more at Lance.

She pulled her jacket closer around herself when she hit the cold, night air. "It's funny how you think you know someone, but you don't know them at all."

"I know. I was so surprised to hear about John's wife. It makes me... I don't know. I'm not making excuses for him, but I'm sorry for him. I know how it feels to be cheated on," Maricela said.

Gwen looked at her. "Right. That. It does explain things. But, I didn't mean John."

"No?"

"No. I was talking about Lance. I think there's actually a nice guy beneath that handsome exterior. That whole hero thing he did tonight—it made me look at him in a new light."

CHAPTER TEN

ENZO'S WAS CROWDED. The warmth, the noise, the smell of garlic and tomato enveloped Art as he entered the sports bar. He and the kids made their way across the black and white checked linoleum floor to an empty table near the back.

"I want a calzone," Tyler said, sliding into the booth.

"You always want a calzone. Why can't you just eat pizza?" Jason sat next to him.

"I want cheese pizza. No pepperoni." Emily made a puke face when she said the word pepperoni.

Jason poked Tyler. "If we share a pepperoni pizza then Emily can have a little one all to herself."

"Enough." Art felt like a single dad. He was left alone to deal with the kids more and more often, and tonight he was out of patience. He'd needed Gwen with him at that concert, needed her not just as a prop, as she described her role, but as a co-parent. If it hadn't been for Lorelei the evening would have been a disaster.

He was standing on the stage in the auditorium introducing the performance in front of several hundred parents and the entire board of directors when out of the corner of his eye, he saw Jason slap Tyler in the head. He'd left the kids alone in the third row with threats of dire consequences if they got out of line while he was gone.

He stumbled on his words, but then saw Tyler's mouth opened in a silent scream. No harm done. He'd deal with Jason later. He regained his composure, but then saw his second son pull a harmonica from his pocket, wiggle up close to Jason's ear, and fill his cheeks for what could only be a blast of hurricane proportions.

Art lifted a hand as if he could stop Tyler from where he stood, when Lorelei, God bless her, reached over the seat and snagged the instrument from his grasp. She kept a hand on each of his son's shoulders while Art hurried through the rest of his address.

A harried waitress in black jeans and a gray Enzo's T-shirt ran up to the table, pulled a pencil from behind her ear and said, "What can I get you, Mr. Bishop?"

"Hey, Carrie," Art said. Carrie'd graduated from St. Barnabas two years ago and was working her way through college as a server. "One large pizza, half pepperoni, half plain cheese."

"Dad..." Tyler started to say, but Art stopped him with a no-arguments look.

"How's school going?" Art asked Carrie as she scribbled their order on a pad.

"Crazy busy. Mid-terms. I have to write a paper after my shift tonight." She pushed a stray, black hair into her ponytail.

"Sounds like you're keeping out of trouble anyway," Art said.

"I try." She smiled.

"Work going well? You guys are pretty busy." Art looked around the crowded room.

"It's okay. We're all still kind of shook up."

It was a strange comment. "Shook up?"

"Because of Olivia's kid."

Art was confused.

"Getting hit by a truck." She lowered her eyes.

The din of the restaurant faded as Art focused on the girl standing in front of him. He was sure he'd heard the words wrong. Her statement made no sense.

"What are you talking about?"

"Brian, Olivia Richard's little boy. He's in third grade at St. Barnabas." Carrie shifted her weight from one foot to the other and looked up the row of tables.

"I know Brian," Art said.

Carrie gave a small nod to another table and spoke quickly. "I was sure you'd heard. He was in a hit and run earlier this evening. I guess he was suspended from school. Olivia had to come into work and couldn't find a sitter. He was supposed to stay in the house, but he went out on his skateboard..."

Cold seeped into Art's veins. Brian, the terror of the third-grade playground. Brian, the only kid in grammar school who'd stand up to Dwayne Pratt. Brian, whose small, defiant face had peered over his desk at him only a few days ago. Carrie must be mistaken.

"The cops came to the restaurant to tell Olivia. It was pretty awful." She paused. "I'd better go put in your order."

As she moved from the table, Art caught her hand. "How bad is it?"

She stood and looked at him for a moment before responding. He could see her measuring her words, choosing carefully before she spoke. "I don't think they know much yet. I guess it's serious."

His thinking became sluggish. He rested the weight of his head in his hands and stared at the red Formica tabletop visible between his fingers. It looked like blood.

CHAPTER ELEVEN

GWEN JUMPED. The stupid bell with its heavy clapper reverberated through her skull. She was still recovering from her extra glass of wine the night before. Today was Valentine's Day and she'd meant to pick up a few bottles, but all the tension between John Gordon and Lance had driven it from her mind.

Afternoon light from a picture window fell in beams on the bar spotlighting the owner. He spoke into a phone but wiggled his fingers at her in acknowledgment. She walked over to a wall of red wines. Most of the time when she shopped here, Mo followed her from shelf to shelf giving her more information than she wanted about his wares. It was a relief to wander without the education.

What should she bring Maricela? A pinot? She ran her finger over a row of pinot noirs. Maricela's daughter, Julissa, was Emily's favorite babysitter. She was old enough to be responsible, but not old enough to be boy crazy. Usually, she came to Gwen and Art's house, but tonight Emily was spending the night at the Alvarez home. Julissa would take cash. Maricela wouldn't, but she never looked a gift bottle of wine in the mouth.

Jason had an overnight event with his youth group from church, and Tyler was invited to a sleepover at a friend's house. Realizing two of her three children were away on Valentine's Day night, Gwen called Julissa. She and Art had been fighting so much lately, she wanted to make amends, make the evening special.

She selected a pinot noir for Maricela then turned down the aisle with the red blends. She picked out two bottles of her favorite, a Meritage from a small vineyard on the Central Coast. It wasn't easy to find. The Leaky Barrel was the only place that carried it locally. The name was appropriate considering the effect it had on Art the last time they'd shared a bottle. It was called Ravish.

She remembered that night well, because it was also the last time she and Art had sex. Things had been rocky between them for at least a year. The busier she got at work, the more they argued. But somehow, at least two or three times a month, they'd scheduled a date night, made up and made love.

Once he took on the principal job, it seemed they had no time to do anything but argue. And, the arguments were worse. He expected her to support his career decision, even though he hadn't consulted her about it. And, he wanted her to scale back her career, which was just beginning to take off. He seemed to think she should drop everything whenever he needed her as arm candy on campus. She didn't expect him to hold her hand at Humboldt.

But, she missed him. She missed the closeness, the friendship. She could count on one hand the number of times they'd had sex since September. She wanted to roll back the clock. Reconnect. She loved Art even though they weren't seeing eye to eye. She believed he loved her.

Valentine's Day seemed the perfect time to offer him an olive branch. She'd bought his favorite finger foods and planned a picnic in the living room in front of the fireplace. That had been their rendezvous spot for years, until Jason walked in on them one night.

Art was a lowly English teacher then, and he couldn't get enough of her. They hadn't been indecent, just making out like a couple of kids. They'd made lighthearted jokes about it scarring their son for life. They'd laughed about it with close friends. They acted like it was nothing, but they'd boxed up their love life in the four walls of their bedroom after that. Now it was gasping for oxygen.

Gwen brought her purchases to the front of the shop. "Anything else?" The owner smiled. His front teeth were too small in for his incisors. It made his face look like Rocket's when the kids got too close to his rawhide bone.

"Just these." Gwen put her bottles on the counter.

"A lovely blend and it ages well. It's a particular favorite of mine," he said when he rang up the Ravish.

"Yes, it's very good."

"You know what they say, wine and women improve with age."

The words struck Gwen like a slap. She took her bag from his outstretched hand, turned on her heel and walked out the door. Her fortieth birthday was fast approaching, March fifth. Less than a month away. Every reminder filled her with a sense of dread.

She knew it was because of what happened on her mother's fortieth. Gwen told herself over and over, her life wasn't like her mother's. *She* wasn't like her mother.

What happened to her mother couldn't happen to her. She wouldn't allow it to. But the feeling of impending doom persisted.

Her mother had cooked her own birthday dinner that night—chicken, baked potatoes and broccoli. Gwen's father never took them out. He always said, why eat in a restaurant when the best chef in the county lived in his own house. That made her mom smile, but Gwen thought secretly she'd have enjoyed a meal out once in a while.

For dessert, her mother made her famous chocolate layer cake. Gwen bought a pack of candles with her allowance on her way home from school, sneaked into the kitchen during dinner and placed four on its top. Her mother had been so surprised when she'd carried the flaming cake into the dining room singing Happy Birthday at the top of her lungs. It was the last time Gwen could remember seeing her look truly happy.

Later when Gwen got in bed, her parents each came into her room separately to tuck her in. One of the things that stood out most in her memory was how unusually affectionate her father had been. He'd kissed her forehead, smoothed her hair, and told her she was special to him before turning out the light. After he had closed the door, Gwen burrowed under her covers with a flashlight and a book.

She'd only read a chapter when she heard her parents' voices rumbling through the ceiling. Her mother's timbre was what first alerted her something wasn't right. It was louder, more piercing, than her usual peaceful tones. Gwen lay still for several minutes listening to the rise and fall of their discussion before throwing off her covers. She needed to know what they were talking about.

She perched at the top of the stairs where she could hear their words clearly. "Please don't cry. It won't do any good. I've made my decision," her father said.

"How long? How long has this been going on?" Her mother's voice broke with anguish.

"It doesn't matter."

"It matters to me."

How long had what been going on? Gwen couldn't imagine what they were talking about, but a stab of fear ran through her.

"We've been seeing each other for several months. Long enough for me to know how I feel about her."

"So, you're just leaving? Abandoning me and Gwen?"

Gwen sucked in a breath. Abandoning? The word belonged in novels and Disney movies. It had nothing to do with her, with her life.

"Certainly not." Her father's voice was chiding. It was the same tone he used with Gwen when she disobeyed. "I'm not the kind of man who shirks his responsibilities. You know that. I'll take care of all your financial needs. You and Gwen will never do without."

"Only without you." Her mother sounded so sad.

Gwen crept to her bed, crawled under the covers and cried herself to sleep. The recurring nightmare she had so often back then visited her that night with renewed intensity. She woke screaming.

CHAPTER TWELVE

THE VIEW WAS STUNNING—her word, not mine. She stood in front of the large picture window and raised an upturned palm to the sparkling ocean beyond like Vanna White offering a vowel.

"Million dollars, that's what it is." She smiled. The sunlight behind her turned her hair into a halo of gold. I didn't gasp this time, but took it as heavenly confirmation of the decision I'd already made.

"Million dollars, at least," I agreed.

"Would you like to see the rest of the house?"

"Most definitely."

I followed her through the great room into an ocean of granite. She pointed out a breakfast nook, and down a short hall to a laundry room and maid's quarters. *"Everybody Ought To Have a Maid"*, that old Broadway title played through my head.

She must have assumed cooking was beneath me, because the kitchen only received a flap of her hand. I, however, recently discovered I wasn't too bad at slicing and dicing. An assortment of knives on a butcher's block caught my attention. I just had time to find one with a nice heft and pocket it before she rushed me onward.

The dining room was empty except for a chandelier as big as a freighter that marked where the table should go. The thought crossed my mind that I should take her here, under that showstopper of a lamp. It would be so theatrical, so Hollywood. The setting should fit the crime and ostentatious was the word this wheel was spelling.

If there was ever a town that deserved the moniker, Newport Beach, California, was it. When Ms. White pulled up the paved drive in her powder blue BMW—vanity plate "HERBEEMR"—took her Louis Vuitton bag from the passenger seat, and graced me with her beautiful set of ivories, I almost laughed in her face.

She was another gorgon.

Another grasping chit.

Not even the abundance of makeup she wore could conceal her lust for status, her need for significance. The listing was just what you'd expect her to represent. Ostentation was carved into the little-boy-peeing fountain in the front yard and the ivy scrollwork on the huge front doors. The word echoed through all the empty, cavernous rooms and swam in the infinity pool in the backyard. I hated it almost as much as I hated her.

The click of her heels on the hardwood floor grew softer. I had to hurry to catch up.

"The game room is really the best spot in the house in my humble opinion," she said.

I doubted she considered any of her opinions humble.

She walked to the dead center of the space and spun toward me. Her beige skirt billowed. Her deceitfully pretty face devolved into a scowl when she noticed I had been lagging and almost missed the performance.

It was a fine room. Windows lined both west and north facing walls. You could see up the coast for miles. It reminded me of the living room in my father's house.

She was off, down a hall and halfway up the stairs, her non-stop talk trailing behind her like steam. "The master suite is directly above the game room. It is my second favorite space in the house. It has a fireplace too, and the balcony is to die for."

Interesting choice of words. We toured the guest suites, none of which was very inspiring, then descended another set of stairs into a wide hall. The first door led into a library.

One wall was covered in floor to ceiling bookshelves, another with a heavy, mahogany mantled fireplace. The room was too Agatha Christie for my taste. Who-done-its aren't really about murder. They are about the cleverness of detectives, not something I was interested in thinking about at the moment.

After passing a sunroom and a music room, we walked into a theater. It was all done up in maroons and golds like an old time cinema. There were no windows. The only light came from wall sconces that made long shadows of us as we marched toward the small stage. It was the perfect place to make a dramatic statement.

"Amos Johnston, the man who commissioned the house, wanted this theater built for family performances as well as to watch movies—hence the stage," Ms. White informed. "His children were dancers and musicians."

"Do you dance?" I asked. My father's daughter—my half-sister, Fiona—danced in college. Something in the way this woman moved reminded me of her.

She spun toward me in a graceful pirouette. "Not really." Her voice faltered. "Well, that's about it. Only the garden left. We can exit at the end of the hall." She gestured the way we'd come.

"But I'd love to see you dance. Won't you mount the platform for me, Ms. White?"

"White? My name is Purcell, Christina Purcell."

"Yes, of course. It was only a joke."

"The exit is behind you." Her voice lost some of its refinement. A Mid-Western lilt lifted the final words of her statement.

I blocked her way. "The stage is behind you." I detected a whiff of fear hiding in the cloud of perfume floating around her.

"Now, this isn't funny, mister. I'm a married woman and not interested in any shenanigans."

Michigan or maybe Wisconsin? It's odd how people revert to the accents of their youths when they're afraid.

"But I love shenanigans." I took the knife from my jacket pocket and pointed it toward the platform. "Dance."

CHAPTER THIRTEEN

ART CLOSED HIS OFFICE DOOR BEHIND HIM. The halls of St. Barnabas were quiet on Saturdays. He didn't like working on weekends, but he had a report due the next morning for the weekly board meeting. Weekends were the only time he was able to focus on big projects without constant interruption. He'd finished just in time. It was 6:02. He'd promised Gwen he'd be home by 6:30 so he could take Jason to church.

He jogged down the central staircase and out the front doors, locking them behind him. When he entered the parking lot, he slowed. Across the blacktop, he could see the round form of Donald Pratt standing under a street lamp with Amy Partridge, president of the Parent Teacher Association. There had been a basketball game in Santa Ana against a rival school late that afternoon. They both had sons on the team and must be waiting for the bus to return.

Art didn't need this. Not now. He never made it past Donald without being lassoed by a string of questions.

"Speak of the devil," Donald roared when Art stepped into the circle of light. Donald had one volume—loud.

"All good things, I hope." Art walked a little faster.

"We were just talking about the McKibben boy's accident. Terrible thing. We were hoping you didn't feel responsible in any way. His suspension was absolutely necessary. My Dwayne was terrorized. We can't allow bullies to rule the playground."

Donald's praise burned. Art did feel responsible. He'd given that particular punishment all by himself. He should have hauled both boys into the office and dealt with Dwayne as well as Brian. He could have sent them to detention for a week, together. Made them shake hands, try to get along. But, no. He was too anxious to please and appease the board. Condemnation fit him like a tailor-made suit. Art mumbled goodnight and raced home.

He made it into his driveway by 6:28. He stayed in the car for a second of peace. Warm, yellow light poured from the windows of his house. He didn't want to bring bad news into that glow. Not tonight.

He'd never told Gwen about Brian's accident. She'd gotten home late last night and he'd worked all day today. Besides he hadn't wanted to bring it up around Emily. It had taken him an hour to calm her after she heard about the accident at Enzo's.

Besides Gwen always accused him of bringing his work home with him. Her schedule was hectic and unpredictable, but when she was home, she was home. He was beginning to think she was right. He did have a hard time separating St. Barnabas from the rest of his life.

It was all-consuming. It gave him purpose and significance, but it required more from him than anything else he'd ever done. It wasn't just a job; it was a ministry, a family. He even spent more time with his own children at school than he did at home. Tonight, he decided, he'd try to find the separation. He'd try to leave campus concerns on campus.

After he dropped Jason at the church, he returned home for the second time. Strains of French Cafe music met him in the entryway. He dropped his keys and wallet on a side table, petted Rocket, and entered the living room. The lights were low; a fire crackled in the fireplace. A feast of chicken salad sandwiches, strawberries, cheese, and chocolate was spread on the coffee table. A knot formed in his stomach. He was afraid romance was a language he'd forgotten how to speak.

"Hey there," Gwen said in a low voice and patted the couch. She looked beautiful. Her hair was pulled into a loose bun. She wore the blue V-neck sweater that accentuated her eyes. She'd dressed to please him, which made him even more anxious.

Art dropped next to her and accepted the glass of wine she handed him.

"The kids are gone." She smiled.

"Emily?"

"She's at Maricela's." Gwen set her glass down and wrapped her arms around his neck. "For the night." She kissed him.

He ought to be excited. The kids were gone. The air was perfumed with something he'd bought Gwen for Christmas. She was obviously in the mood. But he couldn't shake the weight of guilt he felt over Brian's accident. It rode his back like a jockey bent on a win. He downed half his wine.

Gwen handed him a plate and took one for herself. As they ate, he kept the conversation in safe territory. They talked about Gwen's listings, neighborhood gossip, funny things Emily had said that week.

Art wasn't hungry, but forced himself to eat some food between sips of wine. He poured the last of the bottle into their glasses and took a slow breath. Maybe he could relax and enjoy tonight. His problems were beginning to grow fuzzy around the edges. Gwen opened another bottle of wine.

"So," she said. "What's happening with you? What's the latest at school?"

Not good. The events of the yesterday thudded onto his shoulders. His happy buzz began to sound like the droning of bees.

"Oh," he dismissed the question with a wave of his hand. "Boring." He topped off his glass and drank deeply.

Gwen sat up straighter. He knew that posture. The droning bees became the distant ring of alarm bells. She had a sixth sense when it came to him and the kids. They could never hide things from her. "Nothing?" she said, doubt tinged her tone.

Art shook his head.

Gwen picked up one of his hands in both of hers and toyed with his fingers. "I'm worried," she said after a long, silent minute.

"About what?"

"About us."

He couldn't do this. He didn't have the emotional reserves to joist about their marriage. "There's nothing wrong with us time won't solve."

"I don't know about that." Her lips tightened.

Art removed his hand from hers, slugged the rest of his wine and poured more. He didn't want to bring up the accident, didn't want to think about it, but it slammed around in his mind. "Something happened on Friday— "

Gwen put a hand on his mouth and stopped his words. "I'm sorry I brought it up. I don't want you to stress out about work. I want tonight to be about us." She leaned over and kissed him long and deep. He responded mechanically, hoping that his body would cooperate. Hoping love or lust would kick in and override the guilt and self-recriminations that had held him hostage all weekend.

"I have a surprise for you." She pulled away, slid off the couch and left the room.

Art stared at the red liquid in his glass for several seconds, then drained it. He loved Gwen. That was something he knew to be true. He knew it like he knew the earth was round. He knew it like he knew there were craters on the moon. It was a solid fact. Factual.

His love was factual. It was academic. Not emotional. It hadn't always been that way. It might not have been that way yesterday, but tonight that's the way it was.

It was academic, and he was an academic. Maybe that was his problem. He did have a problem. That was a fact. But he couldn't quite remember what it was. His head felt heavy and full. Much too full to unravel puzzles about love and facts and problems. He leaned it against the back of the couch, closed his eyes and in moments entered a disturbed dream world.

#

Thwack. Art's foot made contact with the heavy bag. Thud, thud. Two right jabs to the ribs. Sweat trickled between his shoulder blades and down his back. Front kick to the gut. Pivot, back kick to the knee. Pivot, uppercut—chin. Left cross—cheekbone.

He could feel his tension and anger transfer to the boxing bag every time he made contact. He danced around it on light feet and volleyed six or seven surprise hits to imaginary kidneys. He'd been pummeling the sand for thirty-five minutes. Ten minutes longer than most mornings.

He welcomed the weariness that settled over his shoulders like a robe. He shook himself, grabbed a towel from his gym bag and mopped his face. He had time for two sets of reps in the weight room before heading to the office for the board meeting.

Art had never fought an actual opponent. He'd dreamed about it when he was a teenager, but understood even then it was a fantasy that would never be realized. He was a pastor's kid. Pastor's kids don't fight, not even the bullies. Pastor's kids turn the other cheek, give away jackets along with their shirts, and eat every bite of their humble pie. But kickboxing was a great workout.

He lay on the bench after pushing one-forty-five, staring at the acoustic-panel ceiling and wondered how he'd make things right with Gwen. Falling asleep on Valentine's Day when she'd tried so hard to make the evening special was probably the worst marital crime he'd ever committed.

She'd only spoken to him in monosyllables on Sunday. He'd attempted an apology at breakfast. She'd nodded, like she was only half-interested in what he was saying, then locked herself in the bathroom. This would take more than flowers and dinner dates. Those things were bandages. This rift needed stitches.

Art racked his barbell, picked up his gym bag and headed for the locker room. The hot water sluiced over him washing away the acrid smell of his sweat. Yes, they'd been having problems, but the other night wasn't about that. He wasn't punishing her for not jumping on his political bandwagon at school, regardless of what she thought.

He wasn't ready to talk to her about the real issue until he worked it out for himself, because he might have to admit she was right. Maybe the job was too important to him. Maybe it was so important it almost cost Brian McKibben his life.

While he toweled his hair and ran a comb through it, he made a decision. He'd face the problem head on. Visit Brian in the hospital. Ask his mother for forgiveness. See what he could do to make things right. Maybe then he'd know how to make things right with Gwen.

CHAPTER FOURTEEN

AFTER THE MONDAY MORNING CATTLE DRIVE to St. Barnabas, Gwen drove to the office. She threw her purse into her desk and grabbed her usual spot on the conference room wall between the potted rubber tree and Maricela. "How's it going?" she said in a hushed tone.

"Same old," Maricela said. "We're heading out to preview everyone's listings as soon as Taryn is done yelling at us for leaving the kitchen a mess."

"Not your mother, right?" Taryn said, nodding her highlighted brown head and looking around the room. "On to happier things, agent of the month. Once more it's Lance." Taryn clapped and all the female agents, except Maricela and Gwen, joined in the enthusiasm.

Lance gave a small bow. John Gordon scowled, and Eric Woo discovered something fascinating in the papers on the table in front of him.

"How does he do it?" Gwen whispered to Maricela. "He's only been here, what, eight or nine months?"

"He's got the bait, chica. You and me, we can't compete. Those housewives, they love his big brown eyes, his little dimples, his—"

"Okay, I get it," Gwen said. "But I'm surprised it doesn't bother their husbands."

Maricela raised her eyebrows suggestively. "It's women who do the shopping."

While Taryn passed out maps to the homes they'd be previewing that morning, Gwen mentally ran through her schedule. It was going to be another busy week. As soon as Taryn dismissed the meeting, Gwen scooted out the door. She wanted to check her email before the caravan left. She had several inquiries about the Sailor's Haven property to return. A hand on her arm stopped her before she made it to her desk.

"Hey there," Lance said.

"Hi." Gwen's voice came out unnaturally high.

"Just wondering if you wanted to drive together. I have something I want to talk to you about."

Gwen noted Maricela was correct, he did have dimples. Pitching her voice a bit lower, she said, "I'm going with Maricela."

"Oh, well. Next time maybe."

"But you could come with us." As soon as she said the words she wondered if she should have checked with Maricela.

"That'd be great. I'll get my briefcase."

He walked away, bouncing on the balls of his feet like an athlete, leaving the spicy scent of his cologne behind.

"What are you staring at?" Maricela asked, coming up behind her.

"Lance is going to drive with us. That's okay, right?"

Maricela's eyes widened in surprise. "Us?"

Gwen shrugged. "He has something he wants to talk to me about."

"It's okay with me." Maricela threw her purse over her shoulder and walked out the front door, hips swinging.

Twenty minutes later they entered Coto de Caza through a manned gated. Gwen described Coto to her out of town clients as a wealthy community for equestrians and others who enjoyed the ambiance of Western country living. She always pointed out the stables, horse trails, and the general store with its period cracker barrels. Personally, she thought Coto was hot, dry, and over-priced, but then she preferred the beach.

The first listing on the tour was Caroline's—a faux farmhouse with dated decor. Gwen passed through several rooms filled with oak furniture and floral prints into a terrific kitchen. The kitchen was the home's saving grace. It was large and bright and had recently been remodeled with stainless steel counters and apple red appliances.

Caroline hurried them forward into a dining room sporting a truly terrible wagon wheel chandelier, out the other side, around a mauve carpeted corner, and up a winding staircase.

"Now this is the real selling point of the house," Caroline said as ten agents filed into the master bath.

The floor and the lower half of the walls were lined in pink Carrera marble. Rose wallpaper covered everything else. Bright brass fixtures sparkled like fool's gold under lush mauve towels. A swimming-pool-sized tub stood on a raised platform. It was one of the largest, most expensive, God-awful bathrooms Gwen had ever seen.

"Horrible." Lance mouthed the word from across the room.

Gwen nodded her head in agreement.

They walked through the master bedroom together. "I have a proposition for you," Lance said. "I don't know if you know this, but I used to be in construction. Behind this smooth exterior is a pretty handy guy."

Gwen waited, wondering what he was getting at.

"It might be too soon to talk to you about this, but I previewed your Laguna Beach listing before..." He let his words trail off.

"Right," Gwen said.

"Anyway, it needs a lot of work."

"Yup." Gwen felt a familiar bristle of irritation. Why was its condition the first thing everyone noticed? Whatever happened to location, location, location?

"I don't know if you have a budget, or if the owner wants to sell as-is, but under the circumstances, I think it would move faster and for a better price if the..." He broke off for a moment, like he was searching for the correct word. "If the creep factor was reduced."

Creep factor. Thank you, Lance. She'd just begun to warm up to him a teensy-little bit, but now she was reminded why he annoyed her so much. He was full of himself. She was about to tell him so, but he spoke first.

"I'd like to offer my services. With a relatively small budget, I know I could make some cosmetic changes that would improve first impressions."

"There's not enough money to pay you and buy supplies. Besides—"

Lance cut her off. "You misunderstand. I don't want pay; I want to list the place together. Fifty-fifty. It'll take a team to move that property. And, you'll be safer, having a man around. I could show it with you. Hold open houses with you."

"What I was going to say was, it's a moot point. The house isn't on the market. It may still be an official crime scene, for all I know. But either way, the owner hasn't contacted me."

Lance frowned. "How would you feel about letting me contact him?"

"Absolutely not." Gwen couldn't believe the temerity of the man. Let him contact her client? She strode out of the house toward Maricela's car. He followed her.

"I didn't mean to upset you. I thought maybe I could move the process along. You know, maybe the owner doesn't want to get a hold of you because he thinks you're still traumatized, or something."

"She," Gwen said.

"She?"

"The owner. She's a she."

"Okay, then maybe she thinks you don't want the listing anymore."

Gwen stopped and turned toward him. He had a point. It was possible Fiona thought the subject was too sensitive to raise. She examined his eyes.

His was a hard face to judge. It was too handsome. His appearance tended to distract her from the emotional cues she caught in plainer faces. She'd read somewhere that good character and intelligence are attributed to attractive people whether they deserved it or not, while homely people are assumed to be deficient. She didn't want to fall into that trap with him.

Lance appeared to be sincere. He didn't look dishonest, or shifty. "I'll think about it," she said.

After leaving Coto de Caza, the caravan headed toward the beach. The next listing was Lance's—a tasteful, four-bedroom in an older Laguna Niguel neighborhood. While Lance gave the tour, Maricela sidled up to Gwen. "So, how was your romantic dinner on Sunday?"

"Anticlimactic," Gwen said.

Maricela cocked an eyebrow.

"He drank a bottle and a half of wine then fell asleep on the couch." Gwen flicked a piece of lint from her skirt.

"Maybe things at school aren't so good," Maricela said.

Maricela was making excuses for Art, again. He'd worked hard to get a scholarship for Julissa so she could continue at St. Barnabas after Maricela's divorce. As far she was concerned, Art could do no wrong.

Gwen shrugged. It hurt to think about Saturday night. She'd bought a new, red negligee to surprise him, but by the time she came out of the bedroom to make her grand entrance, he was snoring.

She was as attracted to her husband as the day she'd married him. He'd aged well. His blond hair had darkened to a golden brown. He'd put on weight over the years, but it suited his well-muscled, six-foot-two frame—none of which was wasted on the soccer moms of St. Barnabas.

"I don't know, Maricela. Maybe it's our jobs. Maybe it's my age. Maybe he's found somebody else, but he's just not interested anymore. It's becoming routine."

Maricela took Gwen's arm and pulled her farther away from the group into a child's pink and yellow bedroom. "When Enrique was cheating on me, he brought me flowers, jewelry, talked about vacations. He was always telling me how beautiful I was, you know? It was all an act. He was covering up his guilt. Art's crazy about you, that's why he could just fall asleep. He has a clear conscience."

"One way to tell if your husband is having an affair is if he loses interest in sex. I read it in *Cosmo*."

"Yeah, or maybe he has the flu. I'm telling you, something bad happened at school. Julissa didn't get the whole story, but she heard there was an accident."

"Why wouldn't Art tell me something like that?"

"I don't know," Maricela said. "Maybe he didn't want to upset you."

Art hadn't said anything about an accident, but of course, she hadn't given him the opportunity. She'd stopped him when he'd tried.

"Are you two planning a major remodel in the second bedroom?" Lance filled the doorway.

"We were saying if you took this wall out," Gwen gestured to the wall that faced the tree lined street, "you could put in a drive through window and sell this place to Taco Bell."

Lance smacked himself in the forehead. "Why I didn't think of that?"

The three of them headed to Maricela's car for the last stop of the day. Maybe Lance was okay. The jury was still out. Gwen wasn't about to give him Fiona's number, but at least he'd come to her. It was possible other agents were already making plans to go behind her back. She wouldn't put it past John Gordon.

Lance was right about one thing; she shouldn't wait around for Fiona to call her. She'd been procrastinating. Her feelings about the property were complicated. But no one ever got ahead by allowing emotion to dictate their actions. She'd call Fiona as soon as she returned to the office.

CHAPTER FIFTEEN

THE NEXT DAY Art pushed open the glass doors of St. Barnabas and was hit by a hot blast of wind. The Santa Ana's blowing in from the high desert brought unseasonable heat. It was a phenomena Art never grew accustomed to, even after living in Southern California for most of his adult life. One day you were wearing jackets and sweaters, the next you were sweating in shorts.

"Art." A voice stopped his descent down the school steps. He turned to see Lorelei Tanaka standing just outside the doors. Her fall of black hair, usually shining and smooth, blew in thick strands around her face.

He smiled. "What's up?"

"Just wondering how things are going with Brian McKibben. If you've heard anything. I was going to call his mother. Let her know I'm here when he's ready."

As school counselor, Lorelei would be responsible for helping Brian readjust to classes, rearrange his schedule, or find a tutor if necessary.

Art walked up the stairs to stand next to her. Several high school students congregated on the lower steps, and he didn't want his conversation translated into tweets and texts. "That's nice of you, but I think it's premature. He's in a coma."

"God. That's terrible. A lot of the kids in his class have come to my office to talk it out. They're so upset." Her pretty face looked pained.

"It's funny how different people react. Emily won't talk about it. After the initial tears, it was as if it never happened. I'm a little concerned."

"I wouldn't worry too much. We all process in our own way. She'll talk about it when she's ready." She gave him an encouraging smile.

"You actually caught me on my way to the hospital. I planned to visit after work yesterday, but Brian was rushed into an emergency surgery."

"Oh, no. What happened?"

"I don't know the details. Hemorrhage or something. I guess I'll find out."

"Olivia must be devastated," Lorelei said.

An image of Olivia Richards, doubled over with sobs, formed in his mind. He shoved it away. It was too painful to contemplate. "I'll tell her you asked about Brian."

"I hope they throw the book at the driver. People are so irresponsible. They race through neighborhoods and expect pets and kids to jump out of their way," Lorelei said, her voice indignant.

"It was hit and run. Only one witness, but she didn't see much. Brian came around a corner on his skateboard and shot out in front of a pickup. The police think the person may have been drinking or on probation. That's why he, or she, didn't stop."

"How could someone do that?" Anger made her dark eyes darker.

"It's beyond me," Art said.

Lorelei paused for a moment, then said, "I hope you're not being too hard on yourself."

He stepped closer and lowered his voice. "I am, in part, responsible for this. I shouldn't have suspended him. It was a mistake."

"You did it for his own good. Donald Pratt would never have agreed to extend his scholarship if there hadn't been consequences."

"In part. But I also did it to protect my chances of keeping this job."

"I don't believe that. You're the most selfless man I know." She put a warm hand on his arm.

The hot, dry air felt suddenly claustrophobic. Art became aware of his shirt clinging to his back, the bead of sweat trailing down his spine. Lorelei was sensitive and lovely, and he'd known for a long time she had feelings for him. Maybe it was her size—she was tiny, smaller than most of the high school students—that made him dismiss the signals as if they were nothing more than a schoolgirl crush. But Lorelei was no schoolgirl. She was a brilliant woman in her thirties with a Masters in Psychology.

He'd allowed a friendship to develop between them because it was convenient. She stepped in where Gwen wouldn't. He wondered now when the relationship had crossed the invisible boundary line from coworker to something more and why he'd never noticed it before. Gwen would say this was another sign the job had become too important.

"You don't know me as well as you think." He removed her hand from his arm, gave it a squeeze, and trotted down the steps.

#

Ahead lay the tremendous, concrete disk that always reminded Art of an alien spacecraft out of a 1950's sci-fi movie. The fountain's cheerful sound used to bubble across the parking lot. Because of the California drought of recent years, it was now quiet and dusty. The winds whipped past him blowing bits of dead leaves into its empty waterspouts.

The lobby of Mission Hospital was cool and hushed. Art asked for Brian's room number at the information desk. Before it was given, he heard a familiar voice. He turned to see Brian's mother, Olivia Richards. She sat in a glassed-in waiting room off the lobby with a small crowd surrounding her. Apparently, the family had gathered after hearing about last night's surgery.

She was a pretty woman even with eyes red from crying. A man with brown hair the same color as Brian's—only his was raked into angry spikes—stood stiffly beside her. Art thought he must be her ex-husband, Davy McKibben. His eyes were swollen also, but it appeared to be more from drink than tears. Art had heard this was his solution to most of life's difficulties, hence the divorce.

Art had no idea how he'd be received. He was, after all, the one who'd suspended Brian. If Brian had been safely tucked away in his classroom on last Friday afternoon, he wouldn't have ended up under the wheels of a pickup truck.

"Olivia," he said when he got close.

Their eyes met. Tears sprang into her eyes. Art stood, still, waiting for an accusation. Several moments passed, then in a swift movement, she left the couch and stood before him.

"Art." She took both his hands in hers. "Thank you for coming. It means so much to me."

Relief washed over him. She pulled him into the group and made introductions. Art nodded to Olivia's mother, Sarah Richards, and to Mike McKibben, Brian's paternal grandfather. He'd met them several times at school events.

"How is he?" Art asked.

"Stable," she said.

"Good." Art's tongue tied in a knot. "Good." It was all he could say.

Olivia returned to the couch and sat next to her mother. Sarah was a tiny, sweet-faced woman, and the author of a series of children's books featuring a scalawag of a puppy named Brian the Bloodhound.

Art knew the stories well. Emily adored them. The dog was allergic to flowers, but he loved their scent, so his nose was always stuffy. Stuffy noses are no good for finding things, including the way home. He managed to make it there safely in every book but not without plenty of adventures.

"I named the bloodhound after Brian because our Brian was always wandering away," she said as if she were continuing a conversation that had begun before Art arrived. "As soon as he could walk, he took off running." She squeezed Olivia's hand.

"I shouldn't have left him," Olivia said and rested her forehead on her other hand.

Mike McKibben spoke in a gruff tone. "Get that out of your mind, Olivia. I've been sending patrol cars out after that boy since he was three years old." Mike had been an investigator with the Orange County Sheriff's Department before his retirement.

Olivia groaned as if in pain.

"Now, I didn't mean it that way," Mike said, alarmed. "I just meant Brian has an adventuresome spirit."

"Trying to keep him in the house is like trying to keep in a cat that's used to roaming. They're always looking for an open door," Olivia's mother said.

Olivia's ex-husband patted her shoulder. She pulled away from him and withdrew her hand from her mother's. She huddled in the corner of the couch, wrapped in her own arms and her grief.

When Art was a kid, he'd shot a dove in a tree outside his bedroom window. Not on purpose. He was messing around with his new BB gun and never saw it until it hit the ground.

He scooped it up and ran for the vet. The BB had broken the bird's wing. Unbelievably, it had lived. He fed and watered it for weeks, and one day it flew away from the shoebox nest on his windowsill. That same feeling, guilt mixed with crazy hope, filled him now.

A shrill voice disrupted the quiet scene. "Olivia, Mike, I'm so sorry." Amy Partridge from the PTA stomped across the lobby toward them.

Olivia rose.

Amy bustled over to her and air-kissed her cheeks. "It's terrible. Just terrible. How is he?"

Olivia explained in more detail this time. Brian had a few broken bones, but brain damage was the doctor's biggest concern. The night before the swelling in his head had reached dangerous levels. After releasing the pressure, they placed him in a medically induced coma to give him a chance to heal. It remained to be seen how he would function when he was backed off the drugs.

"This could have been any of our children," Amy said. "It's a perfect example of why we have to create safe drop off and pickup routes at school. The way it is now, it's just plain dangerous."

Anger rose like bile in Art's throat. Brian was nowhere near the school when the accident happened. He couldn't believe she was using this situation to push Donald Pratt's pet cause. He opened his mouth to say so, but a hand on his arm stopped him.

"Principal Bishop." Brian's grandfather was at his side, speaking low.

Art sucked in his breath. "Mike," he said.

"Thanks for coming, for waving the school flag. Olivia needs the support. She's beating herself up right now."

"Of course. Brian's a favorite of mine."

"I'm glad to hear that. I know he was in trouble, suspended I heard."

"Yes." The word felt heavy in Art's mouth.

"He isn't a bad boy, just impulsive. He needs a father in the home. I try to spend as much time with him as I can but..." The man mopped at his eyes with an old-fashioned cotton handkerchief, balled it up and stuck it in his pants pocket.

"He's a good kid," Art said and stared at the gray institutional carpeting under his feet. He thought of his own kids. Impulsive, foolish, but at heart, good kids. Emily had been after Art to take her camping for months. He'd make reservations for a campsite in Big Bear next week. Spending time with his children suddenly seemed critical.

"Mike, I'm so sorry about your grandson." Amy left the group by the couch, walked right past Art like he wasn't there and offered her cheek to Mike.

He dutifully delivered a kiss. While the two talked, Art's eyes wandered to Olivia. Some of her visitors were saying their goodbyes. He should talk to her; find out what he could do to help.

"So, I heard they were raped."

The strange comment boomed in the hushed room. Art's attention lurched to the conversation between Amy and Mike.

"I'm retired. I get my news from the papers like everyone else," Mike said.

"Oh, come on. You must hear things from your old buddies at the department." Amy's voice took on a wheedling tone.

"Not much." Mike shifted his weight and looked over the top of her head.

"Not much is more than the rest of us." Amy's eyes locked on Art. "Your wife is a real estate agent, isn't she?"

"Yes, she works for Humboldt Realty in Dana Point," Art said.

"You see, Mike, you'd be doing a good service if you let Art in on the details. Now that they've found a third body, there's no doubt is there? It must be the Texas killer, right?"

"What are you talking about?" Art hadn't heard anything about a third body.

"It was on the news this morning, didn't you see it?" Amy's face was solemn, but her eyes sparkled with excitement. "They found another dead agent in a house in Newport Beach."

Art wondered if Gwen knew about the killing but hadn't told him because she was afraid he'd get back on the anti-work bandwagon.

"The poor woman was stabbed to death in a theater," Amy said.

"I thought you said—" Art started to say, but she cut him off.

"It was one of those Newport mansions with a gym and library and theater. This guy likes high priced real estate. First, that Laguna Beach house, then San Clemente, now Newport. If I were an agent, I wouldn't show any beachfront properties that's for sure."

Art was glad the police had kept Gwen and Maricela's names out of the papers. Very few people knew they had been the ones to find the first victim. Letting Amy in on that tidbit of information would be tantamount to announcing it through a bullhorn at the next school basketball game. Gwen wouldn't have a moment's peace. Bored women with too much time on their hands, like Amy, would be pumping her for information every chance they got.

Mike moved away from the couch toward the lobby. Amy and Art drifted with him. He lowered his voice.

"Well, if it makes you feel any better, the women weren't raped. At first, the police thought they had been because their clothing was missing, but the coroner says, no rape."

"They were naked?" Amy's voice carried in the stone-tile lobby. Several people turned to look at her.

Mike took her arm and steered her toward the hospital exit. Art followed. He wanted to hear more. "Yes, and their clothing was removed from the scene," Mike said.

The three stepped outside into an arid gale. A hot wind whistled through the corridor between the hospital's wings. Mike loosened his tie. "And that's all she wrote. Don't know anymore."

"But—" Amy said.

"Thanks for coming, Amy," Mike said.

"Why would the killer take their clothing?" Amy's eyes were wide.

"Who knows? The guy's a psycho." Mike bent and deposited another kiss on her cheek. "Great to see you, Amy. Really."

"I'm sorrier than I can say, Mike. Let me know what I can do. I want to help." Art held out his hand. The older man shook it, turned and walked inside.

Mike was clever. It was pretty smooth the way he got rid of the problem in the room. Must be a talent leftover from his law enforcement days. He'd lured Amy outside with the bait of information, and now she stood staring at the hospital doors like a cow at a new gate.

Art wanted to talk more with Olivia, but after a handshake from a family member it seemed inappropriate. Frustrated, he leaned into the wind and pushed toward his car.

CHAPTER SIXTEEN

GWEN FOLLOWED HER GPS INSTRUCTIONS through the winding hills of Dana Point. A few agents from the office were touring homes that had been recently listed by other brokerages, and she decided to go along.

She parked across the street from the first property. An offshore breeze caught her hair and whisked it into her face. The Santa Ana wind wasn't quite as hot and miserable here as it was farther inland. It was tempered by a hint of humidity from the sea.

Lance pulled up behind her. Damn. She hadn't wanted to see him today. She'd talked to Fiona yesterday, and she was ready to list the Laguna Beach house again.

As soon as the police released the property, Fiona hired a trauma scene cleaning company. They'd whisked and scrubbed away all but the memory of the crime, so there was no reason not to put it on the market. But Gwen was dragging her feet. Returning to the sight of the murder wasn't an attractive prospect, and she hadn't made up her mind whether she wanted Lance involved or not.

On the one hand, it would be great to have help from someone with expertise in construction. Fiona's budget for repairs wasn't big. She didn't want to borrow against the house and be stuck making payments for months if it took a while to sell. On the other hand, Gwen wasn't sure she trusted Lance, and there was always the commission. One and a half percent of ten million dollars was a lot of money to give away. Then again, if she couldn't move the property, she wouldn't get anything at all.

"Gwen." Lance trotted to catch up with her.

She was saved from having to respond by John Gordon who stuck his head out the front door. "Leave this open when you come in, okay? The place stinks."

And stink it did. The home was mid-sized, about 2,200 square feet, and every inch of it oozed cigarette smoke. On the walls were pale patches surrounded by nauseating brown stains where pictures had been removed. Every room was covered in a different hue of old, corroded carpeting. It had been pulled back in one of the bedrooms to reveal an army of mold spores marching across the concrete beneath.

"Some people are pigs," Lance said walking up behind Gwen as she made notes on the guest bathroom.

"Hm..." She grunted.

"I listed a house in Nellie Gail last week. I could probably get two million for it if it were in decent shape, but the owners lived like hillbillies. I'm not kidding. I don't think anyone's taken the trash to the curb in a month. They're calling the pile a 'compost heap'. Crazy."

"Excuse me," Gwen said and looked past him toward the doorway he was blocking.

"Oh, sure." His forehead furrowed.

She slipped by him and headed up the hall to the master bedroom. The smell was slightly better here. A sliding glass door leading to the backyard was open, and the scent of foliage rode in on a breeze.

"What a dump, huh?" John said as he entered through the slider.

"You aren't kidding," Gwen said.

"I don't get it. You have a home worth, what, eight-hundred-and-fifty-thousand? And, you treat it like this? No maintenance, no nothing?" He shook his head.

"Money doesn't equal class, no matter what people say," Gwen agreed.

"Right. Then you take your listing, just up the road in Dana Point. I went by again the other day. The place is a gem. Spotless."

"The Frobishers are classy people."

"They picked a classy agent to represent them." John smiled.

"Thanks," Gwen said. "I bet you say that to all the agents."

"He never said it to me." Caroline Bartlett's disembodied voice entered the room a second before she did. Lance was right behind her.

"Me either," Lance said.

"Some deserve the compliment, some don't." John stalked from the room. Apparently, he was still angry with Lance.

"He's such a poop," Caroline said looking after him. "So, what do you think it would take to put this place in shape—a hundred grand?" She turned to Gwen and Lance.

"At least," Gwen said.

While Gwen and Caroline discussed the home's potential or lack thereof, Lance stood, arms crossed over his chest. Gwen felt his gaze fixed on her like a heat lamp.

"I think I'll check out the yard," she said when they'd exhausted the money talk.

"It's the best spot on the property. Most of the plants are dead, but at least it doesn't reek," Caroline said.

The air, though warm, was refreshing after the stench inside. A large avocado tree occupied one corner of the brown backyard. Gwen stepped under its shade and looked over a rusting metal fence at a crystalline view of Saddleback Mountain. The only nice thing about the dry Santa Ana winds was the clarity of the air left in their wake. There was no humidity or smog to cloud the vistas.

She heard a crunch of gravel, but didn't turn. She knew it was Lance. She smelled cinnamon and allspice—the aftershave he always wore.

He came and stood beside her. The only sound for several minutes was the whistle of wind traveling through the hills into the eaves of the wreck of a house behind them. Lance broke the silence.

"So have you given any thought to my proposition?" His question was simple, straightforward.

Gwen's thoughts were anything but. "I have."

"And?"

"I took your advice. I called Fiona, the owner."

"Good for you. What did she say?"

"The police cleared the scene and she's ready to move forward."

"Great. That's great."

Gwen didn't respond. After a beat, Lance said, "I hope today's news doesn't rattle her."

"What news?"

"The body they found. In Newport."

Gwen felt a sinking in her gut. "What body in Newport?"

"You didn't hear?"

She didn't bother answering him. Of course, she hadn't heard. If she'd heard she wouldn't have asked.

"They found another agent, dead, in a vacant home in Newport. She'd been there a couple of days. I guess nobody had shown the place because of the holiday. It sounds like it's the same guy. Same M.O."

The world spun. The dirt beneath Gwen's feet became a whirlpool. It was as if she stood on an unstable patch of earth about to drop into a dark, subterranean place. A place she didn't want to go. She put a hand to her forehead. Lance caught her arm as she stumbled.

"You okay?" His eyes were filled with concern. "I shouldn't have sprung it on you like that. I'm sorry."

The idea of stepping foot into the Laguna house now seemed an impossible task. He was still out there. The man who had turned Sondra Olsen into a lifeless, bloodied corpse was still out there.

She'd tried to convince herself she was safe. That statistically she and Maricela were the most unlikely people to become his victims since, in some sense, they already were. Lightning didn't strike twice in the same place. A shark didn't attack the same person twice in one lifetime. Unless, of course, a person lived under a lightning rod, or regularly dove in shark-infested waters. This was the truth she'd been avoiding.

The house on Cliff Drive was a lightning rod. It was an ideal habitat for this killer. He was drawn to vacant, oceanfront properties like a shark to chum. What had she been thinking? Art was right. She should go home, become a full-time mom again, get out of what had become a dangerous profession.

But then she thought about calling Fiona to tell her she wouldn't represent the property after all. When she tried to formulate the words she'd use, she couldn't find them. Gwen wanted this listing. She wanted it more than she'd wanted anything since she'd decided not to pursue an acting career.

She couldn't face the Laguna house alone, however. Not now. "It's all right. It's just I hadn't heard." She pulled her arm from Lance's grasp and stood straight. "I want you to help me with the place on Cliff Dr. I'll split the commission with you."

His mouth broke into a grin. "You sure?"

She nodded.

"Terrific. We're gonna make a killer team."

Gwen would have chosen another adjective.

CHAPTER SEVENTEEN

GWEN THUMPED TWO GROCERY SACKS on the kitchen counter.

"What's for dinner?" Jason added three more bags to the assortment.

Gwen began sorting through foodstuffs and putting things away. "How about hot dogs?"

"For dinner?"

"I like hot dogs." Tyler, who had been busy dunking chocolate chip cookies into a glass of milk, spit crumbs across the kitchen table as he spoke.

"Gross. Don't talk with your mouth full." Jason pulled a towel from the refrigerator door and snapped it at his brother.

"Stop!" Tyler scooted sideways to avoid it.

Jason flicked the makeshift whip toward Tyler again and landed a blow on his upper arm with a loud thwack. Tyler howled in pain. Jason began twisting the dishrag for another strike. Gwen reached from behind and yanked it from his hands. "Enough."

Jason turned on her, his face set in defiant lines. She stared into his eyes until he looked at his shoes.

"Do I need to talk to your father?" she asked.

"I'm going upstairs." He mumbled something she was glad she couldn't understand and left.

Tyler sat on the window bench struggling to hold back his tears and rubbed his arm. There was only three years difference between him and Jason, but Tyler seemed much younger. It wasn't only the angelic blue eyes and blond hair that gave him the air of innocence; it was his nature. Gwen sat beside him and pulled him close. No matter how hard he fought against it, he was the sweet, sensitive one in the family.

"You okay, buddy?" she asked.

"Why is he so mean?" Tyler's voice broke.

"Teenagers are... difficult."

"No, he's really mean. A lot meaner than last year and he was a teenager then."

"Yeah, well there are these things called hormones," Gwen said.

She gazed out the kitchen window. Her eyes fell on the rusted swing set in the backyard. She remembered the Christmas Eve Art assembled it in the dark while she held a flashlight. All three of her children had a note from Santa in their stockings instructing them to go to the yard for their gift. Over the years, those swings had been transformed into rocket ships, pirate vessels, and flying carpets. They were good years. Safe years. When had life gotten so difficult?

After a subdued supper, the kids went to their rooms to do homework, and Gwen and Art settled in front of the TV. Art picked up the remote, but left it unused in his lap. "I was thinking."

Gwen waited.

"We should get out of town for a couple of days. Get away from the craziness."

"Just you and me?" She could hear the hope in her voice. It sounded pathetic.

Art looked up. "I thought we'd bring the kids. Emily's been asking to go camping."

Disappointment settled on Gwen's shoulders. He was a good father, an excellent employee, a stellar friend and coworker, but not very interested in being a husband these days.

After previewing property that morning, she'd stopped by the school to drop off the lunch Jason had left on the counter. As she was driving away, she saw Art. He and the pretty school counselor, Lorelei Tanaka, were standing on the front steps deep in conversation. So deep, he never looked up to smile or wave when she drove by. He never even saw Gwen.

The image of them so close together, her hand on his arm, gazes locked onto each other's faces rose in her mind like an unwanted ghost. She was sure it was nothing. She was being paranoid, insecure, but she closed her eyes to shield herself from it the way a child pulls the covers over their head.

Lorelei, although she had the dark hair and Asian eyes of her ancestry, had the same petite, youthful frame as Jenny, her father's second wife. And Art reminded Gwen of her father in many ways. Paul Goddard wasn't a school principal. He'd been a veterinarian before he retired, but he was the kind of veterinarian who volunteered at the local wounded, indigenous, animal shelter, did spays and neuters on a sliding scale based on income, sponsored

Little League teams and never turned away a kid with a stray kitten. He was a local hero of sorts, beloved in their small town, and he'd been her hero.

She didn't blame him for leaving her and her mom, not at first. She was sure her mother had let him down somehow. She must have, or he wouldn't have run off with Jenny.

At twelve Gwen didn't understand the distinction between Jenny's thirty years and her mother's forty. Old was old. Besides, attributing a motive to her father as shallow as trying to bolster his ego by seeking the adoration of a younger woman was unthinkable.

After he married Jenny, Gwen became convinced his new wife had been the problem all along. She hated Jenny with a hatred so pure only a child could manufacture it. But it had done no good. Instead of seeing Jenny for the schemer she truly was, her father had only reprimanded Gwen for her rudeness.

One Friday afternoon she perched on the front steps outside her mother's small apartment, her pink Barbie suitcase by her side. She'd been waiting a long time. It was her Dad's weekend, and he was late. Again.

As she sat, an idea struck her. When she was small, her dad took her on his big animal rounds on Saturdays. He would introduce her to the ranchers as his assistant. He always said, "Don't let her size fool you. She's the best vet-in-training in these parts."

But then at eight, she'd had what her dad referred to as "the close call." After that, she was too afraid to go with him, afraid of dark barns and small pens and big animals that crowded and blocked out the light. When he'd wake her early Saturday mornings, she'd roll over and feign illness. In time, he stopped asking.

The more she thought about it, the more convinced she was this was the reason her dad left them. It wasn't her mother's fault. It wasn't even Jenny's. It was hers. She was the one who'd let him down.

The sun set. The streetlights came on. Gwen waited. The longer she sat, the longer her repentance speech became. She couldn't wait to tell him how sorry she was. Tell him she'd be brave. Tell him she wanted to be his assistant again.

It must have been past suppertime—her stomach was rumbling—when her mother eased herself on the stoop next to her. Gwen's dad wasn't going to make it. Something had come up. In the months that followed, something came up more and more often, until Gwen stopped feeling the ache of disappointment.

Three years after they broke up, Gwen's father and Jenny had a child on the way. Gwen's mother was drinking. And Gwen had learned the devastation divorce could bring.

She wanted to ask Art about Lorelei. She wanted to ask what they'd been talking about that had been so fascinating. But, truth be told, she was afraid to. Sometimes not knowing was best. If you didn't know, you could act like everything was fine and maybe it would turn out that way.

"Sure," she said, forcing a lightness into her tone. "Let's go camping."

"I'll reserve a campsite in Big Bear tomorrow."

The silence resumed. Not the comfortable kind Gwen was used to. The kind in which couples who'd been married for many years could sit companionably, each with their own thoughts. This was a strained, uneasy silence. She broke it. "Art. What's wrong?"

"What do you mean?"

"I don't know. You've been preoccupied. Maricela said there was an accident at school. I was wondering—"

"Not at school. A student was hit by a car near his home."

"I read about a hit and run in San Juan, but I didn't know the boy was from St. Barnabas." Gwen felt a rush of parental horror. "Was he killed?"

Art shook his head. "No. Thank God. But he's in a medically induced coma. No one knows what he'll have to deal with when he comes out of it."

"His poor parents," Gwen said. "I can't imagine."

Art massaged his temples. "That's not the only thing bothering me."

Gwen waited.

"I'm sure you heard about the agent in Newport," he said.

"Yes." Gwen felt her face freeze into an expressionless mask.

"Well? I've been waiting for you to bring it up all night."

She shook her head. "I don't know what to say."

"How about, 'I'm going to take some time off work'?"

"I got the Laguna Beach listing back. I'm putting it on the market again as soon as I can get it ready." The words came out in a monotone rush.

Dismay and incredulity fought on his face for several seconds. "I can't believe it," he said, dismay winning.

"I've co-listed it with another agent from the office. A man. I won't be there alone. I'll have to share the money, but at least I'll be safe."

"I don't care about the money." The statement exploded from him.

Emily stuck her head through the doorway. "What's wrong Daddy?"

"Nothing, sweetheart." He modulated his tone. "Go finish your homework."

"It's done."

"Then get ready for bed."

"I don't have to go to bed until 9:00. It's only 8:30." Indignation filled her voice.

"Then go watch TV."

"But, Jason—"

"Go." Art spun around and shot the word at her. Emily's face crumpled, and she ducked from the room.

"Don't take it out on Emily, Art. I'm sorry you're not happy with me, but I'm an adult. I have a business to run."

He didn't answer. Frustration pricked up Gwen's arms. "Look, I'll handle it," she said. "I'm not going to do anything stupid."

They sat without speaking for several minutes, then Art rose from the couch. "I'm going to bed. I want to get to the gym early tomorrow."

Gwen sat up for another hour, staring into a fireplace that was as cold and dark as her thoughts.

CHAPTER EIGHTEEN

CAROLINE BARTLETT DID DUMB BLONDE WELL, but it was an act. She had all the cunning of a girl who'd grown up with an undiscerning, single mother. I felt a bit of a kindred spirit.

Not that my mother had been undiscerning. She only bedded the wealthy and powerful. They usually left me alone, but my younger sister, Angela, wasn't as lucky. She had been groped and fondled by many "uncles". My mother knew what was happening, but I think she assumed her little girl was being prepared for life, certainly the kind of life my mother led.

That was, of course, the only life she knew. I don't think she was uncaring, just practical. I like to give Mother the benefit of the doubt. But Angela, being as innocent and unintelligent as a mewling lamb, suffered. It was a mercy she died young.

Caroline struck me as one who'd found clever ways to thwart unwanted advances. She wasn't beautiful, not like the lovely Vanna White. But she was attractive in an overblown kind of way. A climbing rose just beginning to drop its petals.

I'm sure she'd had her fair share of pimply boys asking for dates. However, she shouldn't have the innate security alarm I sensed in her based on her appearance alone. Those early warning systems are developed by only the very good-looking, the very rich, and those accosted early. Since she was neither of the former, I assumed she was the later.

"I know the decor is a bit seventies, but just imagine what this place would look like with a facelift." She turned and smiled at me. "Now don't you say you can imagine what I'd look like with a facelift."

"I wouldn't dream of it," I said. I didn't have to force the sincerity in my voice. I sympathize with the humble. It's the conceited, self-absorbed, pampered princesses I feel a need to crush.

"As you know the kitchen has already been remodeled. And that's the most expensive room to re-do." She pushed open the swinging door into the large stainless steel and red space. "I love the chickens—so cute. Don't you think?"

I wisely chose not to answer. The house was tasteless—chickens notwithstanding, but it seems the media had pigeonholed me. They were calling me the "Oceanview Killer" now. I realized my error immediately. There are no oceanview homes in Dallas, and not all expensive property in Orange County is at the beach. I needed to branch out if I was going to maintain my fiction. Obviously, identity theft isn't my strong suit.

"Of course, they don't come with the place anyway. Do you want to see the master suite again?" she asked.

"That's a good idea," I said.

It was the most interesting space in this tacky house. The bed was big enough for a romp and the bath...well the bath brought all kinds of fantasies to mind. I caught a whiff of Opium as I followed her up the stairs. Not the drug, the perfume. I hate Opium.

"Here we are." She threw open the double doors to the bedroom with a dramatic flourish. The bed was wonderful in a horrible kind of way. The size, the placement, the bedding, it was deliciously awful.

"Great spot for a party," I said and moved closer to her.

Killing is a funny thing. The more you do it, the more interesting it becomes. There's a thrill in the hunt, satisfaction in improving one's skills.

Her head snapped around. The smile she'd been wearing left her eyes. I'd said too much. Her sixth sense had been activated. I fingered the box cutter I stuffed in my jacket pocket that morning thinking it might come in handy.

"This bed is big enough for an army of kids and the family dog," I said, hoping to mollify her. Her shoulders relaxed a little.

We crossed a field of rose-colored carpet into the master bath. I withdrew the blade from my pocket and held it behind my back with one hand. I imagined Caroline dancing a different kind of dance than Ms. White had—fewer twirls and more leg kicks.

"Did I already tell you we had the Jacuzzi jets flushed by a professional?" the theme song from *Titanic* interrupted her. She fished in her white, snakeskin purse and withdrew a phone.

"Oh, I better get this." She looked at the screen. "Hi. Sorry, I forgot to leave it for you. Top drawer of my desk," she said into the phone. "I'll be there soon. I'm at my Coto listing."

I held my breath.

"Yes. I'm here with—" She turned and smiled at me, then said my name.

I slipped the box cutter back into my pocket.

CHAPTER NINETEEN

LANCE WAS ALREADY THERE leaning against the front door when Gwen opened the creaking gate of the house on Cliff Drive. She was a bit late, on purpose this time. She hadn't been here since she and Maricela found Sondra Olsen's body.

It wasn't that she believed in ghosts, or curses, or bad juju, or anything like that. Gwen wasn't superstitious. But she didn't want to walk through the claustrophobic entryway with its door that led down into the house's nether regions alone. The thought of going upstairs was even worse. Up was where she'd seen Sondra.

Lance was security. She was going to pay dearly for him, so she might as well take advantage of his presence. He was emotional security as well as physical. She couldn't break down in a panic in front of him. She'd have to act as if everything was fine. She lived by the adage, *fake it 'till you make it.* Act like things are fine, and they will be. But she'd always found it easier to perform with an audience.

"I've already walked the perimeter of the property," Lance said. "This place is a mess."

"Wait until you see the inside." Gwen put on her brightest smile. "It's worse."

"Great."

"Hey, this was your idea." Gwen pulled the key from her purse and inserted it into the front door lock.

"No lockbox?" Lance asked.

"Not yet. I think we need to make whatever repairs we're planning to make before we expose the world to this place."

The same musty smell she remembered from her last visit assailed her as soon as she entered the foyer. It was the moldy odor of old beach homes, lakefront cabins, and ski chalets where snow clothes and sleds were left to drip dry in mudrooms. A scent she used to think of as pleasant. Once it had brought back memories of childhood vacations, of trips to her grandparents' house near Lake Michigan. Now it was forever linked with death and blood.

"Oh, wow. I could totally see Morticia Addams floating down this staircase." Lance patted the handrail.

Gwen laughed. "I think we should make it a selling point, you know, target Goths and Satanists."

"I like the way you think. Instead of *handyman's dream*, or *needs a little TLC*, we go with something like *witch's wonderland."*

"Your own haunted mansion, crumbling crown molding, warped oak interior doors, cobwebs and ghouls throughout."

When they entered the living room, she glanced at Lance so she could watch its impact on him. She remembered when she'd first met Fiona here to write up the contract. She'd been so excited to get a beachfront listing, she'd almost gotten a speeding ticket on her way into town. Then she saw it. Disappointment didn't begin to describe her feelings. That is, until she walked into the living room.

Today the Pacific Ocean sparkled before them through the dusty windows like a diamond in a tarnished setting. Lance took a sharp intake of breath. "This'll sell."

"I think so. We just have to get them past the front door."

"Show me the rest of the place; then I'll start taking notes."

Growing enthusiasm replaced sarcasm as they toured the home. He called the outdated kitchen cupboards *vintage,* the scarred wood floor *distressed* and the cracked plaster walls *authentic.* It was amazing the effect an ocean view had on a person's vocabulary.

Gwen showed Lance every nook and cranny of the lower level, even pointed out the hall to the basement. She was stalling. The dread that had been building in her chest all morning felt like a boulder now, but there was nowhere else to go. Nowhere but the second story.

Her heartrate rose with every stair they climbed. By the time they reached the top, it beat against her ribs like a caged animal bent on escape. The hall leading to the master bedroom, the room she'd once been so proud and excited to show Maricela, lay before her. It looked longer and narrower today, as if someone had stretched it out like a piece of chewed bubblegum.

"You first." She couldn't keep the nerves out of her voice.

Lance gave her a small smile of support. "Let's get the master out of the way. Right?"

"Right."

He strode down the elongated corridor—a knight heading into the dragon's lair to defend his lady. When his hand dropped to the doorknob, Gwen looked away.

"Coast is clear." His voice sounded artificially cheerful.

Gwen's shoulders relaxed. She hadn't realized she'd hunched into a defensive posture. She inhaled deeply and allowed her eyes to follow the stained, floral runner down the length of the hall, wander over the doorjamb, and land on the rectangle of sunlight imprinted on the wood floor of the bedroom. It was clean. No blood. No body. She knew it would be—Fiona mentioned she'd had the room cleaned—but she exhaled in relief just the same.

"Okay?"

"Okay."

"Let's get started on the to-do list," Lance said. "It'll be a push, but I want to have our first open house this Saturday."

"That's only a couple of days away," Gwen said.

"Like I said, it'll be a push."

"I'll order the food and wine."

When they left the house, each armed with a Home Depot list, Gwen felt lighter than she had since she'd agreed to renew the listing. There was a lot to do, but the hardest task was behind her. Today they'd faced down the boogieman.

#

On her way to the office, Gwen decided to stop and order refreshments for the open house at the Barrel. She walked across the parking lot to the wine shop. The proprietor sat behind the counter with a magazine in his hands. He looked up when the bell rang.

"Hi." Gwen made her way over to him. "I'd like to order a few pairing platters."

Mo pulled a menu from under the counter. "What's the event?"

"An open house in Laguna Beach. I was thinking maybe an assortment of cheeses and sweets."

They looked over the menu together. Gwen was impressed with the man's suggestions. He certainly knew his wine.

"I'll come by Saturday morning around 9:00 to pick it up," Gwen said after paying for her order.

"As it so happens, I'm pouring for a bridal shower in Laguna on Saturday," he said. "I'd be happy to drop it off."

"Are you sure?"

"Absolutely."

Gwen fished a home flier out of her purse and set it on the counter. "It's on Cliff Drive."

"Right on my way," he said and smiled.

The clang of the ship bell echoed through the shop as Gwen closed the door behind her. One chore down, ninety-nine to go. The thought made her smile. It felt good to conquer the fear that'd been haunting her for the past weeks. A house was just a house, no matter what had happened within its walls, and this one was going to change her career.

CHAPTER TWENTY

ART SHUT DOWN the Reserve America website. He couldn't wait to see the expression on Emily's face when he told her they'd be heading up the mountain next week. Whenever he thought about Brian lying in that hospital bed, he got an urge to pack up his own children and take them someplace safe, away from Orange County's crowds and fast pace. A weekend in Big Bear might satisfy, at least for a few days.

He wondered how Olivia was holding up. He hadn't seen her since Tuesday, two days ago. He looked at his calendar, and made a quick decision to spend his lunch hour at Mission Hospital.

At 12:13, Art parked his car in the half-empty lot between Mission Hospital and the medical buildings next door. He passed the spaceship fountain and entered through the glass doors.

This time there was no group in the waiting room. A gray-haired volunteer at the reception desk sent him to the Children's Hospital of Orange County Center, better known as CHOC, on the fifth floor.

He fidgeted with a thread hanging from his jacket cuff on the way up the elevator. He was nervous, and that wasn't like him. He was used to being the one in control of parent meetings. They came to him with their worries, and he dispensed wisdom. But the accident had shaken his confidence.

He wondered now if he'd been looking at the world ass-backwards. Instead of protecting a child in his charge from a bully, he'd suspended him for defending himself. And now that child was in a coma. If he'd been this wrong about Brian, what else was he wrong about?

The small body in the big bed halted him in the doorway. Brian was swaddled in bandages and bed sheets. His face—blue-black with bruises—peeked out like a moth emerging from a chrysalis. Olivia sat on a chair nearby, her chin resting on her chest, breathing softly. Art hated to wake her.

He walked to the bed. He wanted to touch Brian, to place a hand on him and pray, but he couldn't see a way through the tangle of tubes growing from the child like wild vines. Instead, he folded his hands in front of him and bowed his head.

"Art?" A sweet voice interrupted his meditation. Olivia's short hair was disheveled, her eyes sunken, but the smile she wore was bright.

"Hi," he said and returned her smile. "How's he doing today?"

Olivia rose from the chair and motioned for Art to sit. She perched on Brian's bed, reached through the tubes and took her son's pale hand. "He's doing a little better," she said. "The doctor has started backing off the coma drugs, but he hasn't woken up yet."

"That's good news," Art said.

"Yes." She sounded hesitant. "But, I'm scared."

"Of what?"

"What's going to happen when he does? What if he can't speak, or move, or..." her smile shattered, "he doesn't recognize me?" Art reached out his hand. She clutched it. "It's easier this way. With him out. I sing to him—hold his hand. I can pretend he's sleeping."

Art opened his mouth to say, "He'll be okay," but closed it. He didn't know that. No one did.

"You know what's crazy?"

He gave a small shake of his head.

"I actually hope he wakes up cranky. That way I'll know he's himself. If he wakes up cheerful, I don't know what I'll do." She gave a small laugh. "I used to complain all the time to anyone who'd listen. I thought my worst problem in life was that he was such a bear sometimes."

"Maslow's hierarchy of needs," Art said.

Olivia looked at him with a question in her eyes.

"Maslow was psychologist. He came up with this pyramid to graph human needs from basic to more complex. His theory was that a person wouldn't experience the needs at the higher points on the pyramid if the needs in the lower categories weren't met.

"For instance, if you don't have food or shelter, or if there is some circumstance threatening your safety, you're not going to be spending a lot of time worrying about your social status. I think it's pretty accurate."

"How does this apply to me?" she asked.

"Don't be hard on yourself for feeling upset with Brian for being difficult. That's normal parent stuff. You were both safe, fed, sheltered. Your basic needs were met. You were trying to fine tune life. Nothing wrong with that."

"I've been leveled." Her eyes grew watery. "Reduced to life or death. Nothing else is important."

"Exactly." Art squeezed her hand. "So, let me help with some of the other stuff. What can I do?

"Just be a friend."

CHAPTER TWENTY-ONE

I'M GLAD I DIDN'T GET IN BED with Caroline Bartlett, as the expression goes. My father's home was for sale again, so I hadn't needed to slay that dragon after all. More importantly, it would've been a reflection of my taste.

That house... Expensive? Yes. Tacky? Yes. I like to think I have some breeding, at least on my father's side.

I went to see him when I was eighteen. My mother knew beyond a shadow of a doubt who impregnated her. When I was conceived, he was keeping her in a very nice little house and paying all the bills, so she had no need for other friends. When he learned of the pregnancy he abandoned her. Oh, he paid dearly for her silence. Gave her the house and a healthy sum of money to keep her in groceries until she got her figure back. But I never saw a dime of it.

I wanted to go to college. I'd had good grades in high school. Not good enough to get a scholarship, but good. I knew my father was quite wealthy. Since he hadn't contributed to my needs up to this point, I figured he owed me something. A college education seemed like the least he could do.

I drove to Laguna and parked on the street in front of his house. I sat and watched and wondered what to do. What was behind door number one?

After a while, a woman with brown hair I assumed was his wife, pulled out of the driveway in a white Cadillac. I took advantage of the opportunity.

When I rang the bell, my father answered the door himself. It surprised me. I'd assumed he had a maid for that kind of thing, but I guess he fancied himself a liberal, open-minded sort of man.

He had no idea who I was. He stood there in his shirtsleeves, smiling pleasantly and asked, "Can I help you?"

"Yes, you can," I said.

He cocked his head to the side and waited. He wasn't going to ask me in. He must not have noticed the family resemblance that was so apparent to me. I didn't want to break it to him on his doorstep. I would rather he was sitting down, but he gave me no choice.

"Hello, Father," I said.

I'm not sure what I was expecting. I'd fantasized about him throwing his arms around me and welcoming me into the family with tears in his eyes, but I knew that was unlikely. More probably, he'd want to maintain the secret of my birth.

I could understand that. Respect it even. He had a wife and a daughter. I would be hard to explain. But maybe he'd want to meet his only son for a drink now and again.

His pleasant, benevolent expression changed in an instant. His eyes narrowed. His face grew stony. "Excuse me?"

"Hello, Father," I said again.

"Who are you?"

"Your son." I shouldn't be a complete surprise. He'd known about my birth.

"I don't have a son." His voice was as cold as his visage.

"And yet, here I am. Can't we go inside?" I said.

He stared at me for a long moment. So long I thought he was considering letting me in, but then he said, "If you think you're going to get money from me by perpetrating a fraud, you're sadly mistaken."

The door began to close. I stuck my foot in the opening.

"This is no fraud, Father."

"Get your foot out of my doorway," he said. I could smell his anger.

"Please..."

His voice grew low and menacing. "Get off my property, or I will call the police."

At that moment, I never wanted anything as much as I wanted to be let into that elegant house. As hopeless as the idea was, I longed to walk through the hall that opened into the sunlit rooms beyond, to chat over a drink, to dine with the family.

"Can't we talk about this?" The words struggled past my tightening throat.

"I'm asking you one more time to remove your foot from my doorway."

There was no point in getting in a wrestling match. I left.

That night I walked down the public stairs to the beach. The tide was high. I sat on the bottom step, removed my shoes and rolled up my pant legs. I waded in the whispering waves down the beach until I stood under the house.

It blazed with light from the French doors and windows that faced the ocean. I could see people moving about inside. The brown-haired woman walked back and forth between rooms. My father, head bent over a book, looked up every so often and laughed at someone I couldn't see. I belonged in that room. It was my birthright.

I'm not sure how long I stayed that first night, but at some point I felt the water climb to the middle of my calves, sopping my pants. I needed to leave if I didn't want to go for a swim. As I turned away, movement in the window caught my eye.

It was a girl.

A lovely, redhaired girl. She stepped to the French doors to look out at the night. In the gleam of the lamplight, her hair glowed like a fiery halo.

Years later, I read in the paper that my father had donated a large sum of money, much more than a Bachelor's degree would have cost, to the college I had hoped to attend. They put his name on a plaque in the wing of the building he helped to fund. His daughter, my half-sister, received a master's degree from the same school.

She also gained the house. It was on the market again, but that didn't solve my original problem—how to remove my inheritance. What I needed most now was time to think, time to plan. If I could put off the sale, I wouldn't have to worry about new owners locking it up tight against me before I was ready to make a move. I became more cheerful as I pondered my options. Maybe there was a way I could get my inheritance, and my sister would get what she deserved.

CHAPTER TWENTY-TWO

THE PAST FEW DAYS on Cliff Drive were productive ones. Gwen developed a whole new appreciation for Lance. He wasn't just a pretty boy after all. With hammer in hand, he reminded her of one of those Nordic gods of wind or waves. She decided there ought to be a hurricane named after him.

He'd located the source of the mold smell in the attic. It was the result of a leaky section of roof. He summarily patched the tiles and moved on to the bathrooms, just in case they were contributing to the home's pervasive perfume. He replaced two toilets, four faucets and a showerhead. Then gave each room a coat of fresh paint. Even the towel racks and electric switch plates gleamed.

Lance installed things as fast as Gwen could purchase them. Which was the reason for her trip to the house this morning. He planned to paint the hallways and put up new overhead lighting as soon as he could get away from the office. She'd shopped last night, gone for an early run on the beach, and stopped by to drop off the paint and lamps.

In the front hall, Gwen noted that bleach and a strong fan—Lance's idea—had worked wonders on the attic mold. The old musty odor had been replaced by the clean, sharp smells of new paint, wood polish and cleaning products. It gave her courage.

If you'd have told her forty-eight hours ago she'd be coming here in the early hours of the day, alone, she'd have laughed. Yet here she was with only a slight jogging of her pulse. The renovation affected more than the house. Gwen's fears became less and less marked with each coat of new paint.

She hefted two gallons of Soft Cotton flat enamel across the foyer and into the living room. The ocean reflected the newly risen sun. Flecks of gold and silver glimmered on its surface. If this were her home, she'd decorate to complement the daily show outside. She imagined herself lounging on a deep maroon couch settled across from both the brick fireplace and the wall of windows with a cup of steaming coffee.

She wouldn't put up curtains or shades. She'd welcome the sky and ocean into the space. Privacy wasn't an issue. No one could see in. Not unless they stood on the sand and peered up, and who would do that?

Lost in thought, it was a minute or two before Gwen noticed the scurrying near her feet. Blinded by the light from the windows, at first she couldn't discern what the black specks scuttling across the hardwood were. When her eyes adjusted, she screamed.

The room was alive.

A brown river of cockroaches streamed from the fireplace. It parted before her and joined together behind. A few of the insects took a detour over the top of her running shoes. Huge water bugs crawled over their smaller cousins like military tanks crushing an enemy army.

Gwen dropped the cans of paint, ran from the room, through the front hall, and slammed the door behind her. She hugged herself, then thinking she may have carried a few revolting bugs out with her, she began kicking and stomping her feet.

She gave her purse three or four hard shakes before sticking her hand inside to rummage for the house key. Disgust made her fingers thick and clumsy. Once she found it, she couldn't seem to fit it into the lock. The key dropped from her hand and clattered onto the stone stoop. When she reached down to retrieve it, she saw two brown insects crawling up her leg. Gwen yelped, slapped them to the ground and trampled them in a crazy jig.

Panting, she turned to the door. Two more attempts, and she locked it. She retreated to the street, brushing down her arms and legs as she jogged. *Get away. Go home. Get clean.* She had a sudden compassion for people with obsessive-compulsive disorder. *Get away. Go home. Get clean.* The phrases revolved mantra-like through her brain.

She climbed behind the steering wheel of her car, and her eyes fell on the two boxes of ceiling lights she'd promised to deliver. She stared at them stupidly for several seconds. *Get away. Go home. Get clean.* The words ganged up on a another thought vying for her attention: *Lance needs those.*

It was another five minutes before Gwen could convince her feet to walk toward the house. Roaches were disgusting, yes, but they weren't dangerous. She'd over-reacted, she told herself, then shuddered. Some people hated snakes; some hated spiders. Gwen had a pathological aversion to roaches. Funny, she'd so recently had a conversation about this at the Barrel, and now here she was facing an apocalypse of the damn things.

She set the boxes on the porch and fit the key into the lock. Her hands were slippery with sweat, but she held on to it this time. The bolt clunked back. She knelt. With one hand, she pushed the door open a crack. With the other, she slid the boxes through. The last thing she saw before slamming the door shut again, was a water bug about a foot from her nose, antennae waving.

CHAPTER TWENTY-THREE

AFTER A LONG, HOT SHOWER and copious amounts of scrubbing, Gwen dressed for the office. She called Lance on her way and filled him in on the infestation at the house.

"That's strange." He yawned into the phone. "I've been over there for thirty of the past forty-eight hours, and the only bugs I saw were silverfish and a couple of spiders."

"There was a roach monsoon this morning."

"Bet it woke you up." Lance gave a small laugh.

"It did."

"I'll call an exterminator as soon as we hang up."

"You don't think we should cancel the open house tomorrow?"

"No. We may have to pay extra, but I'll get someone out this afternoon."

They disconnected as Gwen pulled into the Humboldt parking lot. She hurried past the reception desk toward her office. "Ms. Bishop." A voice stopped her.

Investigator Sylla rose from the visitor couch. "Do you have a moment?"

Gwen, startled to see the woman, paused before saying, "Of course." She led her to the conference room past the curious glances of coworkers and shut the door behind them.

"How can I help you?" Gwen said as they took seats across from each other at the long table. She wondered what she could say that she hadn't already.

"Just a few loose ends." Sylla smiled, her teeth brilliant against her dark skin. Gwen hadn't realized how attractive she was the first time they'd met, but, of course, she'd been distracted. "You said you'd received an email from Sondra Olsen informing you she'd be showing the property on Wednesday, February third, correct?"

"Yes." Annoyance niggled at Gwen. She'd been over this territory a hundred times already.

"You also told us she never said who her client was."

"Correct."

"Does the name *Moray* mean anything to you?"

Gwen shook her head. "No. Should it?"

"It's the surname of the former owner of the property on Cliff Drive in Laguna."

"I thought..." Gwen started to say she'd thought it was Randall, then realized Randall was Fiona's married name.

"Yes?" Investigator Sylla widened her eyes.

"Nothing. My client goes by Randall, but she's married."

"I was referring to her father."

"What does this have to do with anything?" The question snapped from Gwen's lips. The conversation seemed irrelevant, and she had so much to do to get ready for the open house tomorrow.

"The name came up on the schedules of all the Orange County murder victims in the week before they were killed. Seems a bit of coincidence."

Gwen inhaled sharply. "Not the Texas victims?"

"No. Not Texas."

"Moray is a pretty common name, isn't it? Was there a first name?" Gwen could hear the defensiveness in her own voice, and wondered why this bit of news made her throat constrict.

"No. Only an initial on one of the victim's calendars, K. The others just wrote *Moray.* Nothing else."

"What was Fiona's father's name?" Gwen wanted it to be Michael, Bob, or Andrew—anything but Kevin or Kurt.

"Edward. Not a fit. But, we're following all leads. I've already spoken to your client, but thought you might have heard something from another agent."

"No," Gwen said.

"Well," the woman pushed herself away from the table and rose in one fluid motion. "I don't recommend setting appointments to show property with anyone named Moray." Investigator Sylla showed herself out.

Gwen sat and stared at her hands folded on the table before her. The hair on her forearms stood at attention. Tension flickered across her skin like static electricity. Attaching a name, any name, to the killer gave him form, substance. He'd only been an amorphous shadow in her mind before this. He'd become a person. That he shared Fiona's maiden name was even more unsettling. An image of evil, born from the dark basement womb of the Cliff Drive house rose in her mind.

"You okay?"

Gwen jumped.

"It's just me." Maricela leaned through the doorway. "I saw that woman cop driving away when I pulled into the center. What did she want?"

"Do you know anyone named Moray?" Gwen asked.

Maricela shook her head. "Why?"

Gwen filled her in on the conversation. Maricela sank into the chair Investigator Sylla just vacated, worry clouding her face. "What do they think? Do they think it's some relative of Fiona's who's killing people?"

"She didn't say."

"You look upset?"

"I am. For some reason hearing a name terrifies me."

"Everyone has a name, *chica*." Maricela covered Gwen's hand with one of hers.

"I know."

"It seems good to me. Like the cops are maybe getting somewhere, closer to catching him."

"Right. You're right." Gwen said. "It's been a crazy morning."

"You know what you need?"

"What?"

"You need to go shopping."

#

A half hour later Gwen and Maricela were wandering through an antique mall downtown San Juan Capistrano looking for things to dress up their listings. Gwen held up a ceramic Toreador lamp topped by a frolicking bull lampshade. "You could do a Mexican theme."

"Or, I could shoot myself," Maricela said. "We're going tropical. Rosie—she's the decorator my clients hired—said the colors should remind people they're close to the beach. She's really good. You should talk to her about the Laguna property."

"We can't afford an interior designer. Our goal is to clean things up, downplay the house and focus attention onto the views. I just need a couple of vases. Fresh flowers cover a multitude of sins."

"I wonder what's in here?" Maricela stood at the open door of a storage room stuffed floor to ceiling with merchandise. Chairs and tables were piled one on top of another dimming the light from overhead neon bulbs.

Gwen pointed to a "sale" sign with an arrow directing buyers inside.

"Let's check it out." Maricela disappeared down a narrow path between mountains of furniture.

"I'll wait here," Gwen called after her.

"Be right back." Her voice echoed from the doorway.

Gwen browsed the booths near the entrance until Maricela returned with two vases. "How do you like these?"

"Perfect. I'll take them."

"*Chica,* what's with you and tight places?"

"Not sure what you mean," Gwen said. "What do you think of these bowls? You could fill them with sea shells for the coffee table—kinda tropical."

"*Bonita.*" Maricela took them from Gwen. "But don't change the subject."

"I have a touch of claustrophobia, that's all." Gwen said.

"A touch? You wouldn't try on that skirt at the mall because the changing room was too small."

"It was too small. And dark. It was dark too."

"Have you thought about seeing someone?" Maricela asked.

Gwen stopped mid-aisle and stared at her. "You mean like a shrink?"

"No, not *like* a shrink. A shrink. Mine is *excelente*. She's helping me process that day. You know face the fear. Get past it."

"It's no big deal. I don't like to be crowded."

Truth was, she had thought about making an appointment with a counselor. The claustrophobia was getting worse. She'd had plenty of panic attacks in grade school and high school, but in college, she'd gotten control of it through method acting of all things.

When she needed to get into an elevator, she'd put on the role of a high profile lawyer with an office on the twentieth floor. In basements, she imagined *ghost hunter seeking evil spirits.* In closets, attics and other tight spaces, she channeled chimney sweep or Victorian maid. Keeping her mind on someone else's story calmed her.

At least it had. Her trick wasn't working anymore. Seeing Sondra's dead body seemed to set off a cascade of old fears. The memory of the close call she'd had at eight-years-old kept popping into her mind at the most inopportune times, and the nightmares were getting more frequent.

Gwen's phone vibrated. She pulled it out of her purse and smiled at the screen. "Lance needs me to pick up another ceiling light. I'll have to stop at Home Depot."

"Hmmm...," Maricela said.

They wandered a bit farther. Gwen could tell Maricela was itching to say something. Several times, she opened and closed her mouth as if she was considering then discarding words the way she was the items on the shelves.

"Okay, what's the issue?" Gwen asked when she couldn't take it any longer.

"What do you mean?" Maricela turned to her with wide eyes.

"You have something to get off your chest. I can tell."

Maricela toyed with a candlestick she'd picked up. "Art is a good husband," she said after a long pause.

Gwen laughed. "That's it?"

"I don't think you appreciate how few good husbands are out there these days."

Maricela set the candlestick down and moved toward the counter at the front of the store. Gwen flushed with annoyance. Maricela was worried she was getting too close to Lance. She thought her friend knew her better than that.

They made their purchases and emerged into the sunshine. Gwen turned to face Maricela. "There's nothing romantic going on between Lance and me. We have a business relationship. That's it."

"I think Art is stressed about school and about you, but you don't seem very concerned about him."

They walked toward the car. Irritation tightened Gwen's jaw. In Maricela's mind, Art could do no wrong. She didn't understand the reality of living with a man who made responsibility an art form. Art championed the cause of the underdog and played Sir Galahad to all soccer moms in distress. He was every woman's hero. Except hers. The stronger and more self-reliant she became, the less interest she seemed to hold for him. What was she supposed to do, drop a hankie like Scarlett O'Hara and fake a case of the vapors just to lure him back?

There were plenty of women at school willing to play that game, like the lovely Lorelei. She was young and oh-so adoring. Besides, Gwen wasn't the one who fell asleep on Valentine's Day. She'd tried to reconnect. He hadn't been interested. "Yeah, well, I'm tired of feeling single," she said.

Maricela looked at her. "You're not, but you act like you are when you're with Lance."

When they reached the parking lot, Gwen strode across the blacktop toward her car. Maricela jogged to keep up.

"I made you mad. I'm sorry," Maricela said after they belted in. She didn't look sorry at all. "But Lance is a player, you know?"

"No, I don't know," Gwen said, her voice frosty.

"He uses people. I know his type."

"Oh, you do?"

"Yes, I do. I was married to one."

They drove in silence. Gwen churned with anger. Maricela meant well, but she was wrong. Lance was secure in who he was. He didn't need weak women to bolster his masculinity. He was nothing like Maricela's ex. But she wouldn't waste her breath defending him; it would make Maricela surer there was something going on between them.

They arrived at the Humboldt office. Gwen opened the car door. Maricela put a hand on her arm and stopped her from exiting. "Listen, *chica*." Her voice was soft. "You can be upset with me for telling you the truth, but I'm your friend, so I'm telling you anyway. You have a good man at home. You have a beautiful family. Don't screw it up. He's not worth it."

"Lance and I are just business partners. That's it." Gwen slammed the car door behind her.

She and Maricela worked side by side for several hours without the usual banter. Gwen threw herself into her paperwork, ignoring the office noise and her hurt feelings.

"Hm," a deep voice startled her. "That must be riveting." John Gordon nodded at the mountain of paper on her desk.

"Fascinating." Gwen nodded.

"Is your Dana Point house in escrow yet?" he asked.

"No. My Chicago clients bought in Newport." Gwen's voice was flat. It still galled her that old Arnie had bought from another agent after everything he'd put her through.

"I may have an interested party." John thumped her desk with his forefinger. "I'd like to take another look at it before I show it."

"Help yourself," Gwen said and looked at her paperwork hoping to end the conversation. She didn't feel like talking.

"Want to go with me?" he asked.

Gwen looked up in surprise. "There's a lockbox on it."

"I know. Just thought you might want to give me the sales pitch." He smiled. It made him look like a ferret.

She opened a desk drawer, rummaged around and pulled out a piece of paper. "Here's the flier," she said. "Everything you need to know in black and white."

"Oh, okay. Thanks." His smile faded. He started to walk away, but turned again. "How about the Laguna house. Is there a lockbox on it?"

"I think Lance is putting one on tonight, but we're holding an open tomorrow."

He nodded and left the room without speaking. Gwen and Maricela looked at each other, and Maricela rolled her eyes. They went back to work, the air between them warmer. Nothing like uniting over a common enemy.

Another hour passed, and Gwen's stomach growled. She looked at her watch. It was 1:30. No wonder. Her breakfast smoothie had worn off long ago.

"I'm going to grab a salad. Want to go?" She asked Maricela.

"Could you bring me something?" Maricela said reaching for her purse.

Gwen took her order and headed out the door. The day was so bright it blinded her for a moment. The Santa Ana winds had waned, and the afternoon temperatures had dropped into the sixties, but the sky was still cloudless. She donned her sunglasses, and when she could see again she noticed Lance walking across the parking lot.

"Gwen." He waved at her. "I was coming to find you. I finished up the painting. We're on for the open house tomorrow."

"What about..."

"The exterminator came."

"What did he say?"

"He took care of the problem."

Gwen was dubious. "Took care of it how?"

"He checked all the likely entry spots—drains, foundation cracks near the trash area, the basement. They're all clear, but he sprayed anyway. The roaches came in through the chimney. He set off a bomb in the fireplace. I can go in and finish up the odds and ends at," he looked at his watch, "six."

"Why would they come in through the chimney?"

"There was sticky stuff inside it. Sweet sap or something. It was weird. I washed it down with ammonia before he set the bomb off."

"Are you sure they'll *all* be gone. It wouldn't be good if one of those creepy things ran over a potential buyer's foot."

"That's what the guy thinks. He said it's good we jumped on it. Didn't give them a chance to get too attached to the place." Lance's mouth was set in serious lines, but his eyes were smiling.

"How about the dead ones? Are they all over the place? I can't go in if there are dead ones all over the place."

"I'll clean them up tonight. Promise." Lance rested a hand on her shoulder for a brief moment, but the warmth of his touch stayed with her for the rest of the day."

CHAPTER TWENTY-FOUR

SATURDAY MORNING WAS BRIGHT AND COOL. An onshore breeze tossed clouds about in a cerulean sky. The ocean, smooth as glass, reflected the heavenly blue. It was a perfect day to showcase a beachfront listing. Gwen, arms full of flowers, tottered a bit in her high heels on the uneven walkway.

"You okay?" Lance put a stabilizing hand on her back.

Stabilizing. That's what he'd become—a stabilizing force in her life. Despite what she'd said to Maricela, he was more than a coworker. More than a business partner. He'd become a friend.

She understood Maricela's concerns. It was hard not to be attracted to him. To say Lance was handsome was an understatement, but his looks weren't his most dangerous attribute. At least, not as far as Gwen was concerned. It was his dependability that made him perilous. She hadn't known he possessed the trait, so she hadn't hardened herself against it.

"Got it." Gwen hurried forward, away from the intimacy of his hand.

"Let me get the door." He walked around her.

Gwen let him enter first. She'd only been in the house once since the attack of the killer cockroaches, and although at the time she hadn't seen any insects, alive or dead, she was still jumpy.

"The walls look great. I love the color. Just a touch of yellow to warm—" Gwen, eyes on the freshly painted stairwell, walked into Lance's back.

"Oh, God. What is that?" Lance said.

The smell hit Gwen a nanosecond after his words.

Ripe. Sweet. Sickening. Like the smell at the top of the stairs the day she and Maricela had found Sondra Olsen. A wave of nausea broke over her, leaving its moisture on her hairline and upper lip. "I can't..."

"Stay here," Lance said.

Gwen didn't. She backed out the front door and stood under the arms of the fig tree. She took deep, cleansing breaths of ocean air trying to flush away the stench. It wouldn't leave her. Neither would the image of a white, bloodied and broken body.

She buried her face in the bouquet she'd brought to brighten the open house. But hidden under the scent of lilies and mums, she smelled death. It seemed to reach out to her from the open doorway.

She dropped the blooms, ran to the street and began to pace. The reek followed her down the block and back, down and back. It had become a part of her. Infused into her. The memory of death. The smell. Now inseparable.

Who was doing this to her? To them?

It was at least ten minutes before Lance walked out to the street. He stood, hands on hips, lips curled in disgust. "Something is dead, but it's not another real estate agent.

Not unless it's a really small one. It's coming from the stove vent. A bird must have flown down, got stuck, and died. It happens."

"I thought there were caps or traps or something at the top of the vents," Gwen said.

"The cap was missing. I checked."

"Doesn't that seem a bit strange to you? Coincidental?" Gwen had a lot of time to think while she'd been waiting for him to return. "I mean, first the cockroaches, then on the day of the open house, a dead bird in the stove pipe?"

Lance massaged his temples. "Maybe. I don't know. Old places are unpredictable."

"I've never heard of a sudden infestation of roaches from a chimney flue. And how did that sticky stuff get in it?"

"No. It was weird. Definitely weird."

"And this, this, smell thing. You were here yesterday, right?"

"Yeah."

"Did you smell anything then?"

Lance shook his head.

"Wouldn't it have to kind of build up? I mean, it depends on how long the... thing... the animal has been dead. If it's this overpowering today, you'd think you'd have smelled something yesterday. Even if it was faint."

"I don't know. I was touching up the paint. Paint has a pretty strong odor. Maybe it masked it. Or, maybe it's been there for a couple of days and just started to stink."

Neither said anything for a beat, then both spoke at once.

"We have to call—"

"We'll have to cancel—"

Gwen stopped talking.

"We'll have to reschedule the open house for tomorrow," Lance said.

"How do we get the bird out of the vent?"

"I don't know. I'll figure it out."

"Lance," Gwen's voice faltered. "I'm afraid. I think someone is sabotaging us." She told him about the conversation she'd had with Investigator Sylla the day before. "What if it's him, this Moray person?"

The tense lines of his face melted into something softer. "Let's not get paranoid. It's a strange coincidence, granted, but I don't see any connection between the murders and a couple of roaches." He stepped forward and put an arm around her shoulders.

Gwen buried her face in his chest. The spicy scent of his cologne wrapped around her head and drove away the stench of decay.

#

Gwen's phone buzzed from somewhere under her desk. She followed the sound to her purse. She'd stowed it there when she arrived at the office. Someone had called on the Sailor's Haven house an hour ago, and she'd stopped by work to get her lockbox key before heading down.

"Hey." It was Lance.

"Hey, yourself. How's it going?"

"Well, it turned out the critter was a rat, not a bird. That's why it smelled so terrible. The removal guy said rats are the worst."

"Nice," Gwen said with a shudder. Her dislike for rats was only second to her loathing of roaches.

"He hooked the thing and pulled it out of the vent with a rope. Then he sprayed with some biological chemical."

"How does it smell?"

"I aired everything out and burned a few candles. Smelled fine when I left."

"Thanks for handling that," Gwen said, her voice growing soft.

"Not a problem. On my way out, I noticed the flier box on the curb is empty. Is there a chance you could refill it this afternoon? It might help pull people in tomorrow. If not, don't worry about it. We can bring down more in the morning."

"I can do that." Gwen opened a drawer and found the master flier for the house. The color photograph printed on it was lovely. The landscape company they'd hired had done a great job cleaning up the vines and bushes. Lance had repaired the rickety fence. Even the fig tree had been tamed by a good pruning. "The house looks so benign in this picture. No one would believe what's happened there."

"Gwen..." Lance's voice sounded tired.

"I know, I know. You think my view of the place has been tainted by the murder. Of course, it has. You're right. But, things haven't gone exactly swimmingly since."

"I've worked on a lot of renovations. The older the house, the more booby traps it has. I've seen stuff you wouldn't believe."

She wasn't going to argue, especially because she didn't know what to think. The idea that someone was trying to undermine the sale of the house did seem a bit farfetched. But she also had a hard time accepting the cockroaches and the rat were just coincidence. "I'm at the office now, about to head to Dana Point. Someone wants to see Sailor's Haven. I'll swing by Laguna on my way."

"You sure you're okay with dropping off fliers alone? I already put the lockbox on the side of the house, so you don't have to do that. Don't even have to open the gate." She could hear the laughter in his words.

Gwen made a stack of fliers on the copy machine in the office then headed out to her car. A pebble of anxiety dropped into her stomach as soon as she turned north on the Coast Highway. The ripples spread in wider and wider circles the closer she got to Cliff Drive. By the time she pulled up to the curb in front of the house a whirlpool of stomach acids churned inside her.

All she needed was to open the plastic holder underneath the "For Sale" sign and drop the fliers in. She wasn't afraid. Not exactly. What she felt was more a marriage of dread and disappointment.

This listing was going to make her career. That's what she'd once thought. Now she couldn't wait to unload the place. She put the papers into the box, got in her car and turned south. She had fifteen minutes to get to Dana Point.

Before she'd hung up with Lance, Gwen told him her theory about houses. . She believed they were like family dogs—emotional vacuums that picked up the moods and attitudes of their owners. The Sailor's Haven house had been decorated with a loving hand. Mementos of a life well lived were everywhere you looked. The very walls of the house exuded contentment. Cliff Drive was like an abused animal, dangerous in its hunger.

CHAPTER TWENTY-FIVE

GWEN GOT TO LAGUNA EARLY on Sunday morning. If there were going to be any surprises, she wanted to know about them before anybody else did. Shoving down the distaste rising in her throat, she unlocked the front door.

She thought about waiting for Lance before entering, but didn't want to give him any more ammunition. He'd teased her enough about her theory on the similarity between houses and family pets when she shared it with him.

She hurried through the entryway past the baleful basement door and into the kitchen. While she ran water into the vases she'd bought in San Juan, she pulled three bouquets of flowers from a paper sack. Instead of fully staging the house, she and Lance had decided to use some of the furniture he'd found in a basement room, some odds and ends from her home, and flowers to make the place as homey as possible.

Gwen refused to go down to the cellar with him, so she had to trust his judgment. *He did okay,* she thought when she entered the living room. An old sofa table with claw-foot legs sat in front of the picture windows gleaming with polish. Gwen glanced across the expanse of the floor before crossing to it. No bugs. No dead rats. No surprises. Her vase of yellow tulips made a striking contrast to the blue of sky and sea beyond.

A square wood table, gray with age, sat between two black, ladder-back chairs under an ancient crystal chandelier in the dining room. An arrangement of white hydrangeas and roses with celery green grass looked elegant against the severe backdrop.

As Gwen moved from room to room adding a throw pillow here, leaning a picture there, her mood lightened. The bones of the house were lovely. The freshly painted walls hid the scars and bruises of the past. It wasn't cheerful, but it had drama. Maybe they could sell this place after all.

"Hello, the house." Lance's voice rang through the empty rooms.

"In here," Gwen called from the kitchen.

"Hey, our crazed pit bull is looking pretty good this morning."

"Funny."

He dropped three bags onto the counter. "Candles—scented just in case. Crackers—to go with the cheese plates. And toilet paper. We're going to be here all day."

"Good thinking." Gwen opened the package of toilet paper, selected a candle and headed to the guest bathroom off the front hall.

"Have you been upstairs yet?" Lance followed her.

"No. I haven't had a chance."

"I put a few chairs up there, that's it. I didn't want to haul up beds and dressers. But I thought we could add pillows or a throw blanket to warm things up."

"There's a big, plastic garbage bag full of that kind of stuff in the kitchen. Help yourself." Gwen busied herself with the toilet paper holder, taking longer than necessary to insert the roll and make a triangular fold in the first sheet.

Lance watched her for a moment then disappeared into the kitchen. She'd go upstairs, just not yet. She'd used up all her courage credits opening the house by herself this morning. As she lit a candle to leave on the side of the sink, she heard Lance's footsteps on the stairs.

Several minutes later, he joined her in the kitchen. "Can I take those?" He pointed to the last bunch of flowers, bright red gazanias in a milk white jar. "The master needs a little something else."

While Lance finished the second story, Gwen ran to the car for the box she'd packed with coffee pot, cups, cream and sugar. Wine was fine for the afternoon crowd, but she for one wanted to start the day with caffeine.

"Can I help you with that?" John Gordon pulled up to the curb as Gwen lifted the cardboard crate from the trunk. John, Taryn, Eric Woo and Caroline climbed out of the vehicle.

"What are you doing here?" Gwen said.

"That's a nice greeting." John took the box from Gwen's arms.

"We wanted to see the mystery house," Eric said. "It's the highest price listing in the office."

"I brought donuts." Caroline held up a greasy bag.

The group followed Gwen inside and scattered when they hit the front hall. She could hear the click of heels on the wood floor, creaks overhead and raised voices from all around the house while she made coffee. She poured the first cup for herself and carried it into the entryway. "Coffee's ready." From that vantage point, her voice carried into every room.

John walked down the stairs a moment later and accompanied her to the kitchen. The rest entered through the door off the dining room.

"It's a bit beat up, but it's a great location," John said.

Lance moved a bite of donut into his cheek then said, "You should have seen it before we spruced things up."

"The place gives me the creeps," Caroline said.

Taryn looked at her over the top of her glasses.

Caroline's hand fluttered in the air as if she was trying to wipe away her words. "I mean, I'm sure it'll sell. The view is amazing. I just wouldn't want to be..."

Taryn put a fist to her mouth and coughed. Caroline stopped talking.

"I'd better get the signs up." Lance wiped the donut crumbs from his hands onto his pants and walked out of the kitchen.

"Do you need help with anything?" Taryn said.

"No, I think I'm good." Gwen smiled at her. Taryn never showed up at her agents' open houses, but then none of her agents ever had a multi-million dollar, beachfront listing in Laguna before. Gwen could tell she wanted to stay and make sure she and Lance didn't screw things up.

"Let's get going then," Eric said. "I want to stop by a couple of other places on our way out of town if that's okay with everybody."

The watchful silence of the house closed around Gwen when the agents left. She felt the raw edge of claustrophobia and hurried to the living room to look out at the ocean. The view from the windows usually had a calming effect on her, but while they'd been in the kitchen drinking coffee and eating donuts, a fog had blown in. The house was now shrouded in gray. The line between sea and sky invisible. She'd heard a storm front was moving in next week.

Gwen shivered.

Caroline was right. The place was creepy. They could groom it, put a bow on it, but she still didn't trust it. Once you've been bitten, it was wise to be wary.

She wished Lance would get back, but she knew he'd be a while. He had to pound in signs on the highway, north and south, and up and down all the neighboring streets. It was strange how much she'd come to rely on him even though they'd only been working together a short time. Well, not that surprising really.

Art had always been her rock—solid support, the one she depended on. Not lately. The nasty voice she'd been trying to ignore since she'd seen him and Lorelei together on the steps of St. Barnabas earlier that week crept into her mind. *She's younger. She's adoring. He won't be able to resist her.* She was tired of quieting that voice, of fighting it. What if he did leave her for Lorelei?

Gwen was about to sell the most expensive property of her career. Granted, she had to split the commission with Lance, but it was still a hefty sum. One listing at this price point would lead to others too. Real estate was all about groups and communities. Neighbors and buyers with a lot of money to spend would be stopping by today along with the curious and the lookie-loos.

This house, as difficult and traumatic as it had been, was an incredible opportunity. She wouldn't be dependent on the generosity of her ex-husband like her mother had been. Not that she thought Art was actually going to become an ex-husband, but she needed to look at the worst-case scenario, face her fears.

If Art left her, she'd be okay. She'd found a profession she was good at, and she had a partner. Her face softened when she thought of Lance. Not romantic thoughts. He was younger. Probably not interested anyway. But it was nice to have someone to rely on.

"Anybody home?" A voice, loud and male, made her jump. Mo stood behind her under the arched entrance to the living room. She'd forgotten she called and rescheduled the food for today.

"You startled me."

"Sorry. The door was open. I let myself in."

"That's okay. Can I help you carry?" Gwen pulled herself together.

"I've already unloaded."

Covered cheese platters were stacked on the counter in the kitchen next to plates of chocolate covered strawberries and fruit pastries. "There's a case of wine with four varietals in it—three of each. The pinot noir goes with the sharp cheddar, the Riesling with the Camembert. The Cabernet is for the chocolate, and the Viognier for the peach tartlets." He opened the top of a box on the floor to show her the wines inside.

"How long have you been here?" Gwen was surprised she hadn't heard him come in and out. He had to have made at least two trips.

"Long enough to unload." He flashed his teeth in what Gwen supposed was a smile, but it looked more like a grimace. "Well, I'd better be pushing on."

Gwen walked him to the front door and watched him disappear through the gate. She turned and faced the entryway. "It's just you and me again," she said. Her voice reverberated through the still house.

CHAPTER TWENTY-SIX

LANCE RETURNED WITH SOME OF THE NEIGHBORS in tow—an older couple, both with short, tousled gray hair, dressed in running shoes and walking shorts. Gwen watched them as they traversed the courtyard, laughing with Lance as if they were old friends.

"We've been wondering what was going on around here this week," the man said.

"We figured all the banging and buzz saws must mean something good," the wife said.

"There's a lot more that needs doing, but we did fix things up a bit. Come on in." Lance ushered them forward with an extended arm.

"Welcome." Gwen plastered her best real estate agent smile on her face.

"This is my partner in crime, Gwen Bishop. Gwen, meet Bob and Betty, from three doors down." Lance made introductions.

While Bob and Betty toured the lower story of the house, Gwen and Lance retired to the kitchen. Every new agent learned in Open-house 101 that etiquette demanded you allow the potential client to wander through the property alone. You made yourself available to answer questions when and if you were needed.

"I think we're going to be busy." Lance poured himself a cup of coffee. "This house is kind of famous with the murder and all. Lots of curious people."

"That's not a good thing," Gwen said.

"Oh, I don't know. They say all publicity is good publicity. Even if people aren't interested in buying this house, they might want to buy another one. Gives us a chance to charm the heck out of them."

Betty from-three-doors-down popped into the kitchen. "Do you have a flier? My cousin's husband just retired, and they're thinking about moving down to the beach. This place might be too big, but you never know."

Lance handed her paperwork and his business card. "I'd love to show her what's available in the area." His voice dropped to a sexy baritone. Betty simpered.

Gwen used to think he flirted on purpose. Now she thought it was an unconscious act, like a puppy tilting its head and looking adorable when it wanted you to throw a ball, or give it a treat. Somewhere in his life, Lance had learned when he smiled a certain way, talked a certain way, looked at women from the corner of his eye in a certain way, he got what he wanted. It used to annoy her. Not anymore. He was her partner now, so it was as much her secret weapon as his.

Bob stuck his head into the kitchen. "I'm heading upstairs, Betty."

The fascinated expression Betty had been wearing while listening to Lance talk about his experience as a Realtor, faded. "Coming," she said without so much as a glance toward her husband. "I'll give your card to Stella. I'm sure you'll be hearing from her." With that, she turned and followed her husband from the kitchen.

Gwen shook her head at Lance.

"What?" he said.

"You."

"What?" His voice rose a half-octave.

"You know what."

"I don't."

"Drink your coffee," Gwen said.

Footsteps sounded in the foyer. It was Gwen's turn to meet new prospects. She left the kitchen. This time it was a mother-daughter team. The daughter lived in the area. Mom was visiting and thinking of moving. Based on their accents, clothing, and the awe the property inspired in them, Gwen was sure neither woman could come close to affording the home. She invited them to look around. They disappeared down the hall toward the living room.

She was just thinking about heading to the kitchen to refill her coffee cup, when a loud cry and a thud echoed through the stairwell. A moment later, Bob from-three-doors-down appeared on the landing.

"I think you'd better come up here," he said.

Gwen hesitated. She wanted to run for Lance. Send him instead. But she grabbed the newel post and climbed.

Betty leaned against the wall outside the master bedroom, a hand covering her mouth. Bob stood back to let Gwen walk by. Neither spoke.

Gwen looked at her feet. They were clad in expensive pumps she'd gotten on sale at Nordstrom's. They looked confident. They took one bold step after another. She tried not to think about where they were taking her, or what she'd see when she got there. She just focused on her self-assured shoes. When her feet reached the end of the hall, Gwen forced her eyes to enter the bedroom.

At first, she didn't understand what she was looking at. She saw only colors—white and red—no distinct shapes. It was modern art. Something that gave the effect of a thing without being that thing.

The interpretation came to her all at once, like one of those pictures you have to stare at for several minutes before you can see the dragon hidden in it. It was an impressionistic tableau depicting the death of Sondra Olsen. The last thing Gwen saw before a wash of black covered her vision was the milk white vase of scarlet gazanias sitting on a small table under the window.

#

Gwen lay on the floor in one of the small bedrooms atop a throw blanket she'd brought from home. A pillow was under her head. Betty from-three-doors-down sat next to her, a glass of wine clutched in her hand.

"Want some?" she said, lifting her glass a couple of inches.

Gwen eased herself onto her elbows. "Where's Lance?"

"He's... cleaning things up."

A wave of nausea pushed Gwen back.

"Who would do a thing like that?" Betty said.

Who would do a thing like that? A rhetorical question. No real answer, so Gwen didn't say anything.

"The poor cat. I'm not a cat person. I have a Pekingese. But, really, who would do that to a defenseless creature? It's unconscionable," Betty said.

Unconscionable, good word. The kind of person who would kill a cat and leave its body on display exactly where Sondra Olsen was found had to be without conscience.

"Someone must not want this house sold, that's all I can think. But such a cruel prank. There must be other ways to stop the sale of a house." Betty gulped her wine.

Something switched on in Gwen's frazzled brain. Why hadn't she thought of it before? Occam's razor: The simplest explanation is probably the correct one. Someone didn't want the house sold. That someone had planted the roaches and the rat, and when that didn't scare her and Lance off, they resorted to killing Sondra Olsen again in feline effigy.

"This house used to be such a nice place." Betty was still talking. "Lilly Moyer was a lovely person. When she was alive, the front yard was immaculate. I was only inside once or twice, but the decor was stunning. I thought she'd used a professional decorator, but she said no. She'd done it all herself."

The name *Moyer* made Gwen flinch, but she pushed the emotion aside. K. Moyer, whoever he was, probably didn't give a fig if they sold this place. So who did? Gwen's mind spun with possible narratives. Could there be an insurance policy that would yield more than a sale? She rejected that idea almost at once. This property commanded a huge price tag in the current market. Insurance companies would use comparable sales. Nothing had sold in this neighborhood for at least a year, giving an adjuster an excuse to lower the payout. Besides, why would Fiona hire her, sabotage the sale, then risk arson or something else illegal? A sale was a clean, legitimate path to income.

"When Lilly died, Edward let the place go. He was bereft, the poor man. Almost a hermit. I think the only person he saw regularly was his daughter—the dancer. She would come by on Sundays. It was a shame." Betty prattled on, but Gwen no longer listened.

Another agent. Another agent was the only kind of person who could want Lance and her to lose the listing. An agent who wanted it for him or herself. Gwen had met some competitive Realtors in her time, some who would sink pretty low to get a good listing, but killing a cat and leaving its bloodied corpse in the master bedroom? It strained the imagination.

"When Edward couldn't manage alone anymore, his daughter put him in a nursing home in San Juan. I don't know what was wrong with him. Hazel, next door," Betty pointed right, "thought he had Alzheimer's. Anyway, the place fell into disrepair after he left."

"Maybe I should have some wine." Gwen didn't really want a drink, only a moment to think in peace.

"Certainly, dear." Betty patted her arm and left the room.

Gwen stared at the ceiling and began to sort through possible suspects. Taryn didn't work with clients anymore and stood to gain when the property sold. She was out. Caroline was ambitious, but too flighty to carry off the kind of complex campaign that had been waged. Besides, Caroline was a soft touch for animals. She'd wouldn't kill a rat, never mind a cat. One by one, Gwen evaluated all the agents in the office and dismissed them, until she got to John Gordon.

John was a possibility. He couldn't stand Lance. He was competitive, mean-spirited, and he was a man. Gwen thought the attacks seemed masculine in nature. Women didn't like to get their hands dirty. A woman would be more inclined to use slander, innuendo, or psychological assaults.

The more she thought about it, the more pieces of the puzzle fell into place. She sat up. She was sure. John Gordon must be the culprit.

Fury revived her. She pushed herself off the floor and came to her feet in one motion. She needed to talk to Lance. If John thought he could intimidate them, get them to walk away from the listing, he was wrong. Dead wrong.

She traversed the hallway in long strides, her aversion to the master bedroom washed away in a flood of outrage. She found Lance squatting next to a bucket full of pink, sudsy water scrubbing the wood floor with a large sponge. He looked up at her as she entered, concern etched into the lines of his face.

"I know who did this," she said

Lance rocked back on his heels. "You look like you're feeling better."

"John Gordon."

Lance's eyebrows rose, but he didn't speak.

"Think about it. This... this person," Gwen waved a hand at the floor, "must have been trying to stop the sale of the house. What other motive could they have?"

"You think John wants that top salesman plaque so badly he'd resort to this?" Lance's voice was skeptical.

"No. I think he wants the listing. Money is a big motivator."

"He might want the listing, but even if we lost it, or walked away from it, what's to say he'd get it?"

"If he's the one sabotaging us, he knows what's happening behind the scenes. He thinks he can predict what we're going to do, when we're going to do it." A surge of anger coursed through Gwen like caffeine. She marched to the far wall and back. "He's probably had his pitch to Fiona prepared for weeks, so he can swoop in as soon he gets the word."

Lance dropped the sponge into the bucket and stood. "I'm not crazy about John, and I know he's not the most ethical guy in the world, but this seems like a stretch."

Gwen threw up her hands. "Who else then? Who else could possibly have done this?"

"I don't know, Gwen, but it's not our job to figure it out." Lance's voice was annoyingly soothing.

"You're not talking about getting the police involved?"

"I don't think we have a choice. Sondra Olsen's murderer might have been the one who did this."

"Sondra's murderer is long gone. Have you forgotten the killing in Newport and the one in Huntington?" Gwen stopped pacing and faced him. "I know I've been the one terrified he'd show up again, but I was wrong. You were right. A cockroach infestation doesn't sound like the work of a homicidal maniac. These crimes, or pranks, whatever you want to call them, are motivated by greed. I'm telling you, it's John. The last thing this place needs is more bad press. If we call the police we're playing right into his hands."

Lance didn't say anything but the set of his jaw hardened, and he crossed his arms over his chest. Gwen lowered her voice. "You have to admit; I was right about one thing. When you thought all this was just a series of unfortunate events, I said someone was behind it."

Lance gave her an almost imperceptible nod. "You were right about that."

"Then think this through with me." She held up a hand and ticked off her arguments on her fingers. "John has information the general public isn't privy too. He has motive and opportunity. He was here this morning, wandering around the house by himself."

"How did he get the cat into the house without our seeing him?"

"You put a lockbox on Friday night. He even asked me about it at the office that day. He could have planted the cat in the closet, then pulled it out this morning when no one was around."

"We can check with the security company. See if he's used his key since the box has been on."

"I'll do it on Monday, but meanwhile, let's not call the police. At least, not yet. If John didn't enter the house last night, I'll call Investigator Sylla. Okay?"

Lance inhaled and exhaled slowly. "All right. I guess we can wait a day or two. But, as far as motive goes, I still say it's a crapshoot whether John would get the listing or not. I mean, Fiona could decide to pull the house off the market, or give the listing to a friend or relative who just got a license. Anything could happen."

"True. But John can't stand you. I think he'd be happy just to take the listing away from you even if he didn't get it. It's a no-lose situation for him."

Lance picked up the bucket. "Supposing you're right. It's John. What's the plan? We can't confront him. We have no proof."

Gwen followed him into the hallway and down the stairs. "Well, for one thing, we don't cancel the open house."

"The only sign I took down was the one out front. I could put it up again."

"We don't tell anyone. We act like nothing happened."

"That would piss him off." She could hear the smile in Lance's voice. "What do we do about Bob and Betty?"

"Let me handle them," Gwen said.

Lance headed outside to clean the bucket, and Gwen went in search of the neighbors. She found them in the dining room. Bob sat in a chair and Betty stood, a wine glass in each of her hands. "You must be feeling better," she said when she saw Gwen.

"I am, thanks." Gwen took one of the glasses from her. "Can we talk?"

Betty sat across from her husband and folded her hands on the table like a schoolgirl waiting for instruction.

"I'm so sorry you were exposed to this. I feel responsible." Gwen held up a hand when they began to protest.

"How could you be responsible?" Bob said. "This was obviously the work of a reprehensible deviant. The price of the homes may make this neighborhood exclusive to live in, but you don't have to present a credit statement to visit. There is constant coming and going of all sorts, scuba divers in the mornings, beach bums and tourists all afternoon. I have to tell you; I've been thinking about selling. Moving to a gated community."

A small smile tickled at the corner of Gwen's mouth. It would be a wonderful irony if all of John's efforts to steal this listing from her and Lance resulted in their acquiring another one. "If you're thinking about selling, you'll understand when I ask you to please keep what happened here today quiet. For Fiona's sake."

"Fiona?" Bob repeated the name.

"Ed's daughter," Betty said. "I assume she owns the property now."

"Yes," Gwen said. "She was very shaken by the death that occurred in the house. She might be afraid this incident was directed at her in some way. I don't think it was. I think your assessment of the situation is the correct one. It was a random act by a transient, or some kid taking a dare. But it might be hard to convince her of that."

"I'd hate to upset her, but..." Betty let her words trail off.

"Plus, you know how people are," Gwen said. "If word got around about this, it could affect the sale of the house. Actually, it could affect values in the whole neighborhood, your house even. Nobody wants to spend several million on a home and then have to worry about vandals."

Bob and Betty looked across the table at each other, communicating without words the way people who've been married for many years do sometimes. The way Gwen and Art had done until recently. Seeming to come to an agreement, they rose as one.

"I believe you're right," Bob said. "It's not like there's a crime wave on Cliff Drive. No need to involve the police, or the gossips."

"Exactly," Gwen said. "Now, you have my card, right? I'd love to help you if you decide to relocate."

By the time Bob and Betty from-three-doors-down left the premises, Gwen had them securely in her camp.

CHAPTER TWENTY-SEVEN

ART STOPPED BY THE HOSPITAL on his way to work Monday morning. Brian had woken up, but was still groggy and slept a lot. He was sleeping now, and no one else was in his room. Art offered up a small prayer, and crept out.

On the way out of the hospital, he ran into Mike McKibben.

"He awake?" Mike asked.

"Not yet," Art said.

Mike looked relieved. "I'd better get up there. I'm late. Olivia had to go back to work. The family has been taking turns sitting with him." He headed toward the elevators.

"Wait, Mike. Can I talk to you for a minute?"

They walked out of the main lobby into the smaller waiting room they'd been in the other day.

"I want to do something for Brian, for Olivia. Something practical. What does she need? I can't get anything out of her."

Art couldn't explain why it was so important for him to have a task. Maybe he was reaching for control. Maybe he needed a string of Hail Marys to assuage his guilt.

"Moral support. That's probably what she needs most," Mike said.

"I have to do more. Please."

Mike must have heard the desperation in Art's voice. "Well, she'd kill me if she knew I told you, but she might be getting kicked out of her apartment."

"Why?"

"She was already behind on her rent, and the doctor bills are starting to come in. I have some money. I was going to put the rest on my credit card this month, but I can't keep that up."

"Done." Relief rolled over Art. "How much?"

"Eight hundred would really help."

A small penance. Art checked his watch. He could make it to the bank, pull the money out of savings, drop it by and still get to the Monday morning board meeting on time.

Twelve minutes later, he emerged from the elevator on the fifth floor of Mission Hospital. He almost jogged down the corridor to Brian's room. Mike sat in the only chair.

"This is great," Mike said. "I appreciate it."

Art handed him an envelope. "If she needs anything else, more money, anything, let me know."

Mike waved him away. "This is a loan. One of us will repay it."

"Not necessary," Art said.

"It is. Now get out of here. Get to work."

Art left the hospital feeling better than he had since the accident.

CHAPTER TWENTY-EIGHT

THE FAMILIAR SCENT OF CINNAMON AND ALLSPICE overwhelmed the smell of toner. Gwen knew Lance was behind her before she heard his voice or felt his hand on her back. She hadn't seen him since Sunday. He'd taken off yesterday, and she didn't blame him. With all the repairs he'd had to do, he'd worked the better part of five days and nights in a row. The rhythmic drone of the copy machine stopped.

"Hey there," he said. "I didn't want to startle you."

"Hey there yourself." She lifted her four-color fliers from the tray and examined them.

"What're you doing?"

"Baking brownies."

"I have good news." Lance's breath grazed the back of her neck.

She scooted away and turned to face him. "You do?"

"We have an offer."

"What? Already?"

"Remember that couple from L.A.? The ones you thought looked like aging drug dealers."

"The guy in leather and the woman in black?"

"The same. The offer came in this morning. It's low. We're going to have to negotiate and it might not fly but, hey, not bad for only having the place available for a couple of days. Especially under the circumstances."

"The lockbox company sent me an email. A bunch of agents have been through the house."

"Lots of action since Sunday?" Lance grinned. The look on his face reminded her of Jason when he beat a level of Dragon Quest.

Gwen set her fliers on a table and leaned toward him. "John Gordon was one of them."

"Oh, yeah?"

"Yeah. He was in Saturday night." Gwen lowered her voice. "He could've planted the cat."

"I'm still struggling with that whole idea. It's hard to believe he'd stoop that low."

"Why was he in the house the night before the open house then?"

Lance shrugged. "He wanted to see it before everyone else did?"

"He's been acting funny for the past two days."

"Funny how?"

"Funny, guilty funny. He asked me how the open house went."

Lance hunched his shoulders and brought his face closer to hers. "Caroline and Eric asked me how the open house went too. I think they're in cahoots. A conspiracy. Or, would it be a coup? Is it a coup when you're being deposed?"

Gwen slapped his shoulder. "Oh shut up. You're making fun of me."

"Listen, I think Bob and Betty had the most logical explanation. Everybody knows there was a murder in the house. Some whacko from the neighborhood either made a lucky guess about where the body was found or has a friend on the police force. It was a prank. A very mean prank."

"Really?" Gwen folded her arms across her chest. "When did they plant the cat then? I was there all morning, and you said yourself it wasn't there when you went upstairs with the flowers."

"The door was wide open. Someone must have walked in while you were in the kitchen."

Gwen didn't answer. That explanation didn't cover the cockroaches or the rat, neither of which she was willing to chalk up to coincidence. "If you're right we should take some security measures."

"Like what?" Lance pushed her fliers aside and sat on the copy room table.

"Motion sensitive lights. An alarm system."

"We can't put in an alarm system. We have a lockbox on the front door."

"We can. We just set the alarm to go off between the hours of midnight and five. We can do it remotely." Gwen sat up late the night before comparing the perks and prices of home security companies.

"Is there anything left in the budget for all this?"

"Not much."

"If we ask Fiona for more we'll have to tell her what happened."

"Right, but if we clean out what's left in the account and each throw in five hundred dollars, we can do it."

"You think it's going to do any good? If there's a lockbox on the property, agents can get in whenever they want."

"Not without our knowing about it, and not in the middle of the night. Besides, I thought you didn't think an agent was our problem."

He tipped his head in concession. "I guess it couldn't hurt. We don't want a repeat of last weekend."

After Lance left, Gwen went to her desk and pulled her laptop out of her briefcase. She and Art had an agreement. They would discuss any purchases over two hundred dollars before making them. But right now she rebelled at the thought of asking him for money. She would make more on this one deal than Art made in a year. She wasn't a child.

If Gwen had learned one thing from watching her mother's life, it was that she needed to be able to take care of herself, retain some measure of autonomy. Her mom had once been a beautiful, intelligent woman. She could have done anything she chose with her life, and she chose to be a wife and a mother. She excelled at it. No one could out bake her at church bake sales. She was the class mom, Brownie leader, and in charge of fundraising for Gwen's soccer team.

She made all the costumes for the school plays and designed picture perfect holidays. Their home could have graced the pages of Red Book, or Better Homes and Gardens. The birthday parties she threw were the envy of the neighborhood.

When Gwen's father left, her mother had to sell the house she loved and move into a small, sterile apartment.

Gwen's father did his duty by her, as he'd promised. She received an alimony check each month that covered her basic expenses and occasionally a little extra.

She tried to find work for a while, but no one was interested in hiring a forty-year-old woman who hadn't held a job since she was twenty-two. There were no sections on applications for killer banana bread recipes, or elaborate Juliet costumes. Gin became her comfort and then her executioner.

One day in Gwen's senior year of high school, she came home and found her mother passed out on the couch. After that, Gwen watched as she disappeared into the bottle's black hole a piece at a time. She died ten years later of a stroke.

Gwen opened her computer and logged into her bank page. She scrolled until she found the savings account she and Art had created for emergencies. In her mind, this qualified.

Last time she looked, there had been about thirty-five hundred dollars in there. The balance at the top of the page now showed only two-thousand-six-hundred, and change. Strange. She was sure there had been over three thousand. She scanned the list of credits and debits. Her eyes stopped on an eight hundred dollar withdrawal. It was made that Monday.

It took several moments for her brain to compute the implications. Art had taken eight hundred dollars out of their account. He hadn't said a word.

She sat still in her chair, staring at the screen. She reached for her phone and began to punch in his number, but instead of hitting call, she hit cancel. She needed to think this through.

If she asked Art about the money, he'd know she was looking at the account. He'd wonder why. She hadn't told him about the dead cat, and she wasn't planning to. Why would she? He'd just get angry with her for putting the house on the market all over again. He'd want her to give the listing to Lance and stay home.

Her cell phone dinged. She opened her text messages. Funny timing. It was Art. "Can you take Friday off? Want to leave early for Big Bear."

Could he have spent the money on this trip? No. Camping didn't cost eight hundred dollars.

Maybe he was going to take her away as a surprise—the camping trip a ruse? He'd done that before. Once he'd told her they were going to his parents for the weekend then spirited her away after they dropped off the kids. Another time he told her to get ready for a picnic on the beach. The beach turned out to be the one in front of their hotel room at the Hotel Del Coronado in San Diego.

But he'd put a hotel on a credit card. He wouldn't pay cash. Lorelei. The name flitted through her mind. He wouldn't use a credit card if he bought a gift for Lorelei. It would be impossible to hide the purchase of, say, an eight-hundred-dollar necklace from a jewelry store.

Suddenly she didn't want to know where the money went. If it wasn't returned in a month or two, or if any more disappeared from the account, she'd ask him then. She prayed silently her fears were unfounded, that this mystery would have an innocent answer.

She picked up her phone and typed, "Fine." Then she clicked open the bank's transfer form, found the correct savings account number, and transferred five hundred dollars into her personal checking account. Done. If he noticed, he couldn't very well ask her about it. Not without telling her what his withdrawal was for.

CHAPTER TWENTY-NINE

I SAT IN MY CAR in front of the house on Cliff Drive with my windows rolled down and waited for dark. A strong breeze blew off the ocean, and the palm trees at the end of the block bent toward the hills. The neighborhood was solid and established. I liked the stable, old-money feel of the place. So many Orange County homes are like much of the state's fruit—oversized and absolutely tasteless.

There was a picture of Gwen on the house flier. She really was a lovely woman. I've always been attracted to redheads. Fiona is a redhead.

I bumped into my sister by accident one day. I knew it was she even though I'd only seen her from a distance. Her photo was in the local society section of the paper when her engagement was announced. She, of course, didn't notice me.

She was coming out of a department store in Fashion Island loaded down with bags—probably shopping for her upcoming nuptials. The date was drawing close. I had the reaction most people have when they see a celebrity. I stopped and stared, then doubted my eyes. It was difficult to believe we were occupying the same few feet of space. We lived in such different worlds.

She, the beloved. I, the rejected. She, a part of my father's household. I, thrown off his property. She was the north pole of a magnet and I, the south. When I found myself in her field, the pull was irresistible.

I followed her past a fountain, down a row of boutiques, and into a coffee shop. I slipped behind her in line and inhaled her expensive perfume. I listened to the lilt of her voice and felt the warmth of the smile she bestowed on the barista. She was so confident, so happy. A diamond—three and a half or four carats—sparkled on her left hand. It was beautiful. She was beautiful.

I fell under her spell that day. I couldn't get her out of my mind. At first, I only followed her on social media. I attended her wedding on Instagram, then her honeymoon. When the flurry of photos subsided, I began to follow her car.

I trailed her from the dance school where she worked to her house. Once I knew where she lived, I would show up on the street whenever I could. In this way, I learned where she shopped, worked, ate, and played. On five different occasions, I drove behind her to our father's house in Laguna Beach.

One night about a year ago, I sat in my car across the street from her home. From my dark, solitary perch, I could see her through the windows of that bright, open space. I watched her the way I had when she was a girl.

It came to me then. Literally. *It* came to me. I wasn't looking for a counter-spell, an antidote. I didn't believe there was one.

It was getting late. She was sitting at her kitchen table reading. I hadn't seen her husband through the windows in a while. I assumed he'd gone to bed. I was tired and thinking about doing the same, when she stood.

She walked to the doorway of the kitchen. The room went black. In a second, she reappeared in the dining room, crossed it and disappeared into black again. The vision repeated in the office. Then the living room. I watched her disappear again and again.

When the last light was extinguished, my mind was illuminated. She must disappear for me to become visible. She was the black hole, the vacuum. She had sucked all my light and all my worth into herself. That was when I began to make plans.

The streetlights popped on up and down Cliff Drive. The sun had set while I'd sat reminiscing. It was now dark enough for my errand. An older couple with a little thing on a leash that looked more guinea pig than dog strolled down the block. I waited until they turned the corner.

I hefted the black bag from the passenger side of the car. It clanked. The sound echoed down the quiet street. I looked around, but didn't see anyone. I calmed myself with the thought that people in this neighborhood were used to the noise of divers and their equipment. I had to up my game regardless of the risks.

Sunday had been a roller coaster of emotions. I'd been so happy with the way my little present turned out. I'd had enough time to stage it without arousing suspicion. Everything had gone flawlessly.

Imagine my dismay when the open house went forward as if nothing had happened. I'd been so sure

Gwen would collapse from the horror of it all—that she'd run away and never look back. She showed strength I didn't know she possessed.

I had to come up with a new, more aggressive plan. My mind spun in a hundred directions, until it landed on the traps. There is nothing like bodily harm to put a crimp in things. I didn't care who was injured, although the idea it might be my sister was delicious. A dancer's body is her bread and butter. It would be fun to snatch the food out of her mouth for once. But anybody would do.

The traps were old and rusted and looked as if they'd been left out in salt air for years. They could have been planted by a deranged old man bothered by raccoons and opossums. No one could be sure. And I liked that.

I wanted Gwen to wonder if a corporeal being was behind these attacks, or if they were some trick of the house itself. Had the house drawn cockroaches like a corpse draws maggots? Had it trapped a small rodent in its stovepipe like a carnivorous plant captures an unsuspecting bird? Had it beckoned a homeless man and filled his muddled head with ideas of feline death? I smiled and reached for the gate.

Light. Bright. Blinding. I was caught.

I spun around, naked and exposed, in the glare of the spotlight. Any moment I expected the shriek of a siren.

But nothing came. When the pounding of heart calmed, I heard crickets chirping again. The blood cleared from behind my eyes, and I saw the source of the light. There were three halogen lamps hidden in the foliage of the front yard positioned to illuminate the entrance.

I moved into the shadows and stood very still. In a few minutes, the lights clicked off. Until this point, I'd looked at this as an adventure, a game of wits. Now I was angry.

CHAPTER THIRTY

"HOW MANY BEDROOMS DID YOU SAY IT HAS?" Susan Langdon—upper-middle class, fiftyish, surgically enhanced—wanted to know.

"Technically four. The downstairs office counts as one and there are three up," Gwen said. It was Thursday morning, and she'd shown the Sailor's Haven property every day that week. It's funny how things came in waves. After the Pauls walked away from the deal, there'd been no action for at least ten days. Suddenly everybody and their sister wanted to see it, not that she was complaining.

"I really want five, but this place is so nice." Susan stuck a French manicured thumbnail between her front teeth. "Can we look upstairs again?"

"Of course." Gwen led the way up the carpeted steps. The Frobishers were coming home next week. She'd almost given up on her goal of having an offer waiting for them, but now she had renewed hope.

"It's just me and Ron, but I need a room for each of the kids when they visit. And my daughter is having her first baby. I wanted to turn one room into a nursery. I saw the cutest jungle theme crib set at Petite Tresor."

They walked down the hall toward the place Gwen had almost clocked Arnold Paul over the head. The place she'd thought she was about to meet her maker. She smiled at the memory. So many apparently threatening things had happened since the murder on Cliff Drive. Apparently being the operative word.

Some of them were the product of an overactive imagination fueled by a smidgen of post-traumatic stress. The rest, she now believed, were the acts of someone counting on the fact she was running scared. That person had fooled her for a time, but no more. She wasn't going anywhere.

"The front bedroom is big enough for a queen and a crib," Gwen said, allowing Susan to enter before her. She hovered in the doorway leaving as much open space inside as possible.

"It could work." Susan spun in a slow circle. "I'd just have to give up the stuffed giraffes. Nowhere to put them."

They looked at the other guest room, discussed furniture and giraffe placement, then walked down the hall. Susan had been enamored with the view off the balcony of the master bedroom. Gwen wanted her to see it one more time before they left the property—let it be her last impression. Gwen couldn't get enough of the view herself. She loved Dana Point, loved the neighborhood, loved the house.

Sailor's Haven came as close to Gwen's dream home as any place she'd seen since she'd been a Realtor. She fantasized about investing her commission from the Laguna Beach house into this one, but that's all it was—a fantasy. She and Art wouldn't qualify even with a big down payment. They'd incurred too much debt. A house at the beach would remain a dream for a long while.

On the way down the stairs, her phone rang. She glanced at the screen. It was Lance. She'd been waiting for his call all day. He'd sent a counteroffer to the drug lords—her nickname for the couple who'd made the offer on Cliff Drive. Their agent was supposed to respond this morning.

"You can take that. I want to measure the office," Susan said.

"You sure?" Gwen said to Susan's retreating back. Susan twiddled her fingers over her shoulder and disappeared through the doorway. Gwen answered the call on the fourth ring. "What's the news?"

"It's good. They accepted the counter." The excitement in Lance's voice crackled through her phone. "Ten million, twenty-five thousand."

"Fantastic. When are we going to sign the papers?"

"They'll be in town tomorrow morning. We can sign then and put it in escrow on Monday."

"I can do that." Gwen would have to meet Art and the kids in Big Bear later in the day, or go up Saturday morning. This was too important to miss. He'd have to understand.

"Oh, more good news. You remember Betty from-three-doors-down? Her cousin called. She wants to look at property in the ten to thirteen million range. I'm taking her out in about an hour. Want to come?"

Gwen hesitated. They had never discussed continuing their partnership past the Laguna Beach property. It wasn't unusual for agents to join forces. The most common were husband and wife teams, but plenty had a purely business arrangement. There were advantages, shared workload, shared expenses, and so on.

In Gwen's experience, the only disadvantages arose when work ethics weren't a match. No problem there. Lance worked harder than she did. But she hadn't discussed the idea with Art. She wondered how he'd feel about her teaming up with a young, attractive male. Not positively, she thought. But she didn't feel too positively about his relationship, working or otherwise, with Lorelei.

"I can't make it. But keep me in the loop," she said. Whether they established an official arrangement moving forward or not, she wanted a piece of any deals that came because of the Cliff Drive property. It was originally her listing after all.

"I hope you're not too busy to celebrate going into escrow."

"Definitely not too busy for that."

"Friday night?"

"Sure. Dinner, somewhere expensive." She rang off, happiness and relief mingling inside her. She'd head up to Big Bear on Saturday morning. She deserved a night out. She was about to get the largest commission check of her life and at the same time offload a nightmare.

CHAPTER THIRTY-ONE

COFFEE SLOSHED AROUND IN ART'S STOMACH. He set his cup down. He'd skipped breakfast and come in early. It was Thursday. If he wanted to take tomorrow off, he had to clean his slate today. The kids were too excited about leaving the next morning to disappoint.

Only one more task to go before lunch. He picked up the phone and dialed Mission Hospital. He was anxious to see how both Olivia and Brian were doing. He'd heard Brian was talking and walking, and the prognosis was good.

Olivia wasn't there. The nurse on duty, who also happened to be the mother of a St. Barnabas student or he'd never have gotten the information, told him she thought Olivia had gone to work. She'd been in earlier wearing her Enzo's uniform.

A good sign. If things weren't going well with Brian, Olivia would never have left his side. Art pushed away from his desk. He'd celebrate with pizza for lunch and get the news directly from her.

When he got to Enzo's, he peered through the front window into the dim interior of the sport's bar. He saw Olivia's blond head flitting between tables in the back.

He entered, stood by the "Please wait to be seated" sign, and watched her efficient movements.

She dropped two beer mugs at one table, a pizza tray at another. She darted from customer to customer, her face tight and controlled.

When she saw Art, she nodded. After she finished scribbling on an order pad, she wiped her hands on her apron and came toward him. "Hi," she said, picking up a plastic menu. "Just you?"

"Just me. I came in to see how you and Brian were doing."

Olivia stared at him expressionless for a long moment. Art's mouth tipped into a tentative smile. She dissolved into grief, threw her hands over her face and sobbed.

CHAPTER THIRTY-TWO

GWEN HUNG UP THE PHONE and glared at Maricela. "Some people are just so..."

"What happened?" Maricela's forehead wrinkled with concern.

"Susan Langdon, the woman I just showed Sailor's Haven to, called to tell me she's canceling our appointment tomorrow because she's in escrow."

"What?"

"Yeah. She made an offer on another house last weekend, but wanted to hedge her bets, so she dragged me out today. Talk about a waste of time."

"It happens." Maricela said.

"I know. It's one reason I want to work with higher end clients. I can't handle all these flaky people."

"Totally, I get it." Maricela nodded gravely. "The rich are so much more stable. No flaky people in those high-income brackets."

"Ha. Very funny. Okay, they're not any better, but at least the commission makes it worth putting up with their crap."

"Do me a favor, *chica*. Don't forget us little people when you're a broker to the rich and famous."

Gwen escaped the office to go home for lunch. She'd just turned onto her street when her phone dinged. She pulled into the driveway and read the text from Tyler. He'd forgotten his Government book and paper. The paper was due today. Could she, pretty please, stop at home, pick them up and bring them to the school? He'd mow the lawn on Saturday.

Since the family was going to be camping Saturday, this wasn't much incentive, but she was sitting in the driveway and school wasn't far. She returned the text. "Next weekend. And pick up dog poop."

"Yuck. Yes," came back.

After delivering Tyler's book and paper to him, Gwen found herself in the hall outside Art's office. She hadn't intended to stop, but there she was at the door. She hesitated with her hand on the knob.

What was she hoping for? That his face would light up when he saw her? That he would drop everything, take her to lunch then home for a quick dessert like he used to? Nostalgia ached in her chest.

Millie sat at her desk in the front room as she had for the past thirty years. She'd become as much a part of the school as the statue of St. Barnabas standing in the courtyard. When she saw Gwen, she smiled.

"Hi, Millie," Gwen said.

"He's not here. I'm sorry."

When Millie referred to Art as "Him" or "He" it always sounded as if she used a capital "H", like there were no other "hims" or "hes" worth talking about.

"Oh, well, it was nothing important. I was dropping off a book for Tyler and thought—"

"How is everyone doing at home?" Millie asked. "I've been concerned about *Him*."

"We're fine. Art's fine."

"I'm not sure *He* is." Millie's face became solemn. "*He* hasn't been *Himself* ever since Brian McKibben's accident."

"Is that the third grader who was hit by a pickup two weeks ago?" Gwen said.

"Yes." Millie's eyebrows rose in surprise.

Should Gwen be more aware of the story?

"It's hit *Him* hard, for obvious reasons," Millie said.

For obvious reasons, what would those be? Art cared about all his students. Why was this one special? Gwen fiddled with the strap of her purse while she wondered how to ask what the obvious reasons were, without making the state of their marriage obvious.

"He does take responsibility for everything that happens at St. Barnabas, whether he should or not," Gwen said, fishing.

"Yes." Millie nodded her head emphatically. "And it's hard to get through to *Him* when *He's* blaming *Himself* for things that aren't *His* fault."

What wasn't his fault? Gwen tossed a little kindling onto Millie's fire of indignation. "It's great to be a person of character, but you can't take the weight of the world on your shoulders," she said.

"Exactly," Millie agreed. "But you know what *He's* like."

"I do." Gwen thought for a moment. "But I'd like to know your opinion. You know him better than anyone outside his family."

Millie inclined her head in modest agreement.

Gwen continued, "What do you think about his reaction to the incident. I mean, not the broad strokes. I get that." Gwen waved a hand to illustrate. "But the day to day stuff. The details."

Millie inhaled deeply through her nose and adjusted her glasses. "I've told *Him* over and over it's not *His* fault. It's tough for single mothers to find sitters, I understand that. But the principal of a school can't be held responsible for problems at home." She peered over the top of her bifocals, searching for understanding.

Gwen nodded, but was even more in the dark than before. How could it be Art's fault that Brian's mother didn't have a sitter?

"Children are suspended all the time," Millie continued. "Well, not all the time, but frequently enough. Brian had been in three fights on the playground."

The pieces of the puzzle were beginning to fall into place. Art had suspended Brian. Gwen hadn't known that.

"Just because Dwayne Pratt is a bully doesn't give Brian a pass. He should have asked for assistance from his teachers." Millie was on a roll now. "The child, poor soul, needs to acquire some self-discipline. I only pray he comes out of this well enough to learn it."

Understanding and sympathy welled up within Gwen. Of course, the Pratts, the bane of Art's existence. He had probably already been questioning his motives for suspending Brian; then the boy had gone and gotten hit by a truck.

This explained so much. Art was in pain, and she knew from long experience when he was in pain he withdrew. She had assumed the distance between them was all about her, or all about Lorelei.

Shame burned her cheeks. They say blondes think the world revolves around them. In fact, this redhead had done a pretty good job of setting herself up as the planetary axis. She wanted to find Art, to ask his forgiveness.

"Do you know where he is, Millie?" Gwen asked.

"*He* said *He* was going to Enzo's to grab a slice of pizza for lunch."

"Thanks." Gwen rushed from the office and pulled out of the parking lot in the direction of Enzo's.

#

The parking lot was full with lunch crowd vehicles. Gwen circled several times before she remembered there were spaces behind the building. She cut between Enzo's and a florist shop into a service alley and parked next to a Honda with a pizza-shaped flag attached to its passenger side window.

She picked her way around cast-off cardboard boxes and stacks of pallets. The bright sunlight dimmed as she made a right into the shade of the narrow passageway between the establishments. It took her eyes a moment to adjust. A few yards in, she saw a door opened to the alley. It must be the restaurant's rear exit. As she drew closer, she heard murmurs coming from the doorway—a man's voice low and pleading, a woman crying.

Gwen stopped, not wanting to intrude on what sounded like a lover's quarrel. She stood in indecision, wondering if there was another path around the building, or if she should clear her throat and let the couple know someone was coming. Before she could do either, they came into view.

The woman was petite, blond, and attractive, even with mascara tracks decorating her cheeks. She was dressed in black jeans and an Enzo's t-shirt. She looked familiar. Gwen thought she had waited on them once or twice when the family had gone in for dinner. The man's back was to her, but she had no trouble recognizing him.

It was Art.

Art.

What the hell was Art doing in an alley with a blond waitress whose name Gwen couldn't remember? She couldn't hear their conversation. But based on the emotion on the woman's face and her tears, it seemed intense and very personal.

Neither of them had noticed Gwen. She stepped behind a Dumpster located against the wall of the flower shop. She needed a minute to process.

Art. In an alley. With a waitress.

Was Art was having an affair after all? She put a hand to her chest and covered her heart. She might have imagined Art running around with the school counselor, but this was so in her face. For some reason a fling with a complete stranger seemed an even greater betrayal.

A waitress did make a weird kind of sense, however. Art liked to be the hero. He loved to champion the cause of the underdog. If he were to be tempted into adultery, it would most likely be disguised by a virtuous cause—a damsel in distress. Based on the emotions echoing through the alley, this damsel qualified.

Even though the idea he was cheating had teased around in her brain, Gwen hadn't believed it. Not really. Seeing her husband with another woman didn't compute. It was surreal.

Think, Gwen. Think. Her hand moved from her chest to her forehead and massaged her temples. She'd spent the ten minutes it had taken her to drive here berating herself for jumping to hasty conclusions, for being self-centered, for taking five hundred dollars out of their savings without telling Art. It had been a very uncomfortable ten minutes. She didn't want to repeat them.

Gwen had no idea why Art was in deep conversation with the waitress. Maybe she was the parent of a St. Barnabas student who wasn't doing well. Probably not. Private school generally wasn't an option for someone at the bottom rung of the service industry. Besides, your kid's poor grades didn't usually make you sob in an alley.

Maybe the woman had applied for a teaching position at the school, and Art had told her she wouldn't be getting the job. That was a possibility. It was pretty unprofessional of her to get so emotional, but who knew what her financial situation was? The point was, there were any number of scenarios that would cover the scene before her. Why assume the worst?

Gwen's hand dropped to her side, and she straightened her spine. She would step out from behind the Dumpster and greet them as if nothing was wrong. Because as far as she knew, nothing was. Think the best. Believe the best. Wasn't that Biblical? She'd step out and...

Wait. How would she explain why she was hiding behind a Dumpster?

She slumped against the wall of the florist shop and stared at her feet. The sound of Art's voice rose and fell. She caught a word here and there: "sorry", "my fault", "important to me", "anything for you". It was that last phrase, "anything for you", that revived her fears.

She and Art used to perform a little stand-up routine, a private vaudeville shtick, when they were feeling romantic. Art would say, "I was so stuck on you, baby, I'd have done anything for you. Anything in the world to make you mine."

Gwen would respond, "Too bad I didn't know that when you asked me to marry you. I'd have held out for more than a half carat and a honeymoon in Arrowhead."

They hadn't had that conversation in years.

The odor of rotting flower stems permeated the air. Gwen knew, in the future, whenever she dumped a vase of old blooms, she'd be transported to this horrible moment. Smell, strong emotion, and memory occupied close territory in the brain. The scent of decaying vegetation was right now linking arms with regret, fear, indecision, and embarrassment and trotting into her neural pathways. She had to get out of there.

The alley had grown quiet. Gwen realized she hadn't heard Art's voice or the woman's sobs for several minutes. Maybe they had gone inside the restaurant, and she could escape unnoticed. She longed for time alone in her bedroom to figure all this out before she had to pick up the kids. She pushed herself off the wall and crept to the edge of the Dumpster. The noise of her heels on concrete sounded like drumbeats in the dead air.

She peered into the alleyway where she'd first seen Art and the woman, expecting it to be vacant. But they were there, spotlighted by a patch of sunlight. Art's arms enveloped her. Her face was buried in his chest. They stood in a silent embrace.

CHAPTER THIRTY-THREE

GWEN SLAMMED HER CAR DOOR. She wanted to scream. Instead, she inhaled deeply. Rage rode on the oxygen from her lungs into her bloodstream and was carried to every inch of her body. Her muscles vibrated with it. How could he?

She started the car and swung onto Ortega Highway, tires squealing. Was it only two weeks ago she'd tried to stage a romantic evening for the two of them? The wine, the food, the red negligee, each was now a dart to her pride. Humiliation scorched her face. He'd probably been dreaming about the skinny waitress when he fell asleep on the couch.

She'd been an idiot. How had she not seen it? The distance he'd put between them, the disinterest in sex, the moodiness, the brooding silences. He'd been acting like a lovesick teenager. And the money he'd sneaked out of their bank account. She didn't want to think about what he'd spent it on.

To think she'd been on the fence about becoming Lance's partner because she was afraid it might bother Art. He wasn't worried about bothering her. Decision made. She'd let Lance know tomorrow.

Art had crossed the line. She could tell by the way he was stroking that woman's back, by the disgusting way the tramp was burrowing into his chest. They had a thing going. A real thing, not just a friendship like she had with Lance. There was nothing casual about what she'd seen in the alley.

A car horn startled her out of her thoughts. She'd cut off an SUV. An angry finger appeared through the driver's window as the car jerked around her. She returned the blessing. She drove five miles and exited the freeway on autopilot, lost in misery. She came to herself when she parked in the Humboldt Realty lot not remembering how she'd gotten there.

She thought about driving right back to the school and confronting Art, but she didn't want to give him the upper hand. She needed to get her emotions under control first. When she saw him, she wanted to be cool. No, cold. She wanted to blow into his world like an Arctic wind.

Maybe she should go into the office and find Maricela. She sniffled at the thought of being comforted by her best friend, then rejected the idea. Maricela would defend Art like she always did, come up with some reason for him to hug a blonde in an alley. Then Gwen would let her have it. She couldn't handle the end of two pivotal relationships in one day.

Her eyes traveled the length of the business park and came to rest on The Leaky Barrel. Wine. A bottle of wine and a bath, that's what she needed. First, she dialed Art's office. If he had time to run around with other women, he had time to get his kids.

The phone rang three times before Millie answered. "St. Barnabas. Principal Bishop's office."

"Hi Millie, it's Gwen."

"*He* just got in from lunch. I can connect you."

"No, no. Just give him a message for me, would you?" Gwen said. "I have a migraine. It came on suddenly. I'm going home. To bed. Could you ask him to get the kids for me?"

"Oh, you poor dear. My cousin Marilyn gets terrible migraines. They're so debilitating."

Gwen half-listened to several minutes of Marilyn's medical history, her thoughts wandering to her own problems. The familiarity of Millie's voice and the confidential way she spoke would be gone if Gwen and Art were no longer Gwen and Art. The thought of this loss, so small in comparison to the totality of losses that were sure to come, was still painful.

By the time Gwen hung up, her anger was spent. Exhausted and numb, she dragged herself across the parking lot to The Leaky Barrel. The terrible bell clanged when she opened the door, but this time she didn't jump. She entered, her movements mechanical, deliberate footsteps echoing on the weathered-wood floor.

"Hello there," a voice called. Gwen looked up to see the shop owner grinning behind his graying beard. "What can I get for you today?" he said.

"Nothing, Mo. I've got it." Gwen didn't want him following her from wine to wine, prattling on about noses and bouquets. She was looking for something to dull her pain, not pair with pot roast.

"If you need me, I'm right here." He winked.

Gwen turned and walked behind a wall of Malbec's. His cheeriness was an affront. She found the shelf with her favorite blend. The last time she'd splurged on a bottle of Ravish was the night Art fell asleep while she was slipping into something a little more comfortable. She might as well have gotten a bottle of Boone's Farm at the grocery store.

She gazed at the other varietals, but nothing sounded appealing. She reached out and picked up a bottle of Ravish. She'd be damned if she'd let Art steal this pleasure from her too. Tonight she was buying the wine for herself, not to impress, not for romance. Tonight it was for comfort. She wondered if one would be enough.

"Gwen. I thought that was you." Lance walked around the stack of wine. His hair was disheveled from the breeze outside, his eyes and his handsome face all smiles. "I saw you park, but you didn't come into the office. We're meeting at 10:00 am tomorrow to sign papers."

Gwen couldn't find her voice. She was so touched to see someone who cared about her, someone who was genuinely glad to see her, she burst into tears.

Fifteen minutes later, she was seated at a high table in the corner of the tasting room with the remnants of a glass of Cabernet in front of her. Lance's hand rested lightly on hers. His eyebrows were knit in concern.

He had held her while she cried and listened while she ranted, but he hadn't yet spoken. After several minutes of silence, he said, "I think you're misinterpreting the facts, Gwen. Based on what you described, it sounds like Art was breaking it off with the woman. That's probably why she was crying. I'm sure he still loves you."

"Loves me? Then why would he have a fling in the first place?"

Lance shrugged one shoulder and gave her half a smile. "He's a guy."

"I'm so sick of hearing about how guys can't control themselves. Like they have some corner on the lust market. Women lust. Women have desires."

"This could be a blessing in disguise," Lance said.

"A blessing?" Her voice rose. Mo, who was unpacking a case of white wine, looked across the room at them. Gwen dialed down her volume. "Maybe you can look at it that way. You don't have children. You haven't been married for fifteen years. I don't see this as a blessing."

"Sometimes you don't appreciate what you've got until you try something else." His voice was soft.

Gwen looked at him horrified. "That's not comforting."

"Hear me out." Lance stroked her hand. "You may disagree with me, but I don't believe people are naturally monogamous. Just look at the culture. People get married. They have children. Then within ten years, they're getting divorced. Why? Because they're restless. The honeymoon is over. They start looking for another mate."

"So marriage is a farce? That's what you're saying? We're all destined to cheat and break up?" The words spit from Gwen's lips.

"No, that's not what I'm saying. I'm saying the institution of marriage should be more flexible. If people would bend with their biology, relationships might not break so often."

Gwen pulled her hand out from under his and sat up straighter on her stool. "Bend with their biology? Like my father bent with his biology? He screwed around on my mother then left her for a younger woman."

"You're putting words in my mouth again." Lance's voice was soothing. "If you're going to have an external relationship you have to pick the right person. It has to be someone who has the same goals for the relationship. Someone who's okay with not being first in your life. Someone who respects the institution of marriage."

"That makes no sense. If I respect marriage, the last thing I'm going to do is have an affair with a married man—or an unmarried one for that matter." Gwen gulped her wine. It was beginning to take effect. She felt calmer despite the disturbing conversation.

"What if marriages were better off, lasted longer, and were happier when they had... outside help?"

"I don't buy—"

"I've seen it, Gwen. A woman I dated in L.A. was on the verge of divorce. She credited me with saving her marriage."

"Ha," exploded from her lips.

"It's true. She said she was refreshed by what we had together, and she brought that refreshment into her relationship with her husband."

"Yeah, well, I think Art's had a little too much refreshing," Gwen said. "Call me crazy, but I'm pretty sure the waitress isn't trying to help our marriage."

"Maybe you can help your marriage, Gwen."

Lance's eyes searched her own. They were so soft, so brown. She could lose herself in those eyes. She shivered.

"How are you suggesting I do that?" she asked.

Lance trailed a finger across the back of her hand. "You're upset. You don't feel appreciated or loved. If you had your tank filled, you might be able to look at this situation more objectively."

Gwen needed objectivity, she'd give him that. She felt like a sailboat tossed in a tempest.

"Art made a mistake, but obviously he still wants you, even though he could have her." He dropped his hand beneath the table. A second later, she felt its heat on her thigh.

"Another round?" Mo appeared at their table with an open bottle like a servile apparition. Lance snatched his hand from Gwen's leg. She jumped and spilled the last drops of her wine.

"Now you definitely need a bit more," the proprietor said wiping the table, his white rag turning blood red.

"No, I—" Gwen said.

"Just a little. On the house." He poured a few ounces into each of their glasses. "This cab is lovely, don't you think?"

"It's great," Lance said without expression in his voice.

"I picked it up on my last trip to Napa. That's cab country you know. Wonderful vineyards." Mo shifted his weight to one leg, as if digging in for a long conversation. "However, I have to say the Zinfandels coming out of Paso Robles are superior to Napa Zins. The Central Coast has come a long way in recent years."

Lance turned his gaze on Gwen and gave a small shake of his head. He mouthed, "Drink up." Gwen took a deep draft from her glass. Lance pulled his wallet from his pocket. The shopkeeper continued to regale them with wine wisdom as they finished and paid.

"The man can talk," Lance said when they stood in the sunlight again.

"He can," Gwen agreed, and for once she was glad he could. His chatter had dissipated the confusion she'd been feeling like an open window sucks the smoke from a room. She had come very close to jumping from the frying pan into the fire, as her grandmother used to say.

Lance walked her to her car, took both her hands in his and leaned forward for a kiss. Gwen gave him her cheek.

"Call me if you need me," he said and squeezed her hands.

"I will," she said, but she had no intention of calling him.

CHAPTER THIRTY-FOUR

ENZO PLACED A COMFORTING HAND on Olivia's shoulder as he passed the table where she sat with Art. After the worst of her sobs had subsided, Olivia insisted she had to get work. But as soon as they got inside the restaurant, Enzo took one look at her face, led them to a back booth, set mugs of coffee before them, and bustled off to manage her tables.

"The crazy thing is, I had a sitter all lined up. She got food poisoning at the last minute," Olivia said in a shaky voice.

"If he hadn't been suspended—" Art began.

"You have to stop blaming yourself." Olivia's voice was weary. "Only one of the hours Brian was home alone was a school hour. The rest were after school. It was my decision. I never work nights, but I switched shifts with another server. It was her birthday."

"No good deed goes unpunished," Art said.

"I left him with a pizza, video games, and told him not to open the door to anybody until his grandpa got there. Mike couldn't make it until five."

Mike did arrive at five as planned, but Brian wasn't there. He didn't panic. The family was used to Brian wandering. First, he called neighbors and other family members. When that didn't turn up any leads, he called a buddy in the Orange County Sheriff's Department.

The officer got back to him within the hour. He'd found a child in intensive care who matched Brian's description. Mike raced to Mission Hospital. After he identified his grandson, two officers were sent to inform Olivia and bring her to wait with Mike while the surgeons did what they could.

"It was horrible." Olivia wrapped thin arms around herself.

"He woke up, and it looks good. Right? Looks like he's going to be okay. Think about that."

She wiped her eyes and nodded. "It sounds terrible, but now I don't want him to get better too quickly."

She had received a phone call on her way to work that morning. There are no latchkey kid laws in California that specify what age a child must be to be left home alone, but national safety organizations recommend twelve as the youngest. Because she had left a nine-year-old unattended, Olivia was now under investigation for child neglect. Child Protective Services was threatening to take Brian from her when he was ready to leave the hospital.

She dropped her arms to the tabletop and clutched her coffee cup like a child does a teddy bear after a nightmare. Blue veins stood out on her small hands. The fingernails were bitten to stumps. Art reached out and touched her.

"The charges won't stick. You're a terrific mother," he said.

"I'm not. I wouldn't have left him alone if I was, but I'm better than foster care. I may deserve whatever the court decides, but Brian shouldn't be punished." Olivia's eyes filled with tears again.

"Listen, the reason Brian has a scholarship to St. Barnabas is because you impressed the board of directors. They could tell you loved your son and were willing to do whatever it took to get him a good education," Art said.

"I wonder how they feel about me now. Pretty sorry they wasted their money. Not on Brian, he really tries. He's a good student. But on me." Tears spilled down her cheeks again. She was drowning in a whirlpool of pain, and his heart ached for her.

"We're going to fight this. I'll be there as a character witness, so will half the school staff."

She stared into the murk of her mug as if she hadn't heard. She'd been through one emotionally wrenching situation after another for weeks. This seemed like the final straw. She looked exhausted.

Art would call Mike as soon as he returned from the Big Bear camping trip and see if together they could come up with a plan to clear Olivia. Mike probably still had some sway with local law enforcement. Art would marshal whatever forces he could at St. Barnabas. He'd raise money for a lawyer. He'd do whatever he had to do.

#

Art arrived on campus just as classes were getting out for the day. He found Tyler and Emily in the parking lot waiting by his car, but Jason was nowhere to be seen.

"I got an E for Excellent on my report," Emily said, standing on her tiptoes and waving a paper in Art's face while he tried to scan the surrounding area for Jason.

"That's great, honey." Art took the paper from her hand and dropped it to his side out of his line of vision.

"Why's Jason late? He's always late," Emily said.

"He's not always late," Tyler said.

"Is too. Mom says so. She says—" Emily pursed her lips, sucked in her cheeks and said in her best adult imitation, "Jason will be late to his own funeral." She dropped the act, then asked, "How could he be late if he's dead?"

"It's just a saying, sweetheart." Art put a hand over his eyes and turned toward the trees that sheltered the small stream at the end of the property.

"I have ballet at four. He better be here soon, or we'll have to leave without him." Emily circled a lamppost to amuse herself.

"We can't leave without him," Tyler said. "Dad, want me to go inside and see if I can find him? He had math last. I know where his room is."

"No. Hold up, buddy," Art said. "I think I see him."

The sun was in his eyes, but Art could make out two silhouettes slipping out of the trees and crossing the grass. He was pretty sure the one with the long, skinny arms and awkward gait was his son. With a sinking feeling, he noted the other looked like the older Pratt boy.

After everyone was belted into the car, Art said, "What were you doing down by the water?"

"Nothing," Jason said, his tone sullen.

"You were late," Art said.

Jason shrugged and looked out the window.

Art was too tired to deal with teen drama right now. The conversation with Olivia had added another layer of problems to his life. He felt drained. Nobody spoke for the rest of the ride home, not even Emily.

"You guys keep it quiet, okay?" Art said as he opened the front door. "Mom's got a headache. She might be sleeping."

The kids scattered, the boys to the kitchen to forage for a snack and Emily to her room to change into her leotard. Art walked to his bedroom and opened the door a crack. The bed was empty, but light slid out from under the bathroom door.

He walked across the room, put a hand on the knob and spoke softly. "Gwen."

"What?" she said, her voice muffled by the wood.

"How're you feeling, honey?"

"My head hurts," she said.

"Can I come in?"

"Why?"

"So I don't have to talk to you through the door," Art said with a small laugh.

"K," she said.

The bathroom was warm, steamy, and smelled like lavender. Art closed the door behind him. Gwen was submerged in a mountain of bubbles. A glass of wine rested on the rim of the tub and a half-filled bottle was on the floor. Her eyes were closed.

"Are you sure wine is good for a headache?" he asked.

"It's good for this headache," she said, her words clip and distant.

"Something bad happen? Your day okay?"

"Fine," she said, then fell silent.

Gwen wasn't prone to headaches. If she did get one, it generally had its roots in stress. Over the years, he'd learned to let her percolate when she got like this. It made things worse if he pushed her to talk. She'd tell him what happened eventually.

Maybe she'd open up when they got to Big Bear. Jason was old enough to watch the younger ones at the campsite for an hour if they went for a hike. They always communicated best when they were out walking. It would be good to leave town, to get away from people, problems, and pavement even if it was just for a few days.

"I'm going to get the camping gear out of the attic after dinner. I guess we can shop for food when we get up there if you're not feeling well," he said. They'd planned to pack for the trip that night so they could leave early the next day.

"I'm not going," Gwen said and slid lower into the water.

Art thought before he spoke. He didn't want to minimize her problem, but it was only a headache. "I'm sure you'll feel better in the morning," he said, modulating his tone to sound sympathetic.

"It's not the headache."

A tickle of anxiety ran up his neck. He needed to get away. "We talked about this on Tuesday. You said this weekend was fine."

"We didn't talk about it," Gwen snapped. "You sent me a text. And it was fine, at the time."

The anxiety turned to irritation. She could be so self-absorbed. And cold. Gwen could really be cold. "Gwen, the kids are looking forward to this. They've—"

"Take them." Her voice was frosty.

She was the one who said they didn't spend enough time together. Here he was trying, and she could care less. What was going on with this family?

"Jason was hanging out by the water again today with David Pratt. I didn't smell pot, but I don't like it. It's a red flag. We need to reconnect as a family." He couldn't keep the frustration from his voice.

"We're signing an offer on the Laguna Beach house tomorrow. Sorry."

She didn't sound sorry.

"Gwen—"

"It's a lot of money. We need it."

Her aim was perfect. The words hit him square in the ego. He left the bathroom and slammed the door behind him.

CHAPTER THIRTY-FIVE

GWEN STARTED AT THE BANG OF WOOD ON WOOD. Art was mad. So what? So was she. She reached for her glass of wine and drank.

She was glad he was leaving and taking the kids. She needed a weekend alone to think this through. She didn't want to break up her marriage. She'd experienced the devastation divorce caused first hand. She wasn't willing to have her kids go through the pain she had, but she couldn't look at Art right now.

Her glass was empty. "The story of my life," she mumbled.

Gwen leaned out of the bath, dribbling water and bubbles on the tile, grabbed the bottle, and refilled. Lance's perspective on marriage was beginning to make an inverted kind of sense.

It was a far cry from the idyllic visions she and Art had nattered about in the beginning, when they'd had constellations in their eyes. How young she'd been. How idealistic. She'd really believed she'd found her soul mate. Her hero.

She raised her glass to the ceiling in a toast. "To reality," she said to no one and gulped. Maybe a fling would help her cope with Art's infidelity—an eye for an eye. If someone slaps you, turn the other cheek. It didn't say which cheek. She laughed bitterly.

The water and wine warmed and wooed her. She rubbed her tired legs one against the other. Skin, smooth and slippery, brought images to mind of other legs, other skin. She allowed her thoughts to wander down roads they'd never traversed before. Refill her tank, wasn't that what he'd said?

That sounded good. She'd been running on empty for a long time. No tenderness. No love. No lovemaking. Why not pull up to the pump? The idea of sex with Lance, once planted in her mind, began to take it over like weeds in a garden.

She closed her eyes and submerged hoping the surface of the water would create a barrier strong enough to keep her from reaching for the phone. It lay on the floor next to the tub—a serpent ready to strike. When she came up for air—and more wine—she eyed it again. It flickered to life as if she'd willed it. Gingerly, like someone reaching for a hot coal, she lifted it off the bathmat and opened her text messages.

She read, "You okay?"

After several moments she typed, "Not really."

"What are you doing?" came almost immediately.

"Taking a bath."

Gwen sipped her wine.

"Nice," flashed on her phone.

She paused, then typed, "Still on for tomorrow night?"

"You bet," Lance messaged.

An idea had been forming in her mind while she soaked. "Let's not go to a restaurant," she typed.

"No?"

"Picnic."

"Where?"

"My listing in Dana Point." Arranging a rendezvous there felt adventurous and rebellious, and she reveled in those emotions tonight.

He didn't respond for a full minute and a half. It seemed an impossibly long time. She stared at her silent screen until the light dimmed. Had she said the wrong thing?

She knew she was sending a dangerous message, one she had no business sending. But he was the one who brought up bending biology and empty tanks and all that. She was just playing along. She didn't plan to have an affair, but she could flirt. She could imagine. She could try on the role of the wanton woman like a costume for one night. See how it fit.

The phone reanimated. "Is that safe?"

"Yes. They're gone until next week."

Another long pause. "When?"

"Seven." Her heart thudded against her ribcage.

"Okay."

It was done.

CHAPTER THIRTY-SIX

I WASN'T SURE WHY I WAS THERE, parked across the street from the house on Sailor's Haven, other than that it was Gwen's listing. Maybe I was hoping it would prove to be a place of vulnerability, her Achilles' heel. I'd had success with other agents in other empty properties. The prey tended to be distracted by their own hunt. They lusted for a sale, while I, you could say, lusted for blood. But I had other plans for Gwen.

"Hello."

The voice startled me. I looked up to see a lanky, old woman with a knobby, gray head of hair striding up the street toward my car, sweater flapping in the wind.

"Excuse me," she said.

I sat up straighter and waited for the inevitable. I knew the type. Every neighborhood has one. A bored, senior citizen who reads too many amateur sleuth novels out looking for a crime to solve.

"Hello there," I said and graced her with my most melting smile.

"Can I help you?" she asked.

I gave her a quizzical look.

"I couldn't help but notice you've been parked here for..." she looked at her watch, "twelve minutes, thirty-two seconds. I thought maybe you were lost."

"That's very gracious of you," I said. "But I'm not lost, just looking at the flier on this house."

"The Frobisher's house? It's a very nice place, but they're out of town."

"Oh, are they?"

"Are you looking for something in Dana Point?" she said.

"Possibly. I'm considering several beach communities." Then, digging for more information, I added, "This seems like a nice, safe neighborhood."

"Oh, it is. We have a very active neighborhood watch committee. I'm on it. I live right next door." She pointed to a house in bad need of a paint job.

"Your neighbors must be grateful to have someone like you on the block."

She threw her shoulders back and displayed a set of crooked teeth. "I'm sure you could get Gwen Bishop, she's the agent, to show you the house."

"Maybe I will," I said. "Maybe I will."

I glanced in my rearview mirror and saw a silver Honda advancing toward me. Gwen had a silver Honda. I didn't want to be seen here. Not yet. The darkening sky opened, and a sprinkle of rain hit my windshield.

"I'd better get going, and you'd better get inside where it's dry," I said. "It's going to be a nasty night."

CHAPTER THIRTY-SEVEN

THE SUN WAS SETTING. Deep magenta clouds bloomed above a midnight blue sea. They were the same color as the roses Gwen had bought on impulse on her way out of Gelson's Market. It was a romantic, fairytale sky—a perfect setting for a fantasy. She was in free fall, hurtling toward a storybook land, parachute unopened. The classical station she kept her car radio tuned to played a Leclair violin concerto. The music added to her Cinderella's-ball mood.

She exited the 5 freeway and turned onto Pacific Coast Highway. Her cell phone rang-hunting horns jarring through the strain of strings from the radio. The foxhunt clarion was Art's ring. She felt anger rising in her chest. She wouldn't answer. She didn't want to mar her evening with images of Art and the waitress.

The horns sounded again. She looked at her phone and bit her lower lip. She didn't want to talk to him, but maybe it was best to get it over with. She answered on the fifth ring. "Hi."

"Hi, honey. How're things back at the ranch?"

"Fine. Did you make it up the mountain in one piece?" She struggled to keep her voice even and controlled.

"Yeah, no problem. We stopped at In-N-Out on the way, but we still got here in time to pitch the tent before dark. The kids are scrounging for kindling now."

"Don't let them wander too far. There are bears up there."

Art laughed. He had a nice laugh. A round laugh that used to roll out of him often. She'd almost forgotten what it sounded like. "They're fine. The only bear they'll see this weekend is the one in the Big Bear Zoo. Emily wants to visit tomorrow."

"Humor me and keep an eye on them." Gwen's voice sounded peevish, even to herself. She cleared her throat.

"So, what're you up to tonight? Working?" Art asked.

"Yes, I told you that. I may stop by Maricela's later if I get my paperwork done." The lies came so naturally, it made her a little nervous.

Art's voice softened. "Well, we wish you were here. Emily is missing her mommy already."

A parental hand reached around Gwen's heart and squeezed. Doubt and fear dropped like a pebbles into her belly. Yesterday she'd been so positive about what she'd seen in the alley. Now, listening to Art's familiar chatter on the line, she felt unsure. Yesterday, she hadn't known him. It was like he'd been body snatched. Now, he sounded like her husband.

"I gave the boys the talk, you know, 'Be nice to your sister. You're the big guys. You need to include her in what you're doing and keep an eye on her.' Tyler is taking it almost too seriously. He hasn't let her out of his sight since we hit the campground."

"Good for him," Gwen said.

"Hey, Jason, put that down," Art yelled. "I gotta go. The natives are restless."

"Okay, have a good time."

"Will do. Call you tomorrow." His voice went deep and throaty. "Love you, babe." The line went dead.

The car felt hollow.

Love you, babe.

Did he?

A dark, Wagnerian symphony had replaced the violin concerto. Gwen reached out, shut off the radio and heard the rumble of thunder. They'd been threatening rain all week. Art had almost canceled the camping trip.

She returned her phone to her purse and her arm brushed the roses lying on the passenger seat, releasing their scent. Unexpected memories of her grandmother's funeral came to her mind. She shook them off.

As Gwen pulled off the freeway into Dana Point, the first fat drops hit her windshield. The magenta clouds looked like they were bleeding. Morbid thoughts. Tonight was supposed to be about celebration. She'd lick her wounds tomorrow.

CHAPTER THIRTY-EIGHT

"I GIVE UP," JASON SAID, threw his flint and steel down and crossed his arms over his chest. "There must be something wrong with it. I did it just like the package said."

"It's pretty damp out." Art rested a comforting hand on his son's shoulder. "We can try again tomorrow." Art pulled a Bic lighter out of his jacket pocket and soon had the kindling the kids had collected blazing. Jason slumped onto a tree stump and began thumbing through his Boy Scout Camping Merit Badge book.

Art was glad they'd made the trip even though Gwen hadn't joined them. He needed to spend some father-son time with Jason. The sullen attitude his oldest had adopted since the beginning of the school year, peeled away with the miles. By the time they'd pitched the tent, Jason seemed to forget he wasn't supposed to be excited about dumb things like camping, or nature, or having fun with his family.

"I'll find something else to do. Most of this stuff is pretty easy," he said.

"How about campfire stew?" Emily said, wiggling onto the log next to him. "We did campfire stew in Jenny Andrew's backyard for Brownies, but I didn't eat any." Emily stuck a finger in her mouth and mimed barfing.

"Nah, I don't want to do any cooking stuff." Jason turned some pages. "How about this? Dad, could we build a shelter out of twigs and things? Then me and Tyler could sleep in it."

"I want to sleep in it," Emily's head jerked up, her blond braids bounced, and her voice rose to the whining pitch she'd perfected since starting third grade.

It was nice to be here, away from St. Barnabas. Art was already feeling a perspective shift. Since he'd been angling for the principal job, he'd lost his focus on his family.

Thunder rumbled through the night air. "Well, I don't." Tyler's chin tilted to the treetops. "I want to sleep in the tent." Rocket must have felt the same way. Art watched their brave defender slink across the dirt on his belly and disappear into the Coleman six-man tent.

"Me too. I want to sleep next to Daddy." Emily jumped from the stump and wrapped her arms around Art's waist. Emily didn't like storms almost as much as Rocket didn't like storms.

"I'll sleep in the lean-to by myself. It'll be cool, like Survivorman." Jason started to walk toward the edge of the campsite. "Every man for himself."

Every man for himself. That was the problem. Art and Gwen had been living like independent agents under one roof. They'd become roommates, instead of husband and wife.

"Hey, J-Man, not so fast. Let's all sleep in the tent tonight. Rocket's upset enough. He'll freak if we don't stay together. Tomorrow we can make the lean-to and you can take a nap in it. It doesn't say you have to sleep all night, just sleep." Art held out the merit badge book

Jason had dropped. The sky growled again, and Jason returned to the fire.

"I don't want Rocket to be scared." Jason squared his jaw.

"Thanks. I need you, buddy." Art ruffled his son's hair. Jason looked like a male version of Gwen at this age. He was tall and a little too skinny. He had her thick auburn hair, the same sprinkling of freckles across his nose and her jump-first-look-later attitude. Art's chest squeezed. He missed her. When he got home, he was going to make the past six months up to her.

"S'mores time," Tyler said carrying a bag of marshmallows out of the tent. Rocket's nose followed. It was obvious the dog was divided between fear and food.

"Yay. S'more s'mores please." Emily let go of Art's leg and danced over to her brother.

"You haven't had any yet, so you can't say 's'more s'mores'." Jason said.

"Hey, who has the graham crackers?" Art hoped to deflect the argument he saw growing behind Emily's wrinkled brow. Having two older brothers made her a tough little thing. She didn't back down easily.

"Me, me, me," Emily called out. Insult forgotten, she shot into the tent to find the crackers. Seconds later Rocket emerged with her and the graham crackers—sugar induced courage.

"Make sure Rocket doesn't get the chocolate. It could kill him. I learned about it in health class. It has bro... bro... something in it that's like poison to dogs." Tyler said.

"Poor Rockety-Rocket," Emily said hugging the dog's neck. "I'll make you a marshmallow."

Art looked up at the night sky. Wisps of clouds wrapped around the moon. He wondered how many marshmallows the kids would get to roast before rain put their campfire out.

CHAPTER THIRTY-NINE

GWEN PULLED UP IN FRONT OF THE HOUSE on Sailor's Haven, disabled the lockbox, popped the key out and entered. There was just enough light coming through the windows to see. She carried some of her bundles inside and dropped them on the granite counter in the kitchen, turning on lights as she went. By her second trip to the car—she'd really brought too much—it was pouring, a hemorrhage of water. Thunder rolled again.

The house was chilly. The rain sluicing down the windowpanes blocked the last of the sunset. Gwen shivered. There was a fireplace in the living room with gas and imitation logs. She lit it. It didn't throw much heat, but the glow improved the atmosphere.

Gwen turned to her bags. First, she opened a bottle of Ravish and filled a wine glass she found in the cupboard. She'd stopped by the Barrel again that morning to buy more. She felt so guilty; she'd told Mo she was buying it for an open house at her Sailor's Haven listing in the morning. As soon as the words were out of her mouth, she realized how ridiculous she sounded. Mo didn't care why she bought wine. He was just happy she did.

She downed a third of it in the time it took to unpack oysters, strawberries, artichoke salad, a loaf of French bread, Brie, and a chocolate ganache cake—all foods she and Art used to share in the days when they picnicked at the beach.

Gwen lit a few candles and set the table in the dining room with the homeowners' lovely dishes then walked to the warmth of the fire. She stood at the picture window watching the storm clouds undulating across the water, and the harbor lights popping on one by one. A flash of lightning lit the room for a moment and illuminated the clock on the mantel. It was almost seven. A moment later came a clap of thunder so loud it sounded like it originated on the second floor of the house.

Her cell phone pinged from another room. She hurried to the kitchen, rummaged through her purse, found it and read, "Running a little late. Be there soon." Good, she had more time to prepare. She sent a smiley face.

She found a cut-glass vase in the cupboard above the refrigerator for the roses, arranged them and placed them on the table. She set an unopened bottle of Ravish next to the vase. It was suddenly important to her that he like the wine. Too important. As if his like or dislike of it portended something about their future. She wiped her hands on her jeans and walked into the kitchen.

Her cell vibrated in her pocket. "On way," she read.

"Good." Her fingers felt thick and clumsy as she typed.

Gwen finished off her first glass of wine and poured another. The twinkling candles, the warmth of the fire, and the heat of the wine combined to drive away the chill she'd been feeling since she'd talked with Art.

She hummed to herself while she cut the loaf of bread. It would be okay. Tonight was a festive occasion, an opportunity to commemorate the biggest deal she'd ever participated in, nothing more. It was an evening to relax, enjoy herself and explore future options. Things were a bit up in the air. That's why she felt jittery. Tomorrow she'd be back on solid ground.

Gwen put the bread into a napkin-lined basket and brought it to the table. As she set it down, she heard a rap on the front door. Lance was on time after all.

Her hands tingled as if she'd grabbed a low voltage electric fence. She walked into the entryway with careful, measured steps. The door stood before her, dark brown and solid. She reached across what seemed a great expanse of tile for the gleaming, brass doorknob, turned it and threw open the door.

"Oh, it's you." A thin woman with tufts of gray hair poking out from under her umbrella squinted at Gwen and blinked twice.

#

"Mrs. VanVlear. Can I help you?" The words rushed from Gwen's lips.

"I saw lights and wondered if the Frobishers were home." Esther VanVlear tilted her head to the side, trying to see into the house. Gwen held her arms wide to block as much of the view as possible.

"I'm getting ready for an open house," Gwen said.

"You have candles lit." It was not a question. It was an accusation.

"Yes," Gwen said. Sometimes the less said at these times, the better.

"Trying to create some ambiance, I guess?"

"Yes." Good response. Gwen wished she'd thought of it.

"You're drinking wine?" Not an accusation, a request.

"Yes." Gwen couldn't invite her in. Lance would be there any moment.

Mrs. VanVlear stood, dripping rainwater, on the front stoop like a stray cat looking for a warm hearth. The standoff lasted an uncomfortable thirty seconds. She pursed her lips and wrinkled her forehead, but before she could come up with a reason she should be allowed in, Gwen said, "I've got a lot to do before I can head home. I'd better get busy. Thanks so much for stopping by." She began to close the door and heard her cell phone ping from the dining table.

"I could help," Esther said.

"No, really. That's so sweet of you. I've got it." Gwen's pulse danced with impatience.

"No trouble." Esther VanVlear put one foot inside the house. Gwen's phone chimed again. "Do you need to get that?" Her other foot slid over the doorstep.

Gwen dropped her arms in defeat and went to retrieve her phone. The screen read, "Need anything?" *Yes. Help getting rid of a nosy neighbor,* she thought but slipped the phone into her sweater pocket unanswered.

Mrs. VanVlear was eying the spread on the dining room table. "You go all out don't you?"

"Yes."

"If I ever sell, I'll make sure to call you." She licked her thin lips and looked longingly at the half-empty wine bottle and the chocolate ganache cake. "In fact, I'll make sure to tell the Frobishers' what a wonderful job you're doing for them. Setting the table with their best china, lighting candles all over the house, having wine and food. It's so welcoming. Just like you were getting ready for a...," she looked at the ceiling for a moment. "An intimate tête–à–tête."

Was there a threat hidden behind that waterfall of words? Gwen couldn't be sure, but thought a small bribe might ingratiate the woman. "Would you like a glass of wine, Mrs. VanVlear?"

"If you have enough. I don't want to put you out."

Gwen reached for the glass she'd set on the table for Lance, filled it a third of the way and handed it to the old woman. Then she stood, arms crossed, and restrained her foot from tapping. Her phone jangled in her pocket again, but she didn't dare read it. Every time she looked away, Esther VanVlear slid a little farther into the house.

"I hate to leave you standing in the doorway, but I don't want to get the Frobishers wood floors all wet," Gwen said.

"I understand, dear. I understand." The woman looked at her empty glass and back to Gwen. Gwen's face settled into the mask she wore with the kids on the candy isle of the grocery store.

"That was a lovely wine. It will fortify me for the trip home," Mrs. VanVlear said without enthusiasm. Why she needed fortification for a trip next door was anyone's guess.

"It was so nice of you to stop by." Gwen herded her outside.

"I always strive to be a good neighbor. One can't be too careful these days." Mrs. VanVlear opened her umbrella. "Vagrants are known to move into empty homes when the owners are out of town. When the family returns, they have to evict them. Can you imagine?"

She turned toward the street and made her way around the puddles that had formed on the path. "I read about it in the paper. Sometimes it takes months to get rid of them. Squatter's rights, I think they call it," she yelled over her shoulder.

"Yes," Gwen said.

"Terrible. It's just terrible. I don't—" Gwen shut the door on the final words and pulled her phone from her pocket to read the new message.

"Well? I'm passing Ralphs?"

"No. I'm good." She typed. She took Mrs. VanVlear's glass into the kitchen, put it in the sink and reached for a clean one.

The phone lit up. "Too late anyway."

The clock in the great room said 7:17. The sun was long gone, and the black windows now looked like prying eyes. Gwen turned down the lights. She felt less visible in candlelight.

She sat on the couch, picked up her wine, and tried to slow her racing heart. Why did she feel so guilty? She wasn't doing anything wrong. Okay, maybe a little wrong. Flirting wasn't the best behavior for a married woman, but it wasn't an affair. It wasn't whatever she'd seen between Art and the waitress. By the time she heard the knock on the door, she had drained her second glass and was feeling better about the evening.

CHAPTER FORTY

RAIN PUDDLED ON ART'S SLEEPING BAG. The walls of the tent flapped in the wind like the sail of a boat. He couldn't believe the kids slept through the racket.

He lay on his aching back in his damp sleeping bag, the musty odors of teenage boy, wet dog, and dirt filling his nostrils. At the moment, he couldn't remember whose idea this camping trip was.

Emily was restless; her bag knotted from constant twisting. She fussed whenever the noise of the storm hit a certain decibel, but didn't wake. This was not the trip he'd envisioned.

He rolled over to reach into a pocket built into the tent wall, slammed his hip into a rock, and swore under his breath. After groping in the dark, he found his cell phone.

When it lit, the cozy glow made him long for some of the other comforts of civilization, like real walls, a roof that didn't leak, and the warmth of a wife next to him. He pushed the weather app icon and typed Big Bear into the search menu. It came up, and he groaned. It showed rain all day Saturday and Sunday.

He pondered his options for the morning. They could get up and go into town for a big breakfast, buy rain parkas, and soldier on. Or, they could pack it up and try again another weekend. He knew which the boys would opt for. They would happily turn blue from cold if they could stay in Big Bear.

He shifted in his bag. A trickle of cold water seeped through a gap in the zipper soaking the right leg of his sweat pants. Emily flailed and moaned like a trapped animal. Art flopped onto his back and stared at the undulating tent roof, miserable.

The walls of the tent lit with an amber light. Seconds later, thunder boomed like a bass drum. Rocket tried to bury himself under Art's legs.

Great. They were lying in a pool of water. Forget morning; they should leave tonight. The tent was illuminated as lightning struck again. It was close. Too close. A long, menacing rumble reverberated in the air around him, and he began to think through the quickest way to break camp.

The world became as bright as day. A crack exploded near his head. Emily screamed and fought her way out of her tangled bed to a sitting position. Both boys lurched up, eyes wide.

"Daddy!" Emily called out.

"Shh, shh, I'm here," he said reaching for her.

"I don't like this," she said, whimpering.

"What the heck," Jason said. He was leaning on one elbow with a look of excited wonder on his face.

Another crash detonated near the tent. It was like a war zone out there.

"Okay, guys, we're leaving," Art said. The boys broke into an instant argument. Emily wiggled from her bag and climbed into Art's lap. "Listen to me. No arguing. This isn't safe."

"I have to go to the bathroom," Emily whispered with a panicky look on her face.

"I'll take her," Tyler said.

"I want Daddy." Emily tightened her grip on Art's neck.

"Go with Tyler, honey. Jason and I will start loading the car so we can get out of here." Art unraveled her from around him and passed her off to Tyler. "Let's get going J-Man."

CHAPTER FORTY-ONE

LANCE ARRIVED TEN MINUTES LATER. Gwen pulled him into the house, away from Esther VanVlear's spying eyes, and closed the door behind him. "Crazy weather," he said, removing a dripping jacket and hanging it on a hook in the entryway.

His hair sparkled with water droplets. A stray lock curled across his forehead. He looked like a disheveled Prince Charming just in from a ride on his white steed.

But this was no fairy tale. He was a real flesh and blood man. The musk of the cologne he always wore filled Gwen's head. Her thighs went weak, but not from passion or longing. It was nerves. Anxiety knocked against her rib cage, making it hard to fill her lungs.

"Come and have some wine." She hoped he didn't hear the breathlessness of her voice.

Lance flopped on the couch, and Gwen went to the dining room. After she filled a glass for him and refilled her own, she joined him in the great room and set the drinks on the coffee table. She took the chair across from him, the one she'd sat in to explain the ins and outs of lockboxes to Mary Beth Frobisher what now seemed eons ago. She studied his face.

It was a stunning face, perfect for the cover of a romance novel. Large, dreamy, espresso-brown eyes sat above high cheekbones. In that genre, his mouth would be described as full and soft and promising pleasure. His gold-brown hair might be compared to tousled bed sheets. It begged to have fingers run through it.

She shouldn't be thinking these thoughts.

Love you, babe. Art's last words to Gwen blared like hunting horns in her mind. *Love you, babe. Love you.*

"The house looks great." Lance sipped his wine.

"Thanks. It's a beautiful place."

"I forgot how beautiful it was. I haven't been here since you first listed it."

An uncomfortable silence muted the easy banter that normally existed between them. Lance finally spoke. "I took Betty from-three-doors-down's cousin out yesterday. She fell in love with a house in South Laguna. I think we'll have another big deal in escrow soon."

Gwen leaned forward and clinked glasses with him. "Lots to celebrate."

"I'm glad you suggested doing it here. Quieter than a restaurant."

"That's what I thought. Better for conversation."

He raised his eyebrows. "Conversation?"

"Yes, I wanted to talk to you about our... partnership. I mean, moving forward. I want to know your thoughts."

He looked at her over the top of his glass while he drank, then lowered it. "I'd like to make it an official partnership, if that's what you're asking."

"What would that look like?"

"What would you like it to look like?"

Gwen stared at the water cascading down the black windows. Thunder rumbled in the distance. Turmoil outside and inside. A business partnership with Lance made sense. She could achieve more in her career with his help. She would make more money. More money was better for her family. So, why did she feel like she was being disloyal to Art by considering it? For that matter, why should she even worry about loyalty? Art hadn't. Sitting became impossible. She stood.

"Where are you going?" Lance reached for her hand.

"Let's talk about it over dinner."

He held onto her hand like she hadn't spoken. After a beat, she pulled it away. An angry expression flashed across his features marring them for a second.

"How do you like the wine?" Gwen asked, more brightly than she'd intended.

"Not bad." He twirled the stem of the glass between his fingers and stared at the movement. A few long moments passed, then he asked in a resigned voice, "What are we having?"

Gwen led him to the dining table where she'd artfully laid out her picnic around the vase of roses. Art always said you eat first with your eyes. *Stop it*. She was thinking about Art again.

He had been unfaithful—she was almost certain. He didn't deserve her consideration. She shoved him firmly from her mind.

Lance sat and began picking through the plates with a fork. He speared an artichoke heart. "What's this?"

"An artichoke, silly." Gwen sat across from him.

He stroked his five o'clock shadow while his eyes traveled from plate to plate. Gwen had assumed Lance would like the same things she and Art did, but now realized she had no idea what he liked. Whatever it was, it didn't appear to be on the table.

"We should share any deals that come as a result of the Cliff Drive property," Gwen said.

"I thought that was a given." He helped himself to some bread and Brie.

"What about listings we already have, or clients we had before we started working together?"

He reached across the table and touched her hand. "Gwen, are you sure you should be making this kind of decision right now? I want to know how you're doing first. You had a real shock yesterday."

Sympathy wasn't good. Sympathy threatened to bring on tears, or rage, or weakness. "I'm okay. Try the artichokes." She handed him the bowl of salad.

He took a small spoonful and put it on his plate. He didn't take any of the oysters. "I have a deal closing at the end of the month. You have this place. Those are done. I vote we pick a starting date and share anything we get after that."

Gwen relaxed a little. They were on familiar ground, talking unemotional shop. "Should we sign a partnership agreement?"

"Absolutely. I have a buddy who's a lawyer. He'd probably write something up for us cheap. Unless you have someone else you'd rather use?"

They fell into an easy discourse about the details of their real estate union. Excitement began to replace unease. He was so easy to talk to, so amenable. If she hesitated on any point, he was quick to ask how she'd like to alter it. She marveled at how much she'd misjudged him. It must have been envy. He'd done so well in such a short time, she'd resented it. She'd been no different than John Gordon. Her small-mindedness made her cringe.

Gwen sipped her wine, and planned her future. The storm raged outside. It was warm and lovely inside. This was good. She and Lance would be good together. She cut into the chocolate ganache cake and handed him a thick slice.

"Delicious," he said, mouth full, then swigged more wine.

The last time she'd had this cake was on one of the last dates she and Art had been out on. After the restaurant, they came home to a sleeping house, and she surprised him with dessert. Art loved chocolate cake. They'd opened a bottle of red wine, fed each other, licked frosting from one another's fingers, and flirted like teenagers. Later they made slow, luxurious love.

Gwen took a bite of her own cake. It tasted like sugar-coated cardboard. She dropped her fork with a clatter that resonated with a clap of thunder so loud it shook the windowpanes. She wondered if it was raining in Big Bear.

"Okay, then. I'll call my guy and have him write up the paperwork." Lance pressed his fork into the last few crumbs on his plate and washed them down with the end of his wine. Gwen rose from the table, picked up their plates and headed toward the kitchen. He grabbed her arm as she walked by.

"Dinner was great." He pulled her onto his lap and kissed her before she realized what was happening. His lips tasted of wine and chocolate.

She pulled back and looked into his eyes. "I don't think I'm ready for this."

"Don't want to seal the deal?" He gave her a half-smile, boyish and hopeful.

"I'm married."

"I respect that. I told you, I'd never try to come between you and Art. You have a family to think about." He picked up her hand, turned it palm up and kissed it. A nest of butterflies stirred to life in her stomach.

"It wouldn't be good for a working relationship. If we... you know... It would be awkward."

"It's awkward now." He rested his head on her shoulder. "I want to know you, Gwen. All of you."

Need opened its petals inside her. It was like a night-blooming cereus, alive only for one glorious night. A thing of beauty that would be dead by morning. Shouldn't she celebrate it? Shouldn't she exalt in its brief but brilliant display? She lifted his face with a fingertip and met his lips with hers.

Lance stood and picked her up in one movement. If Art did that, he'd put his back out. *Love you, babe.* The clarion call reverberated in her brain, shattering the moment. "Let's take a bath." The words flew out in a nervous rush.

Impatience hardened his features. "Are you getting in there with me?"

"Of course. Just give me a minute to clean up down here. In case someone comes."

"No one's going to come."

"Please. It will help me relax. There's a great tub in the master bathroom. I'll be right up."

He set her on her feet. "Don't be long." He picked up a freshly opened bottle of wine and took three roses from the vase on the table. As he mounted the stairs, he pulled petals from their stems and dropped them behind him. "Breadcrumbs," he said.

CHAPTER FORTY-TWO

ART PUT EMILY IN THE FRONT SEAT next to him even though Ryan called shotgun first. She'd finally calmed down, and he wanted to keep it that way. The sounds of the gale were muffled now, but Art was still tense.

The road snaked down the mountain, serpentine and slippery. Rain pelted the windshield faster than the wipers could clear it. He could see the lights of San Bernardino far below where Highway 18 dropped off on his left. He hugged the hillside and hoped he wouldn't be hit by one of the falling rocks the signs warned of.

Despite their bravado, Art could tell the boys were nervous as they broke camp. Their grumbling about leaving grew less and less as the lightning strikes grew closer and the thunder louder. Art glanced into the backseat. Tyler dozed. Jason stared out the window.

Art thought about calling Gwen, but it was late. She was probably in bed. No sense waking her, she'd just worry about them driving in these conditions.

At twenty miles an hour, the descent seemed endless. By the time he hit sea level, he felt like a stork—talons instead of hands, permanently craned neck, children in tow. He stopped at a red light, massaged his fingers and rolled his head from shoulder to shoulder. All three kids were sleeping now. Even Jason had crumpled onto his brother's hip and was snuffling quietly. It was peaceful in the car. A small space of refuge. He missed Gwen more than ever.

Art turned on the radio. A cheerful sounding newscaster said the storm was one of the worst in years. He reported road closures, evacuations and mud slides like they were plays in a cosmic football game.

Art shook his head. Perfect. He felt a kinship with the dry California soil. He'd been unable to absorb the problems he'd been pelted with since September, unable to find terra firma. Life shifted and shook beneath him.

This trip, as ill-fated as it seemed, stopped the mudslide. Family was what mattered, and Art had been neglecting his. Gwen. The kids. The mantle of that responsibility dropped onto his shoulders. The weight of it grounded him.

Emily mumbled, reached out and touched his leg. Art placed his large hand on top of her small one. The contact seemed to comfort her. She smacked her lips a couple of times and settled into sleep again.

Things were going to change. This camping trip was his first attempt to make it right. And it had been a great idea, until the worst storm of the decade decided to make an appearance.

Next month he'd take Gwen to the cottage on Moonstone Beach they'd visited three anniversaries ago. She loved it there. And it would give them a chance to reconnect as man and wife, as lovers, without the kids around. With a shiver, he hoped the San Andreas Fault wouldn't choose that weekend to sever the state.

CHAPTER FORTY-THREE

GWEN HEARD WATER RUNNING and Lance moving around upstairs while she did the dishes. She imagined him taking off his shirt, his jeans, his boxers. Did he wear boxers? She didn't even know.

She was sure his abdomen would be lean and muscled, his legs strong. She thought about running her hands over his taught back. An ember of anticipation in her belly flickered to life.

Her phone dinged, "Coming?" the text said.

She dried her hands on a towel, "Yes, almost done," she sent back.

"Hurry."

"I'd be there quicker if I didn't have to text," Gwen said to her reflection in the darkened kitchen window, but typed, "Yes." She was hurrying. If she didn't, she might change her mind. A part of her wanted to walk out the front door, leave him alone in the bath until the water cooled, and he realized she wasn't coming up.

"Drinking all the wine." Another text.

Gwen smiled. "Don't!"

"Have to do something."

She put the last of the dishes away, opening and shutting cupboards until she found their mates. It was important to put everything the way it had been.

She had no idea what Mrs. VanVlear was planning to tell the Frobishers about this night. If what she'd done came out, it would be the end of her career. People didn't take kindly to sharing their bath and bed with their Realtor and her boyfriend. Bath and bed. Boyfriend. Her stomach fluttered again. Had she lost her mind?

The phone pinged. "Waiting."

"I know," she answered out loud while she typed the words. She *had* lost her mind. She'd better find it again before Sunday, before Art and kids came home.

Several shots of adrenaline hit her blood stream like espresso. She shouldn't have thought about Art and the kids. She flicked a dishrag at the counters, hung it over a towel rack under the sink, then stood still in the center of the kitchen.

Although yoga wasn't her favorite form of exercise—she preferred something faster paced—she'd taken classes at the gym. She practiced the ujjayi breathing she'd learned until her pulse slowed, then walked into the great room.

"What's taking so long?" her phone demanded.

"Hurrying." Her thumbs stabbed at the screen.

She crossed the room extinguishing candles as she went. Dread replaced excitement as darkness replaced the light. When she reached the fireplace, she turned off the gas and was momentarily blinded by the echo of the flames. A streak of lightning pointed like a finger across the black room to the staircase, thunder rolled.

"Do I need to come get you?" her phone glowed.

"Coming," she typed.

She stood at the base of the stairs and looked into the dark cavern at the top. *Love you, babe.* Art's words rang through her mind. She couldn't go through with this. Maybe she was a fool. Maybe Art had cheated on her. Maybe he hadn't. Either way, it didn't make this right.

She'd lived her whole adult life mourning her mother's death. A death caused by her father's affair. Gwen didn't believe in bending biology, or flexible marriages. It didn't matter how handsome, or dependable or persuasive Lance was. She knew the reality of infidelity.

She made a decision. She would climb the stairs, go into the bathroom, and tell him she couldn't do it. If it cost her a partnership, so be it.

The feeling that something was wrong hit her on the third riser. There was no warning creak like in a haunted house movie. Everything was quiet. Too quiet.

She heard no splashing, no running water, no sound at all other than the murmur of rain against the windowpanes. She picked her way carefully around the rose petals that were already beginning to wilt.

When she reached the top of the stairs, she called out to Lance. He didn't answer. She paused for a moment, then fixated on the trail of petals as if she might lose her way without them. The red path led her down the dark hall and into the master suite.

From halfway across the bedroom, she could see the tile floor of the bathroom shining wetly in the candlelight. Lance must have splashed water out of the tub as he got into it. With a soft, nervous laugh she said, "You're so messy. We're going to have to mop."

Lance didn't answer.

A strand of hair tickled her shoulder. She slapped it behind her as if she could slap away the light fingers of anxiety tickling up and down her spine. She stepped over the puddle into the master bath.

Her eyes followed the wet trail to the wide, ceramic tub. Rose petals floated on the surface of the water like drops of blood. Lance's chin rested on his chest as if he was sleeping. "Lance." Her voice broke like a teenage boy's. She cleared her throat and stepped closer.

His knees rose like bone, white islands. She noticed, in an absentminded way, his legs were skinnier than she'd imagined them. Burgundy clouds floated in the sudsy water.

"Lance." Her voice was pleading now.

She willed him to open his eyes, to smile sheepishly and tell her he'd spilled a glass of wine into the tub. But he didn't stir. Only his fine, brown, chest hairs swayed in the water like kelp.

DING. The light of her cell phone shone blue and ghostly in the dim room.

"Finally."

The phone slipped from her fingers and disappeared beneath the maroon bubbles.

CHAPTER FORTY-FOUR

ART STEERED THE MINIVAN INTO THE DRIVEWAY. Relief untangled his shoulder muscles. He almost pulled off the freeway several times to find a hotel, but was propelled forward by a longing to be home, in his own bed, with his own wife.

The windows were dark. He looked at his dashboard clock, 12:17. Gwen must be asleep. He hit the garage opener and watched as the door struggled up then clunked into place with the groan of an arthritic, old man settling into his La-Z-Boy. That would probably wake her, and she'd be irritated. He'd been promising to replace it with one of those roll-up jobs as soon as he got the job and the raise, or when the door broke, whichever came first.

He'd expected to have to maneuver around Gwen's silver Honda. She never would pull it all the way to the left like he asked her to. But it wasn't there. He looked into his rearview mirror to see if he'd passed it on the street and not noticed. Not there either.

Gwen must have gone to Maricela's. They probably watched a movie, had too much wine, and she decided to spend the night. He opened the passenger side door and put a hand on Jason's shoulder. "Hey, buddy, we're home."

Jason mumbled something unintelligible and stumbled from the car. Tyler woke, gave him a sleepy smile, then followed his brother. Art walked around the car to the passenger side and picked up a slumbering Emily. Her eyes never opened. Her head came up, wobbled on her bird-thin neck for a moment, then thudded onto his shoulder.

He walked through the dark house without turning on lights and climbed the stairs. Emily's bedroom smelled like strawberry candy. He deposited her on her bed. After kissing her forehead and tucking the covers around her, he headed to the bedroom the boys shared.

Jason and Ryan were already sprawled atop their Batman quilts, breathing heavily. Art took off their shoes, then covered them with superheroes and arch-enemies. He remembered scooting a Matchbox Batmobile around his bedroom and shouting orders to Robin when he was a kid. Some things were constant. It was comforting. In a world full of change and insecurity, Batman never died.

After a hot shower, he climbed under his own duvet-covered, down comforter, between Egyptian cotton sheets that smelled of Gwen's perfume. He stared at his phone. Should he call or text? He didn't want to wake her if she was sleeping. He decided on a text.

"Hi, honey. Came home because of the storm. Everyone in bed. You OK?"

He dozed off with the phone on his chest waiting for a response. An hour later, his bed heaved under him. He reached his hand over the side, and a wet muzzle acknowledged it. A few more bumps and Rocket, the fair-weather guard dog, burrowed deeper under the bed.

Art checked his phone. Gwen hadn't answered his text. He hadn't expected her to, but disappointment seeped from the blank screen just the same. Exhausted, he rolled over and fell into a deep sleep.

CHAPTER FORTY-FIVE

GWEN LOOKED AT LANCE'S BLOATED FINGERS bobbing, white and lifeless, in the scarlet water and pressed her hand to her mouth. He hadn't sent the text. She stumbled and turned toward the bedroom. Who then?

The only illumination came from watery moonlight shining through the uncovered windows. Her eyes ran across the expanse of carpet to the doorway leading into the hall. Dark, indistinct mounds loomed between her and the exit. She stepped forward, wary and alert—a deer sidling toward a salt lick.

A shape on the bed rippled in the blackness. Gwen stared. Was it a trick of moonlight? She strained her ears for a rustle of bed sheets. All she heard was the pounding of her pulse.

Lightning flashed. In that split second, Gwen saw an arm cradling a head. Another flash. She saw feet crossed in a relaxed, picnic-in-the-park pose.

"I've been enjoying the Ravish," a deep voice said. The shape rose onto an elbow. An ebony arm hoisted a toast.

Incredulity almost extinguished Gwen's fear. The voice was familiar. The man put his glass on the bedside table and turned on a low lamp. She knew him—knew, but couldn't comprehend. It was absurd. It was as if a Martian, or Abraham Lincoln, or the Ghost of Christmas Past was lying in that bed.

His eyes gleamed, feral in the low light. How had she not noticed those eyes before? He patted the bed. "You look as ravishing as the wine. Come have a glass."

"What are you doing here?" As soon as she asked the question, she wished she wouldn't have. Its answer lurked in the empty house.

"We have things to discuss."

It must be shock. She couldn't fit the pieces together. The events of the day swam in meaningless circles through the squall in her mind. He was here. In her client's home. In her client's bed, where she'd planned to...

Lance, oh God, Lance.

The fact that he was lying dead in the next room burst through the unreality of the scene and struck her like a cold wave. She began to shiver.

Mo sat up. He swung his legs over the side of the bed. Heartbeats scampered around her chest, but she was unable to move. Like a mouse mesmerized by a cobra, she watched as he crossed the room. He came between her and the door to the hall, between her and her family.

A primal instinct took hold of her unresponsive limbs. She broke into a run and launched herself at him. It was like slamming into Mount Vesuvius. She fell back, stunned.

"No need to be hasty. I was coming to you." He grinned.

Gwen dodged right; he blocked her. She feinted left. He spread his arms wide and sidestepped.

"Calm down. I only want to talk," he said.

Gwen tasted the sour bile of panic. She opened her mouth to reason with him, plead if she had to, but all that came was a guttural moan. She retreated up. He followed.

"You're a wheeler dealer. I've been watching you," he said.

Gwen stepped farther away. She inhaled and exhaled slowly, willing herself to control the fear crawling over her skin. If she could humor him, distract him, maybe she could reach the wall switch by the closet behind her. It controlled the bedside table lamp he'd turned on. She had no further plan, just hide in the dark, away from those feral eyes.

"I don't know what you're talking about," Gwen said.

"Oh, you know. You were willing to..." He spread his hands, jerked his head toward the bed and raised his eyebrows. "Just to get ahead."

"It wasn't..." Her words trailed off. She wouldn't defend herself. She had to focus on the light switch. That small piece of plastic became her talisman. It was the only thing standing between her and complete panic, and the only thing in the world that mattered at this moment was diverting his attention away from it. "What do you want from me?"

"Not as much as Lance did, I can assure you. I have a simple favor to ask."

"Favor? You killed Lance because you want a favor?" A hysterical laugh burbled from Gwen's lips. She bit it off. "What kind of favor could you possibly want from me?"

"A small one."

She swallowed the terror rising in her throat and forced herself to calm. *Improv. Use your improv skills, Gwen.* But the only role she could think of that fit the circumstances was "victim."

"Why should I help you? What's in it for me?" She narrowed her eyes and feigned suspicious interest. At least she could pretend she was tougher than she was.

Mo's fingers twitched. He grabbed the leg of his pants and they stilled. "For starters, I won't blow the whistle on you and your boyfriend. The police will think you killed poor Lance, you know. Not to mention how hubby would feel about it if he knew what you were up to. I will swear you were in The Leaky Barrel with me all evening. Wine tasting."

The switch was only feet away now, but he stood too close for her to reach it unnoticed.

"And, of course, there's your life. Help me, or I'll kill you."

Gwen jumped at the word "kill." Her back slammed into the wall. Something hard and small jutted into her hip. "What do I need to do?" Her words came in panted breaths.

"Just your job. Show me a property."

Her fingers walked up the wall toward her low back. "That's it?"

"Maybe one or two other little things." He waved a dismissive hand.

Gwen felt along the plastic ridge of the switch with imperceptible movements. She relaxed her facial muscles into an expression of resignation. "I guess I don't have much choice, do I?"

"I believe I have you over the proverbial barrel." He chuckled at his own joke.

She flipped the switch. Blackness fell. She slipped toward the bed. His arms knocked against the wall where she'd stood a half-second before.

"Oh, very clever," he said into the darkness. "How will I find you with the lights out?"

She found the lamp in the dark, yanked it from the wall and climbed onto the bed. She heard the light switch click uselessly.

Everything was still for a moment, then the noise of his breath, the sour smell of him, the shuffle of his feet moved closer. Brandishing the lamp in her right hand, she used her left to guide her. She crept across the width of the California King mattress.

"Have you ever played searchlight?" he said.

Gwen didn't answer.

She heard the smack of flesh on wood. Mo cursed. A minute passed. He said, "I used to watch children playing on the beach at night. They used flashlights to tag and capture each other. I should have brought one." He sniffed the air like a hunting dog.

Gwen felt the mattress sag under the pressure of his hand. She slid off the far end of the bed and dropped to her knees.

Lightning lit the room, then thunder rumbled. She huddled into a small ball and hugged the edge of the bed.

"Where are you, little Gwen?" Frustration laced his voice.

Gwen, eyes now adjusted to the moonlight, could see the bedroom doorway only yards away. It might as well be a mile. If she could see shapes in the shadows, so could he. She felt the bed heave and heard his steps—more confident this time—coming toward her.

"Come out, come out wherever you are," he said in a sing-song.

Gwen gripped the lamp and drew her feet underneath herself.

"I'm tired of this game." He sounded peevish.

She readied herself to spring and swing at him. He rounded the bed. A wet sheen on his forehead glistened in the gloom.

They made eye contact.

At the same moment, the trill of the doorbell sounded.

Both their heads snapped toward the hallway.

"Gwen Bishop. Gwen. Are you still in there?" Mrs. VanVlear's muffled voice called out followed by hollow, sharp, rapping. The doorbell rang again.

Before Gwen could yell for help, she saw a quick movement in her peripheral vision. Pain reverberated through her skull, then nothing.

CHAPTER FORTY-SIX

THE EVENING STARTED UNBELIEVABLY WELL. I saw Gwen's car coming up Sailor's Haven when I was talking to that noisy old biddy. I was able to pull around the corner without her noticing me. I parked, jumped the wall into the backyard, made my way around the side of the house and hid behind a hydrangea bush. It was raining, but even that worked in my favor. The downpour created a camouflage.

I watched Gwen pull up to the curb and carry several parcels into the house. A moment later she reemerged, leaving the front door open wide behind her. She scurried right past me so intent on getting out of the wet night she never looked my way. I watched until she was bent into the trunk of her car to retrieve more bags and sneaked across the yard and through the front door.

I glanced around. The second floor seemed like the best place to hide until I could establish a plan. I ran up the stairs before Gwen made it through the front door with her bundles and positioned myself in the walk-in closet of the master bedroom. I waited.

At one point, I bumped into a shelf in the dark, and a shoe thudded to the floor. I feared I'd given myself away, but there was an auspicious clap of thunder at the same moment that must have covered the noise. No one came upstairs.

I left the closet door open a crack and could hear movement and voices below. Several times, I almost crept out just to see what was happening, but I'm glad I didn't. Good things come to those who wait.

The scent of roses was my first clue that a splendid opportunity was about to present itself. My second, the view of Lance dropping said rose petals across the bedroom floor. Romance was in the air.

Catching the gigolo with his pants down was almost too good to be true. He was easy to deal with, half-drunk, eyes closed, and naked as a jaybird. His death was as smooth as a good Cabernet.

Gwen was harder to deal with. I hadn't expected her to turn out the lights and bolt, but even that was only a momentary setback. I enjoyed the chase. It proved she was a good choice. She had grit and ingenuity.

Then that stupid, stupid old crone banged on the front door and almost ruined my plans. She made a tremendous ruckus. I was afraid she'd rouse the entire neighborhood, but nothing ever came of it. When she left, I threw Gwen over my shoulder, no small feat, and sneaked her out through the back door.

It bothered me that I had to bring her to my shop. My sanctuary. But I couldn't think of anywhere else at such short notice. I only kept her there long enough to retrieve her car. It wouldn't do to let the police find it and come to the conclusion she'd been a victim instead of a perpetrator. I left the vehicle in a rough area of Santa Ana with the windows down and the keys in the ignition, walked several blocks to an all-night bar, had a glass of abysmal wine to calm my nerves and called an Uber. I had the driver drop me in the Dana Point Harbor, and I walked to Sailor's Haven to pick up my car. .

When I finally returned to the shop, I was so agitated I paced between the shelves for over an hour, running a finger across the bottles—my form of meditation. It calmed me, helped me think. I drew on the strength of the wine.

Every bottle represents an ancient process, a magic formula. Every crop of grapes demands its own unique care. Was it a hot, dry year? Wet and cold? An early or late spring? Nature infuses the grape with a mystery only the alchemist can unravel.

He combines varietals—dark with bright, sweet with pungent—to achieve balance. He adds a pinch of this, a drop of that, then hides his creation away in the dark. The longer it sits, the more deep and complex it becomes. Every wine has its perfect time. Opened too soon, it will be weak and shallow. Too late, and it's spoiled. This was my time.

My sister wouldn't win. She wouldn't steal my light, or my birthright. But I knew I would have to storm the castle soon if I wanted what was mine, and I did. What had started as a hunger for justice had grown into ravenous need.

CHAPTER FORTY-SEVEN

GWEN ROCKED EMILY, back and forth, back and forth, in the white rocking chair with the floral print cushion. It was the same chair she'd rocked each of her babies in. The day she found out the child she was carrying was a girl, she went to Home Depot and purchased a can of bright white semi-gloss. It had taken several coats of paint to cover the once blue rocker.

"Hush, sweetheart. Hush," Gwen murmured and kissed the top of Emily's head. Instead of the smooth, blond, strawberry-scented hair she'd expected, wiry strands poked her lips. She rocked harder. "There now, Mommy's got you."

Emily had dreamed a terrible dream. She'd seen blood in a bathtub, a lifeless body, the black silhouette of a stranger in the dark. At least, Gwen thought, *it was Emily who'd had the nightmare. It was possible that she, herself, was the one who'd dreamed.*

It was cold. She should cover Emily with the blanket she always kept on the chair, but it was hard to move her limbs. Even her eyelids felt like blocks of cement. Straining, she attempted to lift them but couldn't. She tried to bring her fingers to her eyes to rub them awake. Her hands stopped short. They must be tangled in Emily's hair. Exhaustion overwhelmed her, and she dozed again.

She was awakened by violent shivers. The blanket. She knew where it was but couldn't reach for it. Her arms wouldn't cooperate. She opened one eye a slit and looked at her hands to see what the problem was.

They were tied.

Awareness slapped her awake. Her eyes flew open. There was no sweet face haloed by the strands wrapped around her wrists. There was no rocking chair. Gwen was lying, alone, on her side on a wood floor, hands bound with rope.

The room was dim and shadowed. The only light came from under a door. It was a small space, piled high with boxes. A storage room of some kind.

The memory of the night came to her in disconnected bits, puzzle pieces that refused to make a complete picture: Lance's curling hair and beautiful eyes. The Frobisher's great room. The dark at the top of the stairs. Mrs. VanVlear with wine-stained lips. Wine, the smoky taste of Ravish. And something else. Something she didn't want to remember.

She lurched forward, trying to sit up, but couldn't move. Looking down she saw the cords that tied her wrists looped around her waist several times, crisscrossed around her legs and ended with knots at her ankles. She was trussed up like dead deer.

Fear, cold and raw, raked fingers up and down her body. She opened her mouth to scream, then shut it. She didn't want to attract... Who? A face floated in her mind.

Mo.

The wine shop owner.

She remembered the surrealism of finding him in the Frobisher's bedroom. The chase in the dark. Mrs. VanVlear's calls and then blackness. Why?

But then, of course, she knew. Another face surfaced behind her eyes. The dead, white, plastic sheen of Sondra Olsen's face.

Adrenaline, so thick and strong it burned like whiskey, flowed through her veins. She threw herself back, then side to side as far as the ropes allowed. Her ties chaffed and bloodied her skin, but nothing broke loose.

Gwen was no longer cold. Sweat trickled between her shoulder blades. She reached for the bonds with her teeth. No good.

She cried out in frustration, her voice scratching from her throat. Her eyes skittered around the room looking for a solution. A miracle.

The thudding of her heart crashed in her ears. It almost drowned out the other sound. A sound that filled her with dread. The sound of a ship's bell.

#

Tears sprang into Gwen's eyes from the bright light. She blinked. Mo stood in the doorway, silhouetted by a wall sconce in the hall behind him.

"You're awake," he said.

Gwen didn't answer.

"Good. We can't stay."

He walked toward her in short, swift birdlike steps. This was the first time she had seen him without the ship captain's hat. His hair was very thin. It made him look older. Smaller. Less menacing, until she noticed something gleaming in his right hand.

A knife. Gwen whimpered and threw herself on the floor trying to get as far away from him as possible.

He looked at the blade—not a knife, a box cutter—and showed her his teeth like an aggressive dog. Warm liquid trickled down Gwen's thighs. He laughed.

"What? You think I'm going to use this on you?" He slashed at the air. "Relax. All I want to do is cut some of those ropes."

He leaned over her, turning his head away in disgust. "What a stench. Did you have to do that? I would have let you use the toilet."

Mo flicked his blade through the ropes around Gwen's torso and legs. Then he sawed at the knot at her ankles until it snapped, but he left her wrists tied. She sat up and moaned. Pain shot through her head and down her spine.

"We need to leave. I'm going to put you in my car, but..." He put his face close to hers and held the knife between them. "No fun and games. Not now. Understand?"

Gwen couldn't take her eyes from the blade. He grabbed her arm and lifted her to her feet. She cried out. Sitting up was painful. Standing was agony.

"Look at you. Miss Piss Pants. I can't put you in my car like that. I'll never get the smell out."

He moved to the far wall of the room and pushed aside a stack of boxes with his calf. The light from the hallway fell onto the outline of a square cut into the floorboards.

Holding the razor in front of him with his right hand, he grabbed a small wrought iron ring with the other and pulled open the trapdoor.

Gwen thought about rushing him when he bent into the hole to retrieve whatever he was planning to retrieve, but the feeling in her legs was just now returning. She didn't think she could get there fast enough. As if reading her mind, he said, "If you move I'll cut off your pinkie. I don't believe they give you a discount at the nail salon for doing nine instead of ten."

Mo knelt down, his head and shoulders disappearing. When he reemerged, he was holding a large dress box. He set it on the floor and riffled around in it for a moment or two. Gwen caught a glimpse of sky blue fabric, something white with ruffles, then he pulled out a soft beige skirt. "I think this will fit," he said holding it up and eyeballing Gwen.

He tossed it at her. In reflex, Gwen raised her arms as one unit and caught it. She examined the expensive fabric. Why would he have this? In a flash of insight, she knew. His victims had been found naked. Cold scurried up her arms. She flung down the skirt like she was shaking off a cockroach.

"Pick it up," he said, his voice hard. "It's a gift. That's no way to treat a gift."

She'd made him mad. Not smart. Gwen obeyed.

"Now, put it on. Get rid of your underwear too."

She stared at him stupidly for a moment. How was she going to do that? Her hands were tied. She had no privacy.

"Don't be shy," he said. "I have a mother and two sisters. Had, anyway." He leaned against the wall and began cleaning under his fingernails with the tip of the blade.

Gwen turned her back to him and wiggled out of her pants and panties then stepped into the skirt and pulled it up over her hips. She shivered as the fabric touched her skin.

Mo lifted an empty wine crate from the floor and held it out to her. "Put your things in there. I'll get rid of them."

She did as he said. He held the box as far from himself as he could and set it by the door. "Let's go."

Never go with them. That's what the police always say. You may be killed if you fight, but there were things worse than death.

"No," she answered.

He raised his lip in a parody of a smile again. "No? What do you mean no?"

"I'm not going anywhere." Just saying the words made Gwen feel faint. "You won't kill me here, in your shop. It's too messy."

Mo looked at her evenly for several minutes. Finally, he said, "What makes you think I intend to kill you?"

Gwen's laugh was bitter. "I don't know. Maybe the ropes, the knife. Hitting me over the head. The other dead agents."

His face broke in agony for a split second then remolded itself. "Don't get sarcastic with me. I'm not who you think I am."

Gwen stared at her bare feet. She'd done it again—made him angry. "I'm sorry."

"You think I'm a lunatic who slices up poor little Realtors in their listings for fun?" He waved his knife hand in the air. "I am not a monster. No. I am not."

He stopped and wagged the box cutter at Gwen like it was a finger. "My sister owes me. She's taken it all—the attention, the position, the name, the money. Those women died for a good cause, a just cause. Don't waste any sympathy on them." His cheek twitched.

"I don't understand." Gwen's voice was almost a whisper. She needed to know his mind if she had any hope of surviving the night.

He looked at the ceiling. "They were charming to my face, Mr. Moray this and Mr. Moray that, but they didn't fool me. They were grasping, greedy, self-satisfied sluts. I exterminated them in my father's name."

A look of pain crossed his face; he stifled a groan and fisted his hands. Gwen's pulse climbed into her throat. She held her breath for several long moments, hoping his rage would pass.

He breathed through his nose and seemed to get control of himself. "I'm a sommelier, did you know that? Level two. I was born with an amazing sense of smell. Incredible taste buds. My sister, she buys whatever is on sale at the grocery store. She's a plebeian. But she had my father under her spell."

He switched the knife to his left hand and flexed and clenched his right hand several times. "The witch." His hand shot to his head, he gripped a hank of hair and pulled. It came loose in his fingers. He studied the hair, then let it flutter to the floor.

"We need to go." He walked toward Gwen.

"No. I'll scream."

"Don't irritate me." The words were a hiss. He clapped one hand over her mouth and held the knife to her throat with the other. "I thought we were friends. I even protected you from Lance. He was a wolf in sheep's clothing. Did you know that? He came into the wine shop with three other women over the past two months. And, he left with them. Left with his arm around them, whispering in their ears."

Mo tightened his grip and Gwen felt a pinch at her neck. Then he held the blade before her face so she could see the blood on its tip. A sob gurgled in her throat.

"I'll take my hand off your mouth so you can say thank you."

Gwen nodded.

He removed his hand. "Thank you," she said.

"That's better. Now, let's be allies. You scratch my back. I'll scratch yours." He folded his arms over his chest. "You get me into my father's house, and I'll keep all your dirty little secrets."

"What do you mean?"

"My father's house is on the market again. I want in. I have your key." He dug into his pocket and pulled out an electronic key. "But I don't know the code."

"I'll give you the code." Gwen's words were quick. "Just let me go."

"Not so fast." He waggled the device in the air. "I have another teensy favor to ask. Once we get there, I need you to make a call."

"To who?" Gwen asked.

"My sister." His face clouded again. "I need her there. I want you to call and say you were just showing a client the house and there was a plumbing problem, or... maybe electrical." He stared at the dark ceiling. "No, plumbing is better. The basement could be flooding. She'd have to come then."

"Then what?"

"Then?" he looked at her like he'd forgotten she was there for a second. He narrowed his eyes. "Then I let you go, of course."

Gwen gauged her response. He was crazy, dangerous, but it didn't appear his obsession was directed at her. "That's it? All I have to do is get you into your father's house and call your sister?"

"That's it." A crafty look crawled across his face.

She knew he wouldn't keep his word, but playing along might buy her time.

CHAPTER FORTY-EIGHT

MO OPENED THE TRUNK. Rain splashed Gwen's face. She sucked in air like a diver breaking the surface, her heart pounding. During the drive, claustrophobia had wrapped around her throat like a boa constrictor and squeezed. The breathless ride had seemed an eternity.

She calmed herself by looking at the open sky. The sun was still low on the horizon obscured by a blanket of storm clouds, but there was daylight. This had been the longest night of her life. The sun brought hope, most likely foolish hope, but foolish hope was better than the hopelessness of the dark hours.

She scanned her surroundings. Mo's car was backed into a cracked driveway behind a rickety wooden fence. A large, fig tree hovered over her. She knew where she was. What she hadn't known was this had been Mo's father's home. This was why he hadn't killed her then, why he believed his sister would come when Gwen called. Fiona was his sister. And Fiona was Gwen's client.

He dragged her toward the side of the house where Lance had placed the lockbox. He'd put there instead of on the front door so agents would have to call to find out its location, adding another layer of security. She wondered if all their efforts would backfire on her now. They'd made the house a fort.

She and Mo passed the trash area. There was no odor. Even the garbage cans had been abandoned. That she was truly alone with him became a solid reality. This wasn't a bad dream or the last minutes of a television crime drama where the heroine is rescued by a brilliant detective.

A sob built in her chest, but she caught her breath and wouldn't give it voice. She had to play along, befriend him if she could. She prayed a silent prayer he wouldn't kill her as soon as she gave him her code.

She toyed with the idea of giving him the wrong number, then pleading ignorance when it didn't work. No. Then he'd have no need for her. He'd probably slit her throat right here by the garbage cans.

He pulled the electronic key from his pocket. "What's the code?" he said.

It was the month and day of Emily's birthday. Her throat ached as she repeated it. A fissure of longing for her children, for Art, opened in her chest. It was suddenly clear, whatever she'd seen in the alley alongside Enzo's, it wasn't betrayal. In the deep places of her being she knew her husband. He loved her, and he was a man of integrity.

Mo turned toward her with the house key in his hand. Gwen braced herself for an attack. Maybe she deserved it. Her stupidity had put her here, in this dangerous place. But she didn't want to die without explaining things to Art, without telling him she hadn't slept with Lance whatever it looked like. Without asking his forgiveness.

"Let's go in, shall we?" Mo said.

She exhaled in relief. He must not realize using the key would send a notice to the security company. The hope she'd felt earlier began to revive. If someone was looking for her, surely they'd check her e-key records. But the hope quickly wilted. Why would anyone look for her?

Art and the kids were gone for the weekend. Even Maricela wouldn't notice her absence until Monday. Gwen had thrown up smoke screens between herself and all the people who cared about her to hide her rendezvous with Lance. Regret and shame billowed over her.

She followed Mo to the front door. A jolt of excitement hit her—the alarm system. It didn't deactivate until 5:00 AM. She looked at the sun and tried to remember what time sunrise was this time of year. It could be before five—maybe just.

Mo inserted the key in the lock. Gwen held her breath. He turned it and pushed open the door. Silence reigned. Her pulse slowed from a gallop to a heavy plod. It was after five.

The fresh coat of paint in the entryway surprised her. For a moment she'd forgotten the time she and Lance had spent here. She'd expected to see the house the way it had been before they'd dressed it up.

The primping seemed so pointless now. The house was damaged. There was cancer in its walls. It was a painted prostitute, promising pleasure but delivering disease. How had Gwen not seen it before?

Mo pulled her down the short hallway to the left of the staircase and opened the door. At first, she could see nothing. He pawed at the wall for a moment, and an overhead lamp switched on. A sickly, yellow light illuminated a steep, wooden staircase descending into blackness. Fear lived at the bottom.

Gwen was transported to a time long past. She was on a road trip with her parents. She was ten. She heard the crunch of gravel under tires. Felt the scorching heat of the summer sun. Smelled hot sagebrush and tar. Saw the green and white sign of Carlsbad Caverns.

"It'll be fun, honey," her mother said. Her voice was cheerful, but her eyes worried.

"The caverns are well lit and perfectly safe," her father said. "I've always believed the best way to get over your fears is to face them. You'll be glad you did it."

They purchased tickets. Gwen was promised an ice cream afterward if she would only be a brave girl. But as soon as the cave walls closed around her and the daylight disappeared, she turned and ran.

That same panic welled up from a cold place deep in her stomach. Just as she had at ten, she bolted toward the comfort of daylight. Mo caught her before she'd gone three steps.

"Where do you think you're going?" he said. "I want to show you something. Downstairs."

"No, no please." Her words came in gasps.

"Don't be stupid. There's nothing to be afraid of." He muscled her toward the doorway.

"If you're going to kill me, don't do it down there." The stairway terrorized her more than anything else had in this terrible night. It was even worse than the closeness of the car. At least in the trunk, she'd known she was above ground. Air and light were seeping in through the metal seams.

"I'm not going to kill you. I told you that. Not if you do what I ask." His voice grew angry.

"I will. I will. But don't take me down there. Please," she said, claustrophobia reducing her to a sniveling mess.

He grabbed Gwen by the hair and yanked hard. "I will pull all this pretty auburn hair out of your head if you don't stop being so difficult."

He led her by her hair to the top of the steps and down. She tripped several times, missing one riser, then two. She fell into him twice before they reached the bottom.

Ahead yawned a hallway, dotted every five feet with murky puddles of light. He dragged her forward. They passed doors on either side as they tunneled deeper into the airless place.

After an eternity of sloping descent, the hallway came to a dead end. A wooden door, charcoal-gray with age, blocked their path. Mo reached forward, pushed, and the door creaked open. The smell of mold and rotting wood sighed from the space like sour breath. Nausea rolled in Gwen's stomach.

"The agent who showed me the house the first time didn't want to come down here either," he said.

He flipped on another amber lamp and pulled Gwen inside. Dusty shelves lined three walls of a room about twenty feet by twenty feet. They were piled high with bottles, round bottoms glinting through a coating of grime.

"It's a treasure chest." His eyes opened wide, their whites jaundiced in the yellow lamplight. "Some of these wines have been out of circulation for years. There's a 1940 Romanee-Conti Domaine de la Romanee-Conti Grand Cru, a Chateau Lafite Rothschild, even an early bottle of Screaming Eagle Cabernet from Napa Valley. It's one of the most amazing collections I've ever seen."

Gwen stared around her at the dirt and decay. "Why aren't they better cared for?" His awe was infectious.

"This place was my grandfather's vacation home for many years. He was the wine connoisseur. His talent obviously skipped a generation. I don't think my father knew what he had."

"Why didn't you tell him?"

Mo's laugh was low and angry. "I only saw him once before his death. We didn't have a... a relationship to speak of." His right hand balled into a fist. Gwen flinched, preparing herself for a blow.

"Because of her." The hand released and clenched three times in rapid succession. "He only cared about her."

The hand moved to his head as if it had a will of its own and fingered a tuft of hair. "My mother wasn't good enough for him. I understand that. I was different, but he never gave me a chance."

Gwen watched in morbid fascination as the hand crawled across Mo's head playing with one lock here, experimentally tugging on another there.

"His wife died eight years ago. I tried to call him then. Tell him I was sorry for his loss. He hung up on me." He addressed his words to the shelves of wine, seeming to forget Gwen presence.

She looked around for a way of escape. The room was bare except for an old table and chair and the walls of wine. There were no doors or windows other than the door they'd entered by.

"I thought maybe if my mother was out of the picture, he would be more receptive to a reunion. Maybe he'd been avoiding me, because he didn't want the complication of having her in his life." He looked at Gwen. "She was difficult."

His fingers stopped traveling and wound themselves into a thick strand of hair.

"So I got rid of her." He gave a quick yank, and his hand came away with the lock. It hung from his fingers like a dead thing. "It didn't change anything. Fiona was the problem, not my mother."

He put the hair into his mouth. He sucked on it and gazed at the wine with a thoughtful expression. He stood this way for so long, Gwen wondered if he'd gone into a fugue state.

She shrank away from him, backing toward the open door—an inch at a time. If she could only make it into the hall before he came to himself. Her plan was sketchy. Not really a plan, more an idea.

She would shut the door, and wedge something—she didn't know what—against it. If she could barricade him in the wine cellar, she would run upstairs, into the world of light and sound and people, and she would find help.

It was as if his hand read her mind. He never took his eyes from the wall, but the hand shot out and grabbed her wrist before she'd gone two feet. He looked at her with eyebrows raised as if he was as surprised as she was by it. The hair dangled from his lower lip like a limp cigarette.

"But the good news is," he said with abrupt cheerfulness, "I don't think anyone knows this treasure trove is here except me, and now you. Based on the coating of dust, no one's been in here for years."

"Why not take it then? I could help you. We could carry it out to the car right now." Gwen tried to keep the desperation out of her voice.

"But I want a family reunion." He flashed a smile. "And this is where you come in. You can get her here. She'll come for you."

Gwen nodded, pushing away her fear and disappointment. "Should we go up and call now?" she asked, making her voice bright.

"No." Mo pulled her toward the chair. "Not now. Tonight. I have to pour wine for a wedding shower this afternoon. It's a big event. I'll be busy all day."

"You're not going to leave me here?" Gwen's voice grew shrill. The thought of staying in this place with the weight of the house bearing down, smothering and suffocating, terrified her.

"You'll be fine." Mo pulled a roll of duct tape from a shelf.

Gwen ran for the doorway again, but Mo backhanded her with such force flecks of light flashed behind her eyes. She staggered into arms that closed around her like a vise. Out came the blade. She felt its pinch in her neck close to her pulsing carotid artery.

"Let's try this again," he said.

She allowed herself to be pushed into the chair and wrapped with duct tape. Tears coursed down her cheeks.

CHAPTER FORTY-NINE

AGATHA OPENED THE DOOR of 278 Sailor's Haven Drive. She'd come to clean every Saturday, come rain or shine, for the past fifteen years. She put her purse on the small table in the entryway and scowled. Someone had made a mess on her stairs, and it sure looked like that someone done it on purpose. Something dirty dotted every single riser.

Now she'd have to vacuum before she did the dusting. She liked to vacuum last, so as to leave the carpet all nice and smooth with no footprints. But she didn't want to risk grinding that dirt deeper into the rug.

She told Mary Beth putting a lockbox on the house was a bad idea. No telling who'd come in or what kind of things they'd do. Agatha heard stories about people putting those boxes on their front doors then coming home to find everything from pot parties to beds full of strange panties. Real estate agents were a racy bunch. Always wearing animal print skirts and spiked heels.

She shook her head, scratched around the mole on her nose, and headed to the broom closet. She vacuumed her way up the stairs. "Jeezum," she said to no one when she reached the top. Piles of dirt like the scat of an over-sized rabbit marked the carpet all the way along the hallway into the master bedroom. She poked at one with the extension hose and realized it wasn't dirt at all. It was a blackened, dried rose petal.

Someone had some nerve. Rose petals only meant one thing, an assignation. Disgusting. Doing the deed in your own bed was bad enough, she couldn't imagine doing it someone else's.

Well, it was no use getting her gorge up. What was done, was done. She turned the suction on, swept the floor with the hose, and dragged the machine behind her. She slowed as she reached the bedroom doorway, worried about what she might find around the corner.

If she saw a pair of black lace panties, or worse, red ones, she wasn't going to touch them. Not with her bare hands. People who leave their underwear in other people's beds are the kind of people that carry diseases. No sir. She loved Mary Beth, but she wasn't touching anything like that.

She took a deep breath and stepped into the bedroom. "Jeezum," she said again. The room was a mess. The bedclothes had been pulled this way and that, the broken bits of what had once been a lamp littered the floor. Mr. Charles' golf trophy lay on the carpet next to a big, brown stain.

The room smelled funny too. She sniffed—Mary Beth's favorite bath salts. Now, wasn't that the cherry on top of the crap heap? "Can you imagine?" she said aloud with her hands on her hips.

Wait until the Frobishers found out. She wouldn't say, "I told you so." Nope. She didn't want to rub their noses in it. They could see for themselves she'd been right. Right as rain.

She picked up what was left of the lamp and vacuumed up the broken glass around it. She started to straighten the bed then stopped. Mary Beth and Charles would be home in a few days. They ought to have fresh, clean sheets for their homecoming. Especially since she was none too sure about what had been going on in that bed while they were gone.

She tore the linens from the mattress and was grateful she didn't find any unmentionables. Then she headed to the bathroom hamper. When she reached the open door, she sniffed again. There was something rotten under the sweet floral scent of the bath salts. Not wanting to look but not daring not to, she dragged her eyes to the source of the smell. The linens fell to the floor with a swoosh. Bobbing in the bloody tub was the bloated, white body of a naked man.

"Jeezum."

CHAPTER FIFTY

"DADDY," AN INSISTENT VOICE BUZZED IN ART'S EAR. "Daddy, I'm hungry." Why Emily felt waking him with a whisper was any better than shouting, he didn't know.

"There's cereal." He rolled to his other side, turning his back to her.

"I want donuts." She climbed on top of him, riding his hip like a pony.

"Later, okay?"

"I'm hungry."

A small earthquake erupted under his bed. A moment later a hot tongue slapped his cheek, and dog breath filled his nostrils.

"Good morning, Rocket," Emily said and hugged the dog to her chest. Rocket attempted to wiggle out of her grip, tongue seeking her face now. She giggled.

Art squeezed his eyes shut, trying to ignore the wrestling match taking place on top of him. It was useless. Sleep was gone.

After settling Emily and the dog in front of the TV with instructions to wake the boys if she needed anything, he left the house in search of breakfast. His first stop was the market for milk, bread and eggs. Then he noticed the fuel gauge in the van. Almost empty. He made it to the gas station and filled up before heading to the donut shop.

When he turned onto his street forty-five minutes later, panic punched him in the chest. Two cars, a police cruiser and a plain sedan, were parked in front of his house. He pulled into his driveway and ran up the walk. A uniformed officer and the same female detective he'd seen at the Laguna Beach crime scene, Investigator Sylla, stood outside his door.

"The kids. Are they—" he said.

"They haven't let us in, so I can't say," Sylla said.

"Gwen?" A new kind of dread filled him.

"Your wife is fine as far as we know, Mr. Bishop. But I need to speak with you. Can I come inside?" Tyler and Emily peered out through the front window.

"What's going on, Dad?" Jason opened the front door.

"I don't know, J-Man," Art said. "But I need you to take your brother and sister into the den. Keep them busy, okay?"

Emily flew out from behind Jason and tackled Art. Tyler was right behind her.

"Dad, we didn't know what to do. You said don't let anyone in, but they're police." Tyler's face crumpled.

"You did just fine, buddy. Don't worry." Art put a hand on his shoulder. "Why don't you and Emily go with Jason? He's going to find a movie or something for you guys to watch."

Art and the police officers settled in the living room. As soon as the kids disappeared, he turned to Investigator Sylla. "So, what's this about?"

"Do you know where your wife is, Mr. Bishop?"

Art's heart beat an arrhythmic measure. "She may be at a friend's. I'm not sure."

"She hasn't contacted you?"

"No." The words made him seem so distant from Gwen. "I was gone, camping," he tried to explain.

"We need to find her. A friend of hers was found dead."

Art's eyes widened. "Who?" Maricela's face flashed through his mind.

"Lance Fairchild. He worked at Humboldt."

"She was working with him on a Laguna Beach house, but I don't think they were close. I'm sure there are other people from the office—"

"The cleaning lady found him in your wife's listing in Dana Point this morning."

"A man? Do you think it's the same killer?" Art asked.

"It doesn't look like it. But we'd like to talk to your wife. As I mentioned, it was her listing."

"Yes, but all the agents have access to the lockbox—"

The investigator interrupted, "Her key was the last to unlock the lockbox, and a neighbor saw her there."

"She was supposed to be doing paperwork. That's why she missed the camping trip," Art said.

Investigator Sylla's face softened. "We believe she met Lance Fairchild at the property and there was an altercation."

Art looked at the woman mutely. Was she implying Gwen and this Lance were planning to... planning to what? "Look, detective, I'm not sure what you're trying to say, but I can assure you my wife wasn't planning to hook up with some guy in her client's home. If they met there, it was for business. Maybe Lance had an interested buyer or something."

"He was found naked. In the bathtub." Sylla's voice was flat.

Art's hand balled into a fist. He wanted to hit something. "So, maybe he met somebody there after Gwen left."

"Maybe," Sylla said. "The sooner we find her, the sooner we can get her side of the story."

"I'll call her," Art said and pulled his phone from his pocket. "Let's get to the bottom of this. I'm sure—"

"We have her phone."

"You have her phone?" Art stared.

"Yes. Several of your wife's personal items were left at the scene."

"Wait. Wait." Art exploded from the couch. "You're saying you found my wife's cell at a murder scene? Did you stop to think maybe the person who killed Lance took her?"

"Anything is possible, Mr. Bishop. That's why we need to speak with Mrs. Bishop—so we can clear things up."

"No, I mean, she could be in danger," Art said, his voice rising.

"As I said, anything is possible. I hope we can count on your assistance in locating your wife."

"I don't know where she is," Art almost screamed. "What are you doing to find her?"

Tyler appeared in the living room doorway, his face creased with worry. "Is everything okay, Dad?"

Art crossed to him and hugged him hard. "Everything's fine, buddy. We're just talking."

"Where's Mom?" Tyler's voice was muffled by Art's chest.

"That's what we're trying to figure out. The police need your mom's help with a case."

"Have you, your brother, or your sister heard from your mother?" Investigator Sylla addressed the boy.

Tyler shook his head.

"Why don't you go into the den?" Art forced himself to speak calmly. "Let me talk to the officers."

They sat in silence until Tyler was out of earshot, then Sylla said, "I understand how upset you must be. I want you to know we're doing everything we can to find your wife. Help us. We need a list of names and numbers, anyone she's friendly with. Anyone she might go to if she were in trouble."

Sylla's voice was sympathetic. She sounded sorry. Sorry for Art that he was married to a two-timing murderer.

#

As soon as the police left, Art called Mike McKibben. Maybe Mike could find out something from his cronies at the station that might shed some light on what was going on. He didn't pick up, so Art left a message. Then he set up the kids with calm words, Saturday cartoons, and donuts and headed to Maricela's condo. He wanted to talk to her before the police did.

He paced the small front stoop while he waited for her to answer the door. Worry, fear, and anger swam through his gut in an acid sea. The door opened. Julissa's face brightened into a sunny smile when she saw him.

"Mr. Bishop."

"Is your mom here?" His tone was clipped. Her face fell. "Sorry, but I'm in a hurry," he said forcing more warmth into his words.

"Come on in. I'll get her." Julissa threw open the door and yelled over her shoulder. "Mom. Mr. Bishop is here."

Art moved into the small living room, but he didn't sit. He was too restless. Maricela entered holding a mug. "Can I get you some?" she asked.

"No, I'm fine. I need to talk to you." He cocked his head toward Julissa who leaned against the doorframe.

"I can take a hint." She pushed off and disappeared down a hallway.

Maricela sat in an overstuffed easy chair, forcing Art to perch on the edge of her couch if he wanted to make eye contact.

"What's going on?" The lines of her face deepened with concern.

"When I got home the police were at my house."

"*Dios mio*." She covered her heart with her hand.

"Gwen's missing. They're looking for her." Art hesitated.

Maricela was still recovering from the shock of finding a body. He hated to upset her, but she would hear soon enough.

"Someone was found dead in her Dana Point listing," he said.

"What? Who?" She paled.

"A man. Lance something. The guy she was working with on the Laguna house." Art watched Maricela's face. He needed to know what she knew.

"Fairchild." She looked at her hands.

"Yeah, that was it. Who the hell is this guy, Maricela?"

"He's an agent. He worked at Humboldt." Her voice was subdued.

"I know that. What I don't know is why the police think Gwen may have killed him."

Maricela's head shot up. "Killed him? That's ridiculous. Gwen wouldn't kill Lance... Wouldn't kill anyone."

"I know that too."

They sat without talking for several ticks of the cuckoo clock on the wall. Art broke the silence. "What aren't you telling me?"

Maricela looked to the ceiling for help. "It's nothing."

Art waited.

"I told her he was a player. I told her to watch out for him."

A stone dropped into the turmoil in Art's stomach. "What do you mean?" He steeled himself for the answer.

"They were talking about becoming partners. A business team, you know?" Maricela's words were hardly more than a mumble. "I don't think anything was going on between them. I don't. They flirted, but..."

Art didn't want to hear more. He would have gotten up. Just left the house. Except Gwen might be in danger. If she wasn't, when he found her, he was going to kill her.

"Thursday or Friday something changed. Gwen was upset, but she wouldn't talk about it to anyone but Lance. You could tell they had a secret."

Art stood and began pacing again, as if he could walk away from her words.

"I kept telling her he was like Enrique, not a good man, but she wouldn't hear it. I'm sorry, Art."

"Is that it?" he said. He didn't think he could take anything else.

"I saw them coming out of The Leaky Barrel together on Thursday. I remember because I thought it was strange. Usually, we only go on Fridays. And it was early. Only like two o'clock."

"So you haven't heard from her? You're not trying to protect her?" Art asked.

"No. I wouldn't lie to you." She reached out a hand and touched his. "I haven't seen her since yesterday afternoon."

Art's cell phone rang. It was Mike McKibben.

CHAPTER FIFTY-ONE

TIME WAS MEANINGLESS IN THE DARK. It could have been three in the afternoon or three in the morning for all Gwen knew. She dozed from sheer exhaustion, but pain from the tape pulling at the small hairs on her arms, pain from forced inactivity, pain from the blow she'd received the night before prodded her awake.

Only the nightmares seemed to last for hours. Every time she slipped into unconsciousness, she entered the same continuous loop. She was on a farm with her father, helping him on his large animal rounds. She stood, a small figure, looking up the barn. It was larger and darker in her dream than it had been in real life.

She entered through the heavy door. The smells of hay and dung and something worse flew at her and clung to her skin like mold spores. On her right was a high window. The hay bales beneath glowed golden in the beams of light streaming from it. Her father was always there in the sunlight, smiling at her.

On her left was a loft shrouded in shadows. If there was a window on that wall, it was blocked by the mountain of hay piled in front of it. Under the loft, tucked into the corner of the barn, was a pigpen. It drew her with an irresistible force.

She had this same dream often when she was a child. Sometimes she'd yell herself awake before she saw the sow. Other times she'd wind up in the pen with wild, red eyes trained on her. Screams and squeals mingled. Small, pink shapes darted around her feet. Brown teeth flashed. A white, hairless mountain of flesh charged her again and again, backing her into a smaller and smaller space until there was no corner left to hide in.

Shivering and panting, she would bolt up in her bed clutching her covers and cowering into the headboard. Then her mother would be there, smoothing her hair, speaking soothing words.

"Finish the story, Gwen. Your father came and banged that pan against the pen wall and yelled at that old pig. You sneaked right past her snub nose, and out through the gate. You weren't hurt. It was a close call, but you are just fine. Think about that, honey. Think about that now."

Gwen's father had warned her to stay away from the sow, who'd just had a litter of piglets, but she begged to see them. He'd relented as long as she promised to stay outside the pen.

She hung over the fence and watched the babies for a long time. They were so cute, like wind-up toys, trotting around on short, stiff legs with their Slinky tails making tiny circles in the air. But pretty soon watching them didn't scratch Gwen's itch. She wanted to hold a piglet. Just for a minute.

She eyed the sow lying there on her side snorting and snoring; she didn't look too worried about her babies. Besides, Gwen wouldn't hurt the little things. Didn't her dad say she was the best vet-in-training in the whole county? She knew what she was doing. He'd taught her how to hold kittens and puppies and chicks. Piglets were much sturdier than chicks.

She slipped past a twinge of guilt into the pen and shut the gate softly behind her. She tiptoed to the closest piglet. It wasn't even a foot off the ground before it let out a shattering, ear-piercing squeal. The sow vaulted to her feet.

Gwen dropped the piglet and slammed against the wall of the pen. The sow charged. She moved with more speed than Gwen thought possible from an animal of that size. Gwen's father, motivated by the same need to protect his young, must have moved just as fast. If he hadn't, she wouldn't be having nightmares about it today. She'd have been torn apart.

Bobby White, one of the boys who lived near the farm where it happened, heard all about it. At school that week, he told her the story of a farmer who went to feed his hogs and never came back. When his wife went to look for him, all she found were bits and pieces in the slop.

Bobby said those hogs would have eaten every last bite of him if their dinner hadn't been interrupted. Sometimes that unnamed farmer showed up in her dreams missing fingers, toes, and other important body parts.

After that, fear of dark, close places became Gwen's constant companion. For a time it seemed she'd shaken off the worst of it when she was in college. It had become manageable at least. But claustrophobia found her again through the dead eyes of Sondra Olsen.

Now whenever Gwen jerked awake, panic waited for her. It scurried from the coal black corners of the room and crawled up her legs and arms. It wrapped itself around her chest. *No one is coming. Nobody knows where you are.*

Her greatest comfort was also her greatest distress. Mo was obsessed with his sister. He needed Gwen to lure Fiona to the house. But the fact that Gwen wasn't the object of his mania was a small comfort. Mo didn't have anything personal against the other women he murdered. They'd been strangers to him.

She had many hours to wonder what he'd do if Fiona came to the house. How did you unravel a mind as tangled as his? He tore his hair out by the handful and rambled about his sister's unnatural powers one minute, then spoke logically the next. Hot rages erupted from his icy calm. His grip on reality was tenuous. She didn't doubt his plan was to kill both of them. At times, she was terrified Mo wouldn't return, that she'd be left here in the dark. But mostly she was terrified he would.

Thump.

Gwen sat as straight as she could and strained her ears. Had she heard something? She listened so long and hard, the silence became a sound. A high-pitched, monotone whine filled her ears. Long minutes passed. The thin tinnitus became hypnotic. Her head nodded.

Thump. Clack. Clack. Clack.

Gwen's chin shot up. She heard muffled voices. A woman's. No, two women. A man's deep rumble. Laughter. There were people in the house.

Gwen tried to scream through the duct tape on her lips. Only a strangled cry emerged, loud to her ears but not loud enough to carry through the ceiling. The footsteps and voices were directly above her now.

Gwen planted her feet on the floor and began rocking the wooden chair back and forth, back and forth. The legs clattered against the stone. She blasted her humming yells. After several minutes, she stilled. Had they heard her? Was help coming?

Silence.

She heard footsteps again—quiet at first then growing louder. They must be coming from the upper story. The house wasn't in escrow yet. It must be a real estate agent showing the property. She was sure she'd heard the click of high heels.

The steps now resonated from the front of the house. If it was an agent, she might show the basement. It was packed with the refuse of years past, but still, it was a selling point.

The door. Open the cellar door. She willed them to find her.

She felt, more than heard, a sound so soft it may only have been a displacement of air. Hope bubbled into her heart. One of the women's voices broke into the stillness. It echoed through the basement hallway. It came so close Gwen could almost make out the words.

She threw herself into a frenzy of rocking, stomping, and muffled screams, then stopped as quickly as she'd started and listened for the effect.

Nothing.

About to give it one last effort, she heard the voices again. Not close this time but faint and muted.

Another thump. A door? The front door?

Minute after quiet minute passed. A tear slid along Gwen's check and pooled in a pocket of duct tape. The high whine of silence filled her ears again. Panic crept up her legs.

CHAPTER FIFTY-TWO

ART'S CAR MADE ITS WAY, almost of its own accord, into the parking lot of Humboldt Realty. He'd been sitting, staring out the windshield at Gwen's office for at least ten minutes. He was waiting for her to walk through the glass doors embossed with the company logo into the sunshine.

It wouldn't happen. Logically, he knew that. For one thing, her car was missing from the crime scene.

The words "crime scene" wouldn't compute. Crime scenes were things in CSI episodes and news stories. He couldn't wrap his head around the idea they also existed on bright sunny days in suburbia, or that his wife had anything to do with one.

Mike McKibben's call hadn't been encouraging. Maricela was correct. Lance was a player. According to many who knew him, he'd had several affairs in recent months. The police were tracking down his various lovers. However, the cops' favorite scenario to date was that Gwen had murdered Lance in a fit of jealousy and was now hiding out.

The fact that both Gwen and Lance were real estate agents and three other agents had recently been murdered was looked at as coincidence. This seemed even more illogical to Art than sitting in front of Humboldt Realty and waiting for Gwen to appear.

A man walked out the front door of a small shop a few doors from Humboldt. He placed an easel next to the entrance and walked inside. A minute later, he came out again carrying a blackboard. He adjusted the board on the easel. Art could read the writing from where he sat. "Wine tasting from 1:00 to 5:00. Flights of five for $15." The name of the establishment was printed in bold, black letters on a sign above a large display window—The Leaky Barrel.

That was the place Maricela said she'd seen Gwen and Lance on Thursday. Art also had a hazy memory of Gwen telling him she'd discovered a red wine she loved that could only be purchased at a small shop near her office. The wine had a funny name, Ravishing, or something like that. It had reminded him of a romance novel.

Mike told him the police found several opened bottles of red wine in the Dana Point house. He knew this was at best a fuzzy clue, but it was the only clue he had. He got out of the car.

He didn't know what he'd say to the proprietor. He had no plan. Social niceties no longer mattered. He placed himself somewhere near the bottom of Maslow's Hierarchy of Needs right now. All he cared about was getting his wife back. He'd worry about what she did or didn't do when he found her. If this was the last place people had seen her and Lance together, maybe he would find out something about what happened.

He opened the door of the shop and jumped. The clanging of a ship's bell rang in his ears. The man Art had seen outside appeared through a doorway behind a small bar and smiled through a neatly trimmed goatee.

Art had never thought about where the word "goatee" came from, but when he looked at this man, it was suddenly obvious. The shopkeeper looked like a well-groomed mountain goat. He was Pan or Bacchus from a classic painting—-appropriate, or ironic depending on how you looked at it, for the owner of a wine shop. Art half-expected to see a pair of horns jutting from the cap on his head.

"Can I help you?" he said.

"I hope so." Art walked toward the bar. "My name is Art Bishop. My wife frequents your shop."

The man cocked his head to one side but didn't speak.

"Her name is Gwen. She works at Humboldt." Art gestured in the direction of the brokerage.

"Oh, Gwen. Yes, I know your wife. She stops in every so often for a bottle of Ravish."

"Right." Art brightened. The man knew who she was anyway. "Gwen is... I'm trying to find my wife. I thought maybe you could help me."

"How would I do that?"

"A friend told me she saw Gwen coming out of your shop on Thursday afternoon."

The goat man looked at the ceiling and stroked his beard. It was a theatrical gesture. Almost as if there was a director in the wings signaling him to strike a pose that would indicate "thinking" or "remembering."

"Maybe she was," he finally said. "She bought some wine last week. It might have been Thursday. I could check my records if you'd like?"

"There was someone with her," Art said. "A man named Lance Fairchild. He's also a Humboldt agent."

"Oh, yes. Yes. I remember now. Gwen, Mrs. Bishop, came in first. Lance, a few minutes later. They ended up sitting at that table over there." He pointed to a high top nearby. "They had a glass of wine and talked for a while."

"Did you hear what they were talking about?" As soon as Art asked he felt foolish. If the man had been eavesdropping it would be the last thing he'd want to admit. Just as Art guessed, a look of horror crossed the proprietor's face.

"No. I wouldn't dream of listening in on a private discussion. My patrons know their privacy is always respected." He turned away and reached for a case of wine sitting on the floor near the register. "I have a party coming in for a wedding shower in an hour. I have to set up. Is there anything else?"

"Listen, I didn't mean to offend you. I'm just at the end of my rope," Art said.

The man stood, holding the case of wine, and waited.

"Gwen is missing. I'm afraid something may have happened to her. I'm looking for information, anything...."

An odd look, a mix of unwholesome excitement, hunger and fear, flickered across the man's face. It happened so fast; Art wasn't sure he'd seen it when he thought about it later. But it was the moment everything changed.

"I'm sorry for you. Gwen seems like a lovely woman, but I don't know what I can tell you. She and Lance Fairchild had a glass of wine and left. That was the last time I saw either one of them."

Art knew he was lying. It wasn't anything he could take to the police, but he knew. Art was a professional when it came to spotting deflection, evasion, and fabrication. He'd been judge and jury at more juvenile crimes than he could count over the past fifteen years. This guy stank, from the top of his stupid ship captain's hat to the bottom of his superior attitude.

Art wanted to shake him. To push him up against a wall and demand the truth. The guy was hiding something, and Art wanted to know what.

"If you think of anything, maybe you'll give me a call?" Art said.

"Of course," the goat man smiled again. It was an unpleasant smile, more like a baring of teeth.

"Here's my card," Art said, placing it on the bar and walking out of the shop.

CHAPTER FIFTY-THREE

I HUSTLED FROM TABLE TO TABLE filling wine glasses and refilling platters of chocolate bonbons. It was demeaning, waiting on a room full of women. I should be served, not serving. Soon, I comforted myself. I would come into my own soon.

I had my first wedding shower at the shop two years ago. Not only did I sell several cases of wine and sign thirteen women to my membership program, but the mother-of-the-bride purchased the wine for the wedding reception from me instead of serving the swill the venue provided.

Since that time I did showers whenever I could get them, but today was decidedly a bad day. I would have closed up the shop if it wasn't for the event. It forced me to open. I guess it was just as well. It would have been a mistake to do anything out of the ordinary, anything suspicious.

The bride sat at a high top table—princess for a day—opening gifts while another girl created a ribbon bouquet from a paper plate. I used to think it was an absurd ritual. As if catching a wad of trash could assure a marriage proposal.

At a shower I hosted a year ago, however, the most unattractive girl in the room rammed through a lineup of women and tackled the festooned plate like a football player. I didn't believe there was a bouquet with magic powerful enough to make a man want her, but she scheduled a wedding shower with me six months later.

I wondered who the poor slob was. What I wouldn't have given to be a fly on the wall the morning the spell was broken. The morning he saw her for what she was—a gargoyle. By then it would be too late. He'd be trapped.

I opened the last two bottles of the white I'd been serving and realized I'd forgotten to bring more from the back room. I was having a hard time concentrating. All I could think about was returning to my father's house.

"Oh, how cute." The bride waggled sheer white panties and a matching bra in the air and all the women cooed.

It was obscene. Why did women feel it was not only fine, but necessary to display their underclothes? If I waved my briefs around like that, I'd be arrested.

I was about to go get the other case of wine when the bell rang. A short, dark woman in khakis and a white blouse entered. She walked across the room with an economy of movement I found both fascinating and disturbing. There was something about her I associated with the male gender, but she wasn't masculine. Still, she was as out of place in this gaggle of giggling females as I was.

"Mr. Cotton?" She wasn't American, at least she hadn't grown up here. Her accent was continental.

"Yes. Can I help you?"

"Investigator Sylla, Orange County Sheriff's Department." She showed me her badge and the hair on the back of my neck rose. I tipped my head to one side and smiled as agreeably as I was able.

"I wonder if I could ask you a few questions?" British. She sounded British.

"I'm right in the middle of a party," I said, lacing my words with an apology.

"I'll only take a minute. Is there somewhere we could talk?"

I started toward my office, but stopped short. Gwen's clothes. They were still there in the wine crate. I hadn't had time to get rid of them. Even if the detective didn't see them, she'd smell them.

"On second thought," I said turning. "I'd better stay out here. Keep the party going."

Investigator Sylla narrowed her eyes. "Very well then. On Thursday, the twenty-fifth, Gwen Bishop met with Lance Fairchild here in your shop."

It was a statement, not a question, so I didn't respond.

"I understand they're both frequent patrons of yours?"

"Yes. They work at Humboldt." I pointed in the direction of the brokerage.

"What did they talk about?"

"I'm not in the habit of eavesdropping on my customers."

"Sometimes we can't help but overhear things," she said in a warm manner, as if we were old friends.

"I didn't," I said.

"What about the tone of the conversation then? Did it strike you as friendly? Angry? You're used to dealing with the public. What were your impressions?"

The more she tried to cozy up to me the warier I became. "What is this about?" I made my tone indignant.

"Mr. Fairchild is dead, and Ms. Bishop is missing." Her voice became flat. "Anything you can tell us would be most helpful."

I was saved from having to answer by the mother-of-the-bride to be. "Mo. More white, please. We're out." For once, I appreciated the high-need women I was waiting on.

"How terrible. What happened?" I attempted to look shocked and dismayed.

"That's what we're trying to discover." Her face was solemn.

I matched her expression. "Let me think about it. I'm a bit distracted at the moment."

"Right." She handed me a card. "Call me if something comes to you."

"Of course." I smiled sadly until the door banged shut behind her, then stumbled into my office. The smell hit me as soon as I entered. Thank God I'd remembered the clothes before I'd brought her here. I had hidden the wine crate with the soiled garments under the floor with the clothes from the other agents. If those had been found... I tasted bile.

I'd burn them as soon as I had the chance.

I pulled myself together, found the case of wine and returned to the front of the house. The bride was holding a black lace thing with dangling garters up to her chest and posing for the camera. I had to set the wine on the bar before I dropped it. The room whirled around me. I put my head in my hands and massaged my temples.

My mother had an outfit like that once. It was the first thing I'd taken. One night when I was about thirteen, she shooed me to my bed over the garage early because a friend was coming over. It had been a hot day, and I'd been out in the sun for hours. I was thirsty.

I knew I wasn't allowed into the house when she had visitors, but all I could think about was water. The more I tried to push it from my mind, the more I craved it. Finally, I couldn't stand it anymore.

I crept from the garage and peeked into the living room window to see if the coast was clear. It wasn't. A man sat on the couch. My mother stood by the mantel.

The black thing she wore fit her like a second skin. It accentuated rather than covered her naked curves. I was horrified to see her dressed like that, but I couldn't look away.

That was when I learned some women have a secret art. Not all women, but some. Those who do use cotton and lace and rayon and chiffon to weave spells that can break a man. I put them on sometimes, the clothing I take. They're like armor. They shield me from lust. The ancient Spartans believed warriors only gave into their more base nature to have children, never to satisfy themselves. It's a sentiment I respect.

I stole my mother's bustier the next day and hid it in an old toolbox under a workbench in the garage. She accused my sister at first and sent her to her room. But after several days of steady denials, my mother shifted the blame to Patty, Angela's only friend, and ended that relationship. My mother ruined most things for my poor little sister.

"Are you okay?" The mother-of-the-bride was at my elbow.

"Just a bit of a headache." I lied.

"Can we make an appointment to taste wines for the reception? I've had too much this afternoon to make a good decision." She giggled like a schoolgirl and touched my arm. I itched to slap her hand, but refrained. I can control myself, which is more than I can say for some women.

CHAPTER FIFTY-FOUR

ART PULLED HIS BASEBALL CAP LOWER. He'd parked under the shade of a crepe myrtle down the block from Humboldt Realty and The Leaky Barrel for an hour and a half. He'd run home and given Jason a frozen pizza and instructions to feed and care for his siblings. At four, he'd returned. The wine shop didn't close until five, but he didn't want to take any chances.

The owner was guilty of something. Art didn't know what, but he felt it in his bones. The last time he ignored this feeling he'd suspended Brian McKibben instead of Dwayne Pratt. He wasn't doing that again. Regardless of how ridiculous he felt, he had learned the hard way to follow his gut. Right now, his gut was telling him to follow the goat man.

While he waited outside the shop, he had plenty of time to research the art of tailing a person on his phone. The first thing he'd learned is that he shouldn't be viewing the building through his windshield. Instead, he should be watching it from a side or rear view mirror. He moved the car.

He also learned it was best to know as much as possible about the person you're following. There wasn't much information online about the goat man. His name was Mo Cotton. He was a level two sommelier. He lived in Laguna Hills in a condo, and he'd opened The Leaky Barrel three years ago.

Art sat up straighter. Five cars full of women pulled out of the parking lot, one right after another. The shop must have closed.

He waited, on alert. A minute stretched into fifteen. He began to wonder if Mo had been in one of the five cars, and somehow he'd missed him.

Just as he was about to get out of the car and wander in the direction of the store, another vehicle appeared in the lot's exit. Art saw a bearded profile in the driver's seat of a blue sedan. He turned the key in the van's ignition and idled the engine.

The sedan made a right onto Golden Lantern and blew through the first stoplight. Art drove in the opposite direction looking for a place to make a U-turn. It was a couple of blocks before he could do it safely. By the time he was going in the same direction as Mo, he could no longer see the man's car.

Art sped up as much as he dared, but didn't see the sedan. Frustration gripped him. Golden Lantern bisected the Coast Highway before it ended in the harbor. Which way should he go?

He breathed a prayer and went south. The Dana Point house was south on the highway; maybe Mo Cotton was returning to the crime scene? He'd always heard criminals did that. Of course, maybe he wasn't a criminal at all. Maybe he was just your friendly neighborhood pervert, and that was the guilty vibe Art had noticed.

His shoulders tightened as he wove through traffic. His hands felt sticky on the steering wheel. What the hell was he doing? He was a school principal. He drove a minivan. He wasn't James Bond. He came to an open stretch of highway and scanned the road ahead. He struck the dashboard with the heel of his hand. The goat man was gone.

#

Art drove to the Dana Point house only because he was out of ideas, not because he believed he'd find anything there. It was barricaded with crime scene tape, forlorn and empty looking. He sat staring at it for several minutes before heading out to the highway. He turned north, toward home.

In a few miles, he saw the sign for Strands Beach. On impulse, he pulled into the parking lot. He and Gwen used to come here often for sunset dinners.

He parked in a space overlooking the ocean and turned off the ignition. The sky was pale salmon, the nightly show only just beginning. He rested his forehead on his arms. She should be here—with him. But he'd lost her.

Not tonight in his inept attempt to tail Mo Cotton. He'd been losing her by inches for the past three years. He'd worked so hard to gain the approval of everyone in the world but the one person who meant the most to him. He'd neglected Gwen to romance people he didn't even like. An ass. He'd been an ass.

He sat, head down, empty and defeated until the salmon turned red, and was shot through with lavender clouds. He would stay until dark. He was putting off the inevitable—facing the kids with no news of their mother.

His phone vibrated on the passenger seat beside him. He looked at the screen. Mike McKibben. A spark of hope flickered to life.

"Mike. News?"

"Actually, yeah. I just heard from one of my guys. I asked him to keep me posted. They just got a lead."

"What?"

"Gwen's e-key was used at a house in Laguna Beach this morning, early. Somebody just got around to checking her account at the security company again." Mike paused for a minute.

"I guess the local guys did a drive by. No action. They didn't see her car. They're waiting for Sylla and a search warrant to check inside. Thought you'd want to know."

"The address, what's the address?" Art put his cell on speaker and opened a maps app.

"Listen, if it was her she's probably long gone."

"Come on, Mike. I'm close. I'm in Dana Point. I'll wait for the cops to show."

"I don't know..." he said.

"Mike, she's my wife."

"It's the same house, Art. The house she found the body in."

Thirty seconds later Art was dodging cars on Coast Highway—pedal to the metal in the minivan.

CHAPTER FIFTY-FIVE

GWEN STIFFENED. She heard the thump of the front door again. This time it was followed by rapid footsteps that grew steadily louder. The door of her cell flew open. She shrank into her chair. Dim yellow light exploded like a solar flare in the blackness.

"Okay," Mo rubbed his hands together like a child. "Next on the agenda." His cheerfulness was as jarring as the light.

The pent-up tension that had built in the dark, burst from its cage. Gwen wept. She felt nothing but relief as he pulled the tape from her arms and chest. She was so happy to see another human being, to be loosed from her bonds, she threw her arms around his neck and sobbed on his shoulder.

"Hey. Hey." He untangled himself looking uncomfortable. "None of that. You're okay."

Gwen wiped at her eyes with her hands. "Sorry."

"Not a problem," he said, but he stood well away from her as if he was afraid she might touch him again.

He waited until she'd gained control of herself then said, "Let's go up and make that phone call, shall we? There's no reception here."

The memory of the past twenty-four hours hit her with unexpected force. For a moment, the joy of release had blotted out the knowledge of who had taken her and left her in the dark. Mo wasn't her savior; he was her captor. She wouldn't forget that again.

#

"I have to use the restroom," Gwen said.

Mo's mouth tightened in annoyance.

"You said to tell you." She'd been holding it for hours.

He pushed her into the basement hallway ahead of him. Her legs were weak and rubbery. Her thighs burned as she climbed the stairs. When she emerged from the narrow passage into the open air she almost wept again. The last rays of the sun lit the foyer and the living room beyond with a rosy glow. She couldn't remember ever seeing anything as beautiful

Mo walked with her to the guest bathroom. The candle she'd placed on the sink the morning of the open house was still there, like a relic of an earlier age. She hurried in, her bladder full to bursting, and tried to push the door shut behind her. Mo stuck his foot in the doorway.

"Can I have some privacy?" she asked.

"I don't want you trying to get away." He pointed at a window in the far wall.

Gwen lifted her hands. They were still tied. He shrugged and turned his back, but left the door open. She was past modesty.

When she was done, she stepped to the window. She managed to unlock it and lifted it open with tied hands.

Sea air brushed past her face, clean and bracing. She swallowed deep gulps.

"What are you doing?" Mo yanked her away from the window.

"I need air," she said.

He dragged her into the living room and handed her a disposable cell phone.

"I'll read you the number." He took a note from his pocket and began reading aloud. "Why aren't you dialing?" he said, when he noticed the phone hanging limply from her fingers.

"I can't." Gwen lifted her roped hands. He snatched the phone and began punching in numbers.

"What am I supposed to say when she answers?" Gwen said.

"What we talked about earlier." His jaw muscles clenched. "Tell her you're here in the house, and there's a water leak."

"Where."

"Where what?" Mo's voice rose.

"Where's the leak? She's going to ask me for details. You want this to be believable, don't you?"

He huffed and walked to the window. "Okay, okay. You're right. I'm being hasty. Let's just calm down and make a plan." He faced her. "What's the plan?"

"It could be a slab leak. That happens pretty often in California," Gwen said.

"No, there's a basement. How soon we forget." His face contorted into a nasty grin.

"Okay then, the basement is flooding." Gwen ignored his cruelty. The conversation was surreal. They were concocting a plan to lure Fiona into danger with as little emotion as if they were making dinner plans.

"That's good. A pipe burst and the cellar is flooding. That will bring her out. There's a lot of storage. She doesn't know what's in the wine cellar, but she may assume there's something of value there. She's a greedy bitch. She'll come for the money."

Mo pushed the call button and handed the phone to me.

"Hello," Fiona's voice answered. Until that moment, the call had been an idea, an abstract. It's easy to throw an abstract to the wolves to save your skin, but now the abstract was someone Gwen knew.

"Hi," Gwen's voice was shaky. Mo would most likely kill her, but she planned to tell Fiona to stay far away.

"Sorry I can't come to the phone right now, but your call is important to me. Leave me a message, and I'll call you back. Promise." A long beep rang in Gwen's ear. Relief mingled with disappointment.

"Answering machine," Gwen said.

Mo's face flared red. For a moment, she thought he was going to backhand her again. Instead, he took the phone and threw it across the room. It cracked into the wall leaving a gouge.

He brought his face inches from hers and screamed. "Why do these things always happen to me?" He jerked away and threw himself against the French doors so hard she was amazed he didn't break the glass. His right hand crawled up his chest and neck and buried itself in his hair.

"Nothing is ever easy. I plan and I plan and I plan and I plan and look what happens. I think I'm... I think I'm cursed." He looked at Gwen, his eyes pleading for understanding. "I always thought curses were superstitious nonsense." His hand flew up and a tuft of hair fluttered to the floor. The hand burrowed again.

"When this place came on the market, I thought my luck had changed. It was perfect. This had been her home. He'd sat with her here." His left hand drew a circle where furniture must have once been placed. His right was busy. Another wisp of hair floated from his head.

"I'd thought it was my mother's fault. That he never accepted me, you know?" His monologue changed course again. Gwen couldn't make sense of his ramblings, but didn't dare speak. She scarcely breathed. He was so volatile; a careless word would be like a match to spilled gasoline.

"I thought it was my mother who cursed me." He stared out the windows at the ocean, his face expressionless. Only his hand seemed alive. It plucked at his hair like it was weeding a flowerbed.

"I was wrong," he said, his head snapping toward Gwen, his words and movements so abrupt she started. "It was Fiona. She took his love, his attention, his money. She took what was mine. You understand what I'm saying?"

Gwen nodded because he seemed to expect a response.

He leaned forward and held his palms to the ceiling. Strands of brown hair dangled from the fingers of his right hand. "The only way to break her power is to get rid of her."

"But, he's gone. Your father's gone. What good would it do?" Gwen believed he was past reason, but she had to try. "You've got the wine. Just take it and go."

"That's what I'd planned to do." He paced across the room in short, quick steps. "I thought it would redeem the lost years, you know, to have something of his."

"It would, wouldn't it?"

"No," he spun on her. "There's no room for me. Not while she's alive." He resumed his pacing. "I don't want to kill you, Gwen; I really don't. I feel we've become, if not friends, at least allies. I helped you. I got rid of Lance. And, I know you wanted to help me with my project."

Gwen's heart knocked against her ribs. She'd come to grips with the idea of dying when she'd been tied in the dark—almost welcomed it at some points. Now that she'd tasted life again the idea of leaving it was sharp and painful.

"We'll try Fiona again." Gwen tried to match his matter-of-fact tone.

"No, it's no good. She knows. Somehow she knows." he said. "You tried. I appreciate that, but I'm going to have to come up with another way." A click punctuated his sentence—the sound of a blade pushing up through the box cutter's protective cover.

CHAPTER FIFTY-SIX

ART HEARD a sharp click.

"I won't say anything. You don't have to do this." Gwen said.

The fear in her voice made him want to leap through the doorway, but he restrained himself. He'd waited for the police as he'd promised Mike, for about three minutes. Then he'd gotten out of his car and walked through the dilapidated wooden gate. Mo's blue sedan sat in the drive, hidden by an oversized fig tree.

He'd found a small window open on the side of the house. It led into a bathroom. It was a squeeze. His stomach was scraped raw, but he got in. Then he heard voices.

He followed the sound to the entrance of the living room. Pressing his back against the hallway wall, he craned his neck around the corner until he could see what was happening.

Gwen and the goat man were engaged in a strange dance. Gwen faced the sea, her hair glowing like a halo in the dying sunlight. She moved to her right. The goat man, eyes fixed on her, circled left. He closed the gap between them with each step. They did a little do-si-do and switched positions. He wasn't wearing his ship captain hat and when he turned, Art could see hairless patches on his scalp. He looked like a dog with a bad case of mange. Disgust mingled with the taste of anger in his mouth.

"But I do," Mo said, his tone resigned.

"Let me go, Mo. I haven't done anything to you." Gwen's hands appeared to be tied, but she held them out in front of herself as if to ward off a blow.

"Only because you haven't had the chance."

Art's throat constricted when he saw the blade. He crept into the room. Gwen's eyes widened when he came into her line of sight. She opened her mouth. He put a finger to his lips, and she clamped it shut again. She forced her gaze to Mo.

"You're a woman. Therefore a thief, a cheat, and a liar. I don't fault you. You can't help yourself." His voice grew calmer with each word. "You're like her—a favored, petted princess. You even look like her. But you must know that."

Art crouched into a boxer's stance, fists raised to protect his face. He relaxed his hips and knees and shook his shoulders. He'd never hit a man before. He knew how it felt when his foot made contact with a sandbag, but he had no experience with flesh.

He launched his first kick—a roundhouse aimed at Mo's knife arm. The impact was softer than he expected.

Mo screamed. The blade skittered across the hardwood. Art righted himself. He'd almost lost his balance. A bag didn't give like a man.

Before Mo could turn, Art delivered a quick jab, then a right cross to his kidneys. His fists plowed through muscle and crunched to a stop at bone.

Better.

That was better.

He'd anticipated the force of the momentum this time.

Mo's knees buckled, and he dropped to all fours with a heavy grunt. No time to breath. Move in. A lightning fast front kick to the ribs knocked the man to the floor.

It was over.

Adrenaline pumped in Art's chest. Energy and rage ran up and down his limbs like electricity looking for an outlet. He took in deep breaths to cool the heat.

"Gwen, is there anything to tie him with?" Art circled Mo, never taking his eyes from the goat man. He wanted an excuse to pummel him. Any excuse.

"Tape. There's duct tape in the basement."

"Get it," he said.

Gwen brought the box cutter to Art. He sliced through the ropes on her wrists. She threw her arms around him for one second then disappeared from the room.

CHAPTER FIFTY-SEVEN

GWEN RAN DOWN THE SHORT HALL, across the entryway and slid to a stop at the top of the basement steps. The jaundiced passageway gaped before her, a live volcano, a lion's mouth.

There must be something else to tie Mo with. The tape seemed as inaccessible as if it were buried at the bottom of the ocean. She couldn't make herself step across that threshold. She walked in rapid circles in the fading light of the foyer, tempted to tear at her own hair.

It was only a basement. Nothing more. The threat lay on the floor of the living room with Art standing guard over him. *Face it, Gwen, face it.*

She walked to the open door and gazed down the stairs. Just stairs. She let her mind descend before her. Mentally, she walked the long, amber-lit corridor, approached the gray door at its end and... She shivered and stepped to the center of the entryway.

"Gwen," Art bellowed. "Hurry."

She raced across the floor and dove down the steps like a child jumping into a cold swimming pool on a hot day. *Don't think. Just move.*

She jogged to the end of the hall and, thank you, God, the door to the wine cellar stood wide open. She stopped for a moment at the threshold to locate the tape with her eyes. Keeping one hand on the door to be sure it wouldn't close behind her, she stretched into the room as far as she could. The tape was just out of reach. She released her hold on the door for an unendurable second and grabbed the roll.

A crash echoed from the upper story. She bolted as fast as her weakened legs would carry her to the living room, to Art.

CHAPTER FIFTY-EIGHT

I CURLED INTO A FETAL POSITION and squeezed my eyes shut. I couldn't believe a teacher could fight the way he did. The man was an explosion.

Think. Think. Think.

Intelligence was my best defense against a physically stronger opponent. I opened my eyes a crack and peered at him through a fringe of lashes. He held the box cutter loosely in his right hand. That was the only thing about him that was loose. He was a hunting dog on point. Riveted. Alert. I could smell his anger rippling toward me in waves.

I forced my muscles to relax and let my weight sag into the floor. My face grew slack. Pain tore through me, but I didn't tense. I made a mental assessment of my body. A couple of broken ribs and a few bruises seemed to be the worst of it.

Possum.

It was all I could think of. Let him think he'd done more damage than he had. He was the type who, once he calmed down, would feel guilty if he'd done anything permanent. I could use that against him.

Sure enough.

Soon I heard his breathing grow shallow and steady. I saw the rigidity drain from his face. Soon, his forehead furrowed. He squinted his eyes.

Closer. Come a little closer.

As if obeying my thoughts, he did. He crouched to examine me, so close I smelled his acrid sweat. I stayed as still as death.

Just two more steps. Come on. Come on.

He obliged.

As quick as a snake, I threw my left leg across the floor in an arch. His feet swept out from under him. The blade flew from his hand. He went down hard. I leaped and pinned his outstretched arms with my knees. Surprise was my only weapon until I could reach the box cutter.

It was only a few feet away. I leaned left. Mistake.

He arched off the floor when my weight lifted from him. I threw myself back on his chest and heard air whoosh from his lungs. He struggled beneath me, but I held my own.

Not for long.

He outweighed me by at least thirty pounds. I had to reach the box cutter. I braced myself for another grab and threw myself forward. My fingers closed over comforting steel.

CHAPTER FIFTY-NINE

ART THREW ONE ARM ACROSS HIS FACE and grabbed for Mo's knife arm with the other. The man was stronger than he looked, his muscles all strings and wires.

Art guarded and feinted, but the box cutter made steady progress toward his face. Where was Gwen? What was taking her so long? "Gwen. Hurry," he yelled into the empty hallway.

If he could get a leg up, he could pull Mo down. But his pelvis was pinned.

He focused on working his right hip, inch by inch, out from under the goat man. Time crawled. He lost all sense of its passing. His world became Mo's contorted face and the blade slashing through the air above him.

His hip popped free. In one swift movement, he kicked up, hooked Mo around the chest and rolled with the momentum. Mo was down now, Art on top.

He reached for the goat man's arms. Before he could pin them, a sting shot through into his right thigh. He slapped at his leg leaving his face exposed.

Silver flashed.

Torture pierced his shoulder.

Art roared.

Fuel injected pain surged through him. He threw Mo off with desperate strength and yanked the razor blade from his shoulder. He smelled iron. Sticky heat covered his hand.

One palm on the floor, one on his injured thigh, and he pushed to his feet. The goat man followed. They backed apart and began to circle.

Mo hunched, readying himself to spring, his eyes crazy.

"I'll kill you." Art warned Mo because he should. He wanted to do it. He wanted to see the light fade from those pale, blue eyes. "Come on."

Mo lunged forward.

A missile whistled past Art's head and slammed into the goat man's. He fell sideways. A roll of duct tape bounced on the floor by his feet, then wobbled across the wood into a corner.

Art saw the next move in his mind. Before Mo could regain his balance, Art pivoted. The heel of his running shoe struck gut and ribs. Mo went down again.

Rage thundered in Art's ears as unstoppable as a freight train. In a second, he was straddling the goat man. He'd taken his wife, held her captive, was going to kill her. He'd killed others.

Bone and cartilage crunched under Art's fists. He didn't stop hammering when a voice yelled, "Police."

He didn't stop while he was being yanked roughly away.

He didn't stop until he was holding the sobbing body of his wife against his chest.

CHAPTER SIXTY

ART'S GOOD ARM ENCIRCLED GWEN'S SHOULDERS. She nestled closer to get out of the wind and lifted her face to the sun. They sat on a blanket in their old spot on the cliffs above Strands Beach—picnic dinner and glasses of wine on a camp table nearby. She couldn't seem to get enough of the great outdoors these days.

"I've had an offer," Art said.

"From Landmark Prep?"

"Yes. The same money I've been making, but the cost of living is so much less in Idaho. I think we'd be fine."

"Maricela could list our house," Gwen said.

"She could. This is a big decision, though. How do you feel about moving out of state?"

How did she feel? She didn't know. She'd spent most of the past month trying not to feel. The night she and Art came home from the hospital, there must have been ten news vans outside their house. It had been hard to count with the klieg lights in her eyes.

The number dwindled over the next week, but she'd worried the food in the house wouldn't outlast the blitz. Even Emily got tired of boxed macaroni and cheese.

Reporters on the street weren't her only problem. Her cell phone had constantly rung until she'd turned it off. Along with media outlets wanting an interview, she'd had two offers for book deals from true crime writers. The producers of the reality show "The Day I Almost Died" wanted to interview her for an episode. She'd hid in her house for weeks and wished, fervently, for her old life.

"A new start could be good," she said, her voice hesitant. She hadn't returned to Humboldt since everything had happened. She couldn't face her coworkers, especially John Gordon. She'd never actually accused him of anything, not even after she had learned he had been in the house on Cliff Drive the night before the open house, but her attitude had been harsh.

She knew he'd noticed it, because he'd confessed he entered the house just to see what a ten-million-dollar listing looked like. He'd confessed he was envious. He'd even tried to apologize for his behavior at The Leaky Barrel the night he and Lance had come close to blows. But Gwen hadn't been gracious, and now she needed grace.

The Frobishers had taken their house off the market and wouldn't return her phone calls. She wanted to say she was sorry, beg their forgiveness, but they weren't interested in talking to her.

Gwen didn't know if she'd ever be able to return to work. She'd started seeing Maricela's therapist. She said they were making progress. But right now, Gwen couldn't make herself park in the same lot as The Leaky Barrel, couldn't imagine showing a house, especially if it had a basement. Running away sounded attractive.

"We'd have to come back for the trial," Art said.

Gwen shivered. He tightened his arm around her. The idea of sitting in the same room as Mo Cotton, even if he was guarded and handcuffed, made her a little ill. "How do you feel about leaving St. Barnabas? They offered you the job. And a big raise. They really want to keep you."

When the news came out that Art had beat the Real Estate Killer to a pulp and delivered him to the police, he became a local celebrity. That was just the kind of publicity St. Barnabas needed. Parents had pulled their children from the school because the prior administration hadn't been able to protect them from sexting and bullies. Now they had a bona fide hero on their hands.

"I have mixed feelings," Art said. "I hate to leave the people who need us."

Gwen knew he was referring to Olivia and Brian. His prognosis was good, but recovery would be a long road. Olivia's mother had been given temporary custody. He would be staying with her until the court decided if Olivia was a fit parent. Mike and Art were rallying a group to speak on her behalf. Gwen wanted to help. It would be a penance of sorts.

"You and the kids are my priority. I want what's best for us," Art said.

Gwen closed her eyes. Sunlight turned her lids crimson. She listened to the sound of the waves crashing on the shore below and remembered.

In her mind's eye, she stood on the cracked patio of the Laguna Beach house before it became a place of nightmares, and listened to the surf from that high vantage point. It was a dream then. A dream of things she wanted so badly she almost lost herself. As painful as it was, it was good for her to revisit this memory often. There were lessons to be learned there.

She opened her eyes and looked at Art. "We don't have to decide tonight, do we? I feel so content. Right here. With you." She reached for his hand and threaded her fingers through his.

CHAPTER SIXTY-ONE

EPILOGUE

FRENCH IS THE LANGUAGE OF WINE. I've been studying it since I now have some time on my hands. It makes me regret I never left this bourgeois republic for the eminently more civilized country of France. Oh, well. *Que sera sera,* as Doris Day sang.

My study of the language is how I happen to know the French word for dungeon. It is *oubliette*. It comes from the verb *oublier,* which means "to forget".

In the Middle Ages when one was thrown into the black underbelly of the castle, the trap door was dropped and the prisoner forgotten—not very humane. He was left to rot in the dark and feed the rats.

The state has deemed my extermination of some of Southern California's vermin as a crime. I see my actions as a public service. We disagree but, unfortunately for me, might makes right.

I've been tossed away like so much rubbish into the *oubliette* of San Quentin. They say it will be for life, if you can call this a life.

My sister sees it as divine retribution for my sins—my own personal Inferno. Like Dante, she hopes I will descend deeper and deeper discovering ever more horrific punishments. But unlike Dante, I won't be an observer. I will feel the pain.

I believe, in her heart of hearts, she thinks my incarceration will assuage her own guilt and embarrassment. She is miserable in the knowledge that someone who shares her DNA has snuffed out a few real estate agents. She must accept I am her family, and she hates it. That's a comfort to me.

I should have been my father's heir. I was never understood or appreciated by him, or anyone else for that matter. I've always lived in a black hole. Fiona sucked up all the light.

It's interesting to me that wine, my passion, is treated in much the same way as I have been—buried in damp basements away from the sun. Out of sight, out of mind.

This is where I find my hope. My *raison d'etre,* as the French say. The richness and complexity of a wine comes during its time in the cellar.

So I sit and write my story. I study French and history and weaponry and herbs and potions and poisons. I learn the ways and wiles of man and woman, and I mature. I prepare myself for the day I'll emerge from the *oubliette.* And I will. And when I do, my sister will drink the wine I've made in dark.

ACKNOWLEDGMENTS

It takes a village to publish a book. Here's to those who've populated mine.

Jodi Thompson, my encouraging publisher, Mary-Theresa Hussey, my tough-love editor, and Michelle Fairbanks, my talented cover designer, thanks for making this novel better than I knew it needed to be.

Lt. Matthew Barr, Laguna Niguel Chief of Police, thanks for taking the time to help me understand the ins and outs of the Orange County Sheriff's Department.

Dan Boris, husband and Commercial Real Estate Broker extraordinaire, thanks for answering all my real estate questions and restricting yourself to minimal teasing about my inclusion in the book of a Laguna Beach house with a cellar. Honey, I know So. Cal. oceanfront homes don't have basements constructed from caves, but how cool would it be if one did!

Gayle Carline and the Orange County Chapter of Sisters in Crime, thanks for bringing in such inspiring and informative speakers.

DeAnna Cameron, mentor and friend, Megan Haskell, partner in crime, and all the members of my very own O.C. Writers community, thanks for being there.

Did you find an error in this book?

Fawkes Press strives to present a perfect product, but being staffed by mere humans, mistakes happen. If you find something we missed, please visit www.FawkesPress.com and click on "bounty program," to submit your find and enter to win our quarterly bounty.

COMING SOON!

THE SCENT OF WRATH

SEVEN DEADLY SINS BOOK TWO

Ten-year-old Brian McKibben is a wanderer. Eight months ago he wandered into the street and was hit by a truck. Olivia Richards, his newly divorced mother, was accused of neglect by Child Protection Services. She's doing her best to prove them wrong, keep Brian safe, and help him heal from brain damage caused by the accident. She creates an airtight schedule to ensure he's never alone. She researches essential oils, and consults an herbalist, a descendant of the medicine women of San Juan Capistrano, for holistic remedies.

But her carefully laid plans begin to unravel when it becomes apparent Olivia's CPS caseworker isn't the only one who's watching her. The walls of the Pilates Studio she co-owns seem to have eyes, especially at night. Cryptic messages of death and danger begin showing up in unlikely places. Someone is stalking her.

Who can she turn to for help? The authorities would inform CPS, and she might never be free of the County's intrusion into her life. She suspects her ex-husband of trying to scare her into giving up custody of their son. Her new relationship is complicated. And old suspicions haunt the herbalist.

For news of new releases, special offers, book club goodies and Greta's event schedule visit http://gretaboris.com

[illegible] begged to see them. [illegible] relented as long as she promised to stay outside the pen.

[illegible] the fence and watched the babies for a [illegible] trotting [illegible] making [illegible] them [illegible] night.

CPSIA information can be obtained
at www.ICGtesting.com
Printed in the USA
FFOW03n0220041017
40562FF